To Lisa

2002

PANIC in the JUNGLE

LENA LEE

BALBOA.PRESS

A DIVISION OF HAY HOUSE

Balboa Press books may be ordered through booksellers or by contacting:

Balboa Press
A Division of Hay House
1663 Liberty Drive
Bloomington, IN 47403
www.balboapress.com
844-682-1282

Because of the dynamic nature of the Internet, any web addresses or links contained in this book may have changed since publication and may no longer be valid. The views expressed in this work are solely those of the author and do not necessarily reflect the views of the publisher, and the publisher hereby disclaims any responsibility for them.

The author of this book does not dispense medical advice or prescribe the use of any technique as a form of treatment for physical, emotional, or medical problems without the advice of a physician, either directly or indirectly. The intent of the author is only to offer information of a general nature to help you in your quest for emotional and spiritual well-being. In the event you use any of the information in this book for yourself, which is your constitutional right, the author and the publisher assume no responsibility for your actions.

Any people depicted in stock imagery provided by Getty Images are models, and such images are being used for illustrative purposes only. Certain stock imagery © Getty Images.

Print information available on the last page.

ISBN: 978-1-9822-7207-4 (sc)
ISBN: 978-1-9822-7209-8 (hc)
ISBN: 978-1-9822-7208-1 (e)

Library of Congress Control Number: 2021917454

Balboa Press rev. date: 09/09/2021

This book is dedicated to my late father,
Jay Henry Lee, a phenomenal father, leader and
teacher. A great Artist and Engineer who taught me
everything I know and always believed in me.

This one's for you, Daddy

Chapter 1

Chicago, Illinois
Thursday morning, October 20, 2016

"Honey, calm down. You'll make it to the airport on time. The limo won't be here for two more hours. Relax!"

Sierra's husband, George, was getting ready for work. He had a big meeting that day with all the department heads at Drum Technology. One of his top developers had created new hardware that would change the game in the computer industry in a major way. Kline Computers was deeply interested in George's proposal, and that day, Kline would decide to either give the contract to Drum or walk away and go with Drum's competitor, Mock Industries. The big meeting was scheduled to take place at eleven o'clock that morning. By that time, Sierra and her friends Lisa, Chloe, and Jenelle would be somewhere over the Atlantic, heading toward the Caribbean on a much-needed vacation.

"I know. It's just that I don't want to forget anything! I haven't been on vacation in over five years, and this is the first time the girls and I are going without our husbands. I guess I'm a little scared, babe!" she replied as she ripped through her dresser drawers, looking for her special hair spray and crème.

"Scared of what, for goodness' sake?" He giggled, shaking his head.

"Not used to going somewhere so far without my security system." She smiled and hugged him around the waist.

"Aw, honey, you'll be fine. Once you get to Aruba, you and the girls are going to be like, 'What husbands? We're married?'" he teased.

"Not true! I love you, George McAllister. But you're right. I need to calm down and relax. Perhaps when I come back, you and I can start working on making a baby," she cooed softly in his ear.

George's demeanor shifted from jubilant to slightly annoyed. His wife had been pressuring him for the past two years to start a family. He wanted children, just not right now. He was at the height of his career at Drum Technology. Being the CEO of a prestigious tech company commanded a lot of responsibilities. It just wasn't the right time, and he had made it clear to his wife that until all was settled with the company, having a child would only be a disruption in their lives. Well, his life, not Sierra's.

Sierra was quick to point out that her friend Lisa had children, and even though she was no longer married, she was doing well in raising her children alone. Jenelle was also a mother. Her husband was an ER doctor in the trauma unit. One couldn't get any busier than that, yet they'd managed to have three children and were doing just fine. Her good friend Chloe was the only one who was single with no kids. She was as free as a bird—and loved it—so Sierra didn't include her in the equation. Why was George neglecting her? Man, did she need this time away. She had stressed herself out on the subject, and perhaps going away for a little R&R would change her mood.

"Listen, babe, I have to get going. I want you to relax. Enjoy Aruba with your friends. Don't think about anything but the sea, sand, and cool drinks in your hand. Do not worry about anything here. When you come back, you and I maybe can discuss family planning." He held her face in his hands and then kissed her on the forehead and lips.

"You really mean it, George?"

"Yes, I do. I love you, Sierra McAllister. Call me as soon as your plane lands, okay?"

"I will, my darling. Good luck today with the contract. See you next week."

As he pulled off in his new Mercedes SUV, she watched from the kitchen window, holding a cup of coffee in her hands. He gave one final wave and turned left from their driveway onto Jasper Road, and then he was gone. She checked her wristwatch: 7:02 a.m. The driver would be there in an hour. Sierra was his last pickup, and then it was off to the airport. All her bags were packed and waiting by the front door. She had her passport, credit cards, and cash—lots of it—safely tucked inside her new designer handbag.

George and Sierra were financially comfortable. They weren't filthy rich, but they were not far from it. A Princeton graduate with money on his mind and success in his pocket, George wanted nothing more than to prove to his parents he could make it golden with or without their old money. His father, Samuel McAllister III, had been a banker back in his day; plus, he owned Trak Airlines. He had thousands of stocks and bonds and made multimillion-dollar investments here and there. He'd become very wealthy over the past thirty years, but he'd vowed never to throw money at his three sons just because he had it. His sons had to earn their right in life by working hard, just as he had. The McAllister boys had to graduate from college, earn a degree, and excel in their career for at least five years. Only then would Daddy McAllister give them a portion of their inheritance from their grandfather, Samuel II, who had owned several steel mills around the United States, including one right there in Chicago, which Sam's younger brother, Ryan, had overseen until he died of a heart attack. Samuel III's intent was to give his sons $1 million every year until they reached forty years old. The payout would start at age thirty-five; then, after his sons had proven themselves worthy, he would bother them no more.

George hadn't even stepped into the race yet. At thirty-two, he had been CEO for only a little more than two years now. He had three more years to maintain his position. Then he would begin getting his millions. That was why he was not gung-ho to start a family with Sierra. George's father did not like that his son had fallen in love with and married a black woman.

George's father was the undercover type of racist. He did his dirt with a handshake and a smile. George's mother was the opposite. She couldn't have cared less what color her son's wife was as long as her daughter-in-law made her son happy, which she did, according to her private talks with George. George worshipped his Nubian queen, but having a child right now was not feasible. He wanted to

3

get that inheritance in case he happened to fail at Drum. If things went well that day, he would tell his father to go take a hike so he could finally live his life with his wife without his father's demands, insults, and hateful talk.

Of course, Sierra knew none of that. She knew only that she loved her husband and wanted babies. He would give her that in due time.

Sierra didn't come from a well-off black family. Her parents worked blue-collar jobs and had struggled for most of their lives. Fortunately for Sierra Jackson, she'd been a straight-A student and had won a full scholarship to Princeton, where she'd met George. They'd dated for a few years and fallen madly in love. After graduating from college, they'd gotten married and moved to Chicago, where George had been offered a job at Drum Technology as a computer analyst. He'd worked his way up, and now he was CEO. George believed his father held back on him because he had brought darkness to the family—a black woman. For that, George would have to wait and suffer a little longer before he got his inheritance.

Sierra was no slouch. She was beautiful, talented, and educated and ran her own business: a small beauty supply company that grossed more than $500,000 a year. It was a small family business that Sierra made sure would be run by nobody but her siblings. She oversaw all the daily operations and did 100 percent of the accounting, which had been her major in college. Sierra had a big family, with five siblings. Each one had a hand in running Sierra's Beauty Supply Company. Her three brothers oversaw the manufacturing and distribution. Her sisters worked the store she had opened in downtown Chicago, filling orders and doing anything else that was needed to keep Sierra's Beauty Supply running successfully. They were close-knit and rejoiced that they finally had been able to put their parents in a beautiful home where they could live carefree after all the struggles and challenges of raising a family of eight. They were a Christian family who put God first and everything else second, and they had been blessed through Sierra's hard work and ambitions.

George's family weren't deeply religious. However, his mother had acknowledged God and faith as he was growing up. He remembered going to church with his mother and brothers. His father never attended, claiming he had a business to run, even on Sunday.

Around eight o'clock, a black stretch limo appeared in front of Sierra's home. The driver got out and rang the bell. Sierra opened the door and was filled with excitement as the driver helped carry her luggage to the limo. She got in and was welcomed by her three friends screaming happily and hugging and kissing her with joy. Lisa poured her a glass of apple champagne, and the awesome foursome toasted to their much-awaited trip as the driver took off toward the airport.

"I can't believe it! We are finally doing the damn thing!" yelled Lisa.

Lisa Hamilton, a divorcée with two kids, a boy and a girl, ages five and nine, was the principal at Lakeside Junior High. She'd earned a degree in early childhood education and then gone back to school to receive her PhD. Lisa had worked as a teacher for eight years and had been promoted to principal only a year ago. Ms. Hamilton was the ass-kicking friend of the group. She could be loud, obnoxious, and a little rough around the edges yet sophisticated and glam all at the same time. She was fearless, not afraid of anything or anyone. Sierra loved Lisa's down-to-earth personality. She had an answer for everything, and she was drop-dead gorgeous. She had beauty, brains, and brawn—the full package. Lisa previously had been married to Marquise Brown, a famous football player, who'd left her for some nineteen-year-old after ten years of marriage. Newly divorced only a year now, Lisa was getting her groove back. Her divorce had left her with a $7 million settlement. She was a rich bitch who was now in the process of opening a preschool not far from Lakeside Junior High School, called Hamilton Day-Care Center. After divorcing, she'd taken back her maiden name, Hamilton. Lisa Brown was gone! Return of the Mack, baby.

"I must admit it feels good to be getting away. I can't wait to be lying on the shores of Aruba." Sierra smiled, closing her eyes.

"Me and you both, girlfriend. I told my husband, 'Do not call me. I will call you!' After I've had a few drinks and several laps in the pool, that is, and I figure that should take about—oh, I don't know—five hours or so. I told Nate, 'Don't wait up for me, honey. See ya when I see ya.'" Jenelle laughed.

Jenelle Collins had been married to Nate Collins, an ER physician, for nine years, and they had two boys and a girl. The boys were eight-year-old twins, and their daughter was just turning four. Jenelle's mother would care for them while Jenelle was away on vacation with the girls. Jenelle was also in the medical field; she was a registered nurse who worked in the ER. Jenelle was the voice of reason and strength among her friends. She was the compassionate type and never ceased to help someone in need—she was a true caregiver. She was not quite as tough as Lisa, but she could hold her own.

Sierra was the meekest and most timid of her friends. She was indecisive most of the time when it came to personal matters and was quick to become frantic when things weren't running smoothly. In business, she was a beast, but her personality was like that of a baby lamb. She just wanted the world to be a beautiful place and wanted everyone get along. She was somewhat delusional but in a sweet way.

Then there was Chloe O'Connell. Irish Italian, mostly Irish, she'd graduated from Princeton with Sierra. She was single with no children. She was a beautiful, intelligent, hyperactive, and somewhat wild and crazy strawberry blonde who viewed Sierra more or less as her sister rather than as a friend. Chloe worked in journalism as a reporter for Channel 7 and was feverishly working her way up to become an anchor for one of the top cable news stations in Chi-town. She would stop at nothing to achieve her goals, even if it meant sleeping with the higher-ups. Fortunately for her, she didn't have to do such a thing. So far, her brainpower, tenacity, and hard work were leading her further up the ladder.

"Well, let me tell all of you this right up front: I am hoping to meet a tall, dark, and handsome man who can put a smile on my face for seven days, and if he is really good, I may bring him home with me!" Chloe said as the rest of the girls laughed loudly.

"You know what they say, Chloe: once you go black, you never go back!" Sierra said, and they all broke out laughing.

"Let the fun begin!" they all said, clinking their glasses together.

The ladies arrived on time at Chicago O'Hare International and made their way safely through the gate to board their plane with no problems. Lisa and Chloe sat together, and Jenelle and Sierra sat together across the aisle from them. They were in first class, of course. Sierra wouldn't have had it any other way. The seats were big and comfortable, and the food was top shelf; plus, they could drink champagne and get giddy. More importantly, Trak Airlines, which was owned by George's father, paid for everything. Trak was a company that prided itself on comfort, class, and excellent service. They were in good hands, according to Sierra.

"Ah, this feels wonderful," said Jenelle.

"We may as well get comfy. It's a five-and-a-half-hour flight. Hey, Chloe, want a pillow?" Sierra asked.

"Sure, thanks. You know, I can't believe we are actually going away, all of us together. We've been planning this for so long," Chloe said as she adjusted the pillow behind her neck.

"And now our plans have become a reality." Sierra smiled.

"My sister, Megan, wanted to come, but she didn't want to intrude," said Chloe, adjusting her headrest.

"She could have tagged along, Chloe!" exclaimed Sierra. "This plane—and Aruba—is big enough for everyone."

"I don't think her husband would have allowed her. She is such a slave to that man. I don't know. I think I will stay single for the rest of my life. Commitment is turning me off."

"You're just a bird whose wings should never be clipped, my dear," Jenelle said.

The plane started its path down the runway, full speed ahead. Minutes later, they were eye to eye with blue skies and fluffy white clouds. About fifteen minutes into the flight, breakfast was served.

"Looks good," Sierra said, twiddling her fingers.

"Now, this is what you call a breakfast. Eggs, bacon, home fries, toast, coffee, orange juice—not bad, Trak. Not bad. Kudos to George's family," said Jenelle as she spread jelly on her toast. "How's everything going with you and George and the, um, baby thing?"

Sierra sighed tiredly, reluctant to talk about the situation. "Well, it's still a sensitive subject with my husband and me. But he promised to talk about it once I get back from our trip. He even said perhaps we can start planning. That's a start, you know? I mean, he says this whole thing about being financially secure with Drum Technology and maintaining his title as CEO for at least four years will put us in the right place to be better prepared to start a family."

"You'll be thirty-six by then. Don't want to start having kids close to forty, CeCe. The body changes, my dear, and your chances of getting pregnant start to diminish. That's the nurse in me talking to you, but I know how much you want a child or children. If you don't start now or at least by next year, things get harder after that. I know you, Sierra, and I know you want at least four children. Correct?" Jenelle said.

"Yes, but I'll settle for two at this point. I mean, you're right about everything. And I agree with you, but my husband doesn't get it. Here I go getting upset about this all over again. I said I wouldn't talk or mention my baby woes."

"I'm sorry. I didn't mean to bring up the subject to stress you out, but we've got to be real here. George needs to take a chill pill and let you have your babies. Hell, it'll be you doing all the work anyhow, during and after. Just keeping it one hundred. You have more time on your hands than he does, so why is he trippin'? I mean, seriously!"

"Don't know, Jenelle. He just doesn't want kids right now."

"But you've been married almost eleven years! Hello! I don't know, CeCe. George is holding back for a reason, and I believe it has nothing to do with finances. Y'all ain't poor, okay? You're very well off. You intentionally slowed down with Sierra's Beauty Supply just so you and George could start a family. You're in the office for, what, three hours in the morning, and then you're home? You're home before the rooster crows twice. I don't get it. You need to leave the birth control pills alone and just do the damn thing."

"Jenelle! I can't trick my husband like that."

"Girl, please! You're his wife, not some hoe off the street trying to trap him. You're married! No trick or trap or any of that mess. George is beginning to piss me off. Eleven years of marriage, and he is still hollering, 'Not enough money!' Come on now. That line is old. Like biblical old. His excuse is as old as Moses!"

"Well, he has some validity to that. I mean, my mother used to tell us it takes more than love and kisses to raise a child. You need to have money," Sierra said quickly, defending her husband.

"And y'all got it! M-o-n-e-y all day every day. Sierra, you're my girl. We've been friends since grade school. There is something your husband is not being completely honest with you about. I don't know what it is, but you know what? Screw this conversation. Everything will be all right. You and George will talk about it when we get back. I bet he will be ready to screw your brains out trying to get you pregnant!" Jenelle laughed.

Sierra laughed with her and agreed. "No more talk of babies, getting old, and all that stuff." She looked over Jenelle's shoulders. Lisa and Chloe were giggling about something. All was well. She just wanted to free her mind and concentrate on Aruba.

After breakfast, Sierra figured she could finally close her eyes for a long nap. She was tired. George had woken her up at four o'clock in the morning just so she wouldn't miss the limo. She loved George for allowing her to go away with the girls for a few days. The two of them had been really going through it, and it wasn't all about baby issues. Sierra was tired of George's father's constant meddling in their lives. She knew Sam hated her, as did George's eighty-seven-year-old grandmother, Ruth. People thought it was hard to be in a biracial marriage. Maybe it was hard for everyone else, but it was not for George and Sierra. The love they shared for each other was genuine and respectful. Sometimes she wished the others would all just go away! His family was mentally draining.

Speaking of feeling drained, her body felt sluggish all of a sudden, so off to slumber land it was. About hour and a half into the flight, the rest of the girls followed suit and fell asleep. Hopefully, when they woke up, they would be close to landing on the beautiful island of Aruba.

***

Drum Technology conference room
11:30 a.m.

Executives from Drum Tech and Kline Computers had been behind closed doors for almost forty minutes. Everyone was waiting for a positive outcome in which Kline would finally sign with Drum Tech on the invention of the newly designed software and hardware engineered by Harry Filmore, Drum's top engineer. It had been the talk around Drum for more than six months now, and it would be a big, shining moment for George McAllister. It would be the biggest deal to close since the cell phone upgrade during the late 1980s. The clock tick-tocked away. George's secretary was called in twice for coffee.

It was one thirty in the afternoon when the conference doors opened, and everyone exited the room. After two hours of negotiating, finally, it was settled. There were many smiles. George's was the biggest. It was done: Kline Computers had signed the contract with Drum for $50 million. George would receive $5 million. The company was looking at major raises for its employees. Mostly, the money would be used to market and produce their new laptop design. The rest would go to the expansion of Drum Technology investments and other important business for the betterment of the company, including better health care, more vacation days for all, and something all the women had been complaining about for years: a day care within the company for all the working moms. Women made up about 60 percent of the workforce at Drum, from secretaries to office cleaners to managers to a few engineers, and of those 60 percent, about 40 percent were young and still of childbearing years. It was a great day at Drum Technology. It was time to go back to work until tomorrow afternoon, when the company was planning to shut down early to party and celebrate.

George couldn't wait to call his father. That he had earned $5 million from the Kline contract before receiving his own inheritance was a major achievement for George and a sweet slap in the face for Samuel McAllister III. Everyone congratulated George and his team as he walked back to his posh office down the hall and around the corner. He sat down in his overstuffed leather chair and exhaled.

"We did it, George!" exclaimed a happy Jim Melton, his CFO and best friend.

"Yes! Man, can I tell you how good I feel right now? This has been a long time coming. When my wife gets back from vacation, we're going to go on another vacation!" He laughed loudly.

Jim popped open a bottle of champagne from the fridge in George's office and poured two glasses of the bubbly. "And now you and Sierra can practice making those babies she's been pressuring you about."

George smiled and nodded in agreement. "Yes. I think—no, I know—we can start that family she's always wanted. I want kids too, Jim, but you know I had to be sure about a lot of things first. This right here will secure our future to be able to start a family. Oh, my baby is going to be over-the-top happy."

"She will be very proud of you, George," said Jim, taking a sip.

George looked at his wristwatch. "They should be landing in Aruba around five thirty. I'll wait until she gets settled in her hotel room before I call to tell her the good news." He could not stop smiling.

"Here's to making babies and making money, George!" Jim toasted as he raised his glass high in the air.

★★★

In flight, Trak Airlines

The ladies awakened from their naps and expected to land in another hour or so, according to their itinerary. Dinner had been served, and now it was time to chatter away, for soon they would be in Aruba, enjoying island sun and contemplating lots of fun.

However, an hour later, they were still in flight.

"It's five thirty, Jenelle. Shouldn't we be preparing to land soon?" whispered Sierra.

"Yes, we should, but no one has said anything. Usually, the flight attendant would have made an announcement by now."

Both were confused that no announcement had been made to prepare for landing.

"We didn't get our time mixed up, did we?" asked a nervous Sierra.

"Of course not. Maybe we are circling the airport. That happens a lot when there is heavy air traffic," said Jenelle, looking for the flight attendants.

Six o'clock came and went, and still, there was no sign of the flight attendants. Sierra began to stir in her seat. There wasn't any turbulence, so what was the problem? Six thirty turned into seven o'clock. Lisa leaned over and told Sierra and Jenelle that she was going to summon a flight attendant. She pressed her call button, but no one came until seven thirty. They were two hours late in landing in Aruba. Something wasn't right. Sierra and Chloe began to panic a little.

"Yes, ma'am, can I help you?" asked the flight attendant. She was holding a drink and a napkin in her hand, heading toward the cockpit.

"Yes, hi. My friends and I are concerned that we have not landed in Aruba yet. It says our flight was due to land at five thirty eastern standard time. It's seven thirty! Can you tell us what's going on?" asked Lisa, visibly upset.

The flight attendant smiled like a Stepford wife and replied, "Oh, I'm sorry. While you and your friends were asleep, we touched

12

down in Miami. Other passengers had connecting flights. There was an hour layover. We should be in Aruba by eight thirty."

As she started to walk away, Jenelle grabbed her arm gently. "Wait a minute! We had a nonstop flight! Here's our itinerary right here." Jenelle pointed out to her their flight information.

The flight attendant's eyes grew wide, but she appeared annoyed, thinking the group of women seated comfortably in first class were going to give her hell. "I'm sorry about that. You must have made a mistake, or you weren't given the right confirmation, but this flight, 5005, is a connecting flight. Listen, try to remain calm. We're only an hour away from landing. Can I get you all a drink or a snack?" she asked sweetly.

Lisa and Jenelle said no, but Sierra and Chloe wanted a glass of wine.

"Be right back with the wine, ladies." She smiled and walked toward the cockpit.

"Something is not right here. I know damn well there were no confirmations regarding a connecting flight," Lisa said as she looked out the window. It was beginning to get dark.

"Can I say I'm scared right now?" Chloe stuttered.

Jenelle touched her arm and rubbed it. "It's okay, Chloe. Just some kind of crazy mix-up. In an hour, we'll be checking into our hotel and sitting by the pool for an evening swim." She smiled, but Chloe was not smiling, nor was she convinced all would be okay.

"I'm with Chloe. I don't feel right," Sierra said, looking around. There were only about twenty people on the plane. When they'd left Chicago, it had been close to a full house.

The flight attendant came back with their glasses of wine and smiled, telling them, "Everything is okay. Simply relax. These things happen."

"No, they don't happen," whispered Chloe. "Someone screwed up our flight information. God, my nerves! Please let this wine calm me down, because I'm feeling really frantic right about now."

★★★

Chicago, Illinois
8:00 p.m.

George had left the office early, around four o'clock. He ordered takeout from his favorite restaurant before heading home. He was ecstatic at the day's events. That day, he had become a millionaire, and he just wanted to go home, open up a bottle of his favorite wine, and wait to hear from Sierra. Six thirty came, and still, no word from his wife. He tried to reach her on her cell, but the call went straight to voice mail. At home, relaxing with their dog, Bo, a beautiful, sweet collie, he waited patiently to hear his wife's voice tell him she had made it safely to Aruba. He'd expected her to be excited, and perhaps she'd unpacked and gone straight to the pool or beach, but not to take one minute to call? It wasn't like her to do such a thing. It had been close to three hours since their plane's expected arrival in Aruba. The clock struck 8:45 p.m. Still, no word from his wife.

He called the hotel where they were supposed to be staying, Dolphin Lagoon Resort, and asked if a Sierra McAllister had checked in. The front desk clerk said no one by that name had arrived, and there were no reservations for a Sierra McAllister or her friends.

"What the fuck?" he exclaimed. *No reservation? Okay, this woman is tripping.* He had specifically watched his wife make reservations at Dolphin Lagoon, and now they were claiming there never had been a reservation to begin with.

He got back on the phone and called once more to have the desk clerk check again. Again, she said, "I'm sorry, sir. No reservation for a Sierra McAllister. So sorry."

George dialed Jenelle's husband, Nate, to see if he had heard anything. He too was awaiting a call from his wife. He was worried because he knew Jenelle was always on time with everything.

George called the head person in charge at Trak Airlines. This was his father's company, and the situation was totally unacceptable. He did not appreciate any type of mix-up or discrepancy when it came to customers, especially his wife. Where the hell was she? One

14

thing was for sure: he was going to get to the bottom of this, and somebody was going to pay royally for the mistake.

"Chris, this is George McAllister. Listen, my wife's plane, flight 5005, has not landed in Aruba yet. They were supposed to touch down at five thirty this afternoon. It's now nine thirty at night, and there's no record of them checking into Dolphin Lagoon Resort either!" he screamed. "What the hell has happened?"

"George, calm down. I have all the information right here. I can't do anything about their hotel reservations; you'll have to call the hotel. But I can tell you this: flight 5005 was not heading to Aruba today. Are you sure your wife gave you the correct information?"

"Yes! I saw the itinerary and confirmation with my own eyes, Chris! So if 5005 was not heading to Aruba, where was it going?"

"Trak Airlines flight 5005 landed hours ago in Paris, France, George! There were three flights around the time you say she was supposed to be on one. Flight 335 was scheduled to land at five thirty in Brazil; 6010 went to Los Angeles, California; and 2444 went to Sydney, Australia. That's it! No Aruba flights, George."

George screamed out angrily, "What! Listen, Chris, something's wrong. Someone messed up somewhere. I don't know how or where, but right now, my wife and her friends are in flight or have landed somewhere they shouldn't be. Please find out where they are. I'll give you an hour, and I'll call back."

"Sure thing, George. I am so sorry. I will find them and find out what happened. Hold tight. I'll call you back, okay?"

George was shaking with fear, practically near tears. "Yes. Yes, please. Call me back. Call me right away the moment you hear something, Chris."

George called Jenelle's husband and told him the bad news that the women were missing. Nate informed him that he was on his way over to his house. The two men, scared and upset, decided to come together to figure out what to do next. The first order of business was to call the authorities. A report had to be made. George and Nate could barely contain themselves. They were wrecks and were panicking.

In the meantime, George kept trying to call his wife on her cell, but each call went straight to voice mail.

★★★

Somewhere in Brazil
10:00 p.m.

Sierra and her friends were hysterical. Sierra looked out her window. It was pitch black outside. She couldn't see anything.

The flight attendant smiled and told them quietly, "Welcome to Aruba." But they were not in Aruba. They were in Brazil.

Immediately after the last passenger left, the flight attendant closed the door and walked to the cockpit. The pilot winked, and the copilot gave her an envelope and a thumbs-up.

The other passengers exiting the plane were happy to be home. Sierra and her friends walked through the breezeway into the airport, which was pretty much bare, on the dingy side, and much smaller than they'd expected. One thing was strange: everything was written in Spanish. A few men and women with vacuums and cleaning buckets passed by. Sierra asked one who smiled at them strangely, "Where is baggage claim?" The lady just smiled and looked at them, for she didn't speak English. She spoke only Spanish.

"Oh my God." Chloe gasped. "Where are we? We are not in Aruba!"

"I speak Spanish; let me ask her. *disculpe señorita, donde estamos?*" Lisa said.

"*Estás en Brasil,*" the woman replied sweetly.

"Oh, sweet Jesus! We are in Brazil! Oh my God. We got on the wrong-ass plane!" yelled Lisa hysterically.

"Okay, listen, y'all. Let's go find a police officer or somebody who can help us. It's going to be all right. We'll get help and get another flight out of here. Come on. Let's go," said Jenelle.

They walked through the small airport, not knowing which direction to follow. Fortunately, Lisa was fluent in Spanish. The rest of the ladies simply followed her lead. When they arrived at baggage claim, a gentleman near the office was locking the door. Lisa asked for a police officer. The man spoke enough broken English to give them some answers.

"Sorry, senorita. The airport closed. No more flights tonight. The police will patrol outside for two hours after the airport closes. They make rounds every thirty minutes. You will need to walk to the other side to purchase tickets, but that's only if there are flights leaving tonight. Those gates are now closed to the main area of the airport. Wait out front here. An officer will be stopping here in about thirty minutes. Be safe. This not a good area to be stuck." He turned to walk away.

"Can you wait with us, sir?" pleaded Sierra. Her hands were sweating and shaking like leaves.

"I'm sorry. I must go home to my wife and family. Just be patient. Police will ride past here very soon." He left.

They waited outside and sat on a bench. It was dark and slightly chilly. Only one streetlight in the pickup zone shone from the sidewalk. Sierra and Chloe began to cry. Lisa cursed heavily. Jenelle was quiet, already in survival mode, something she was good at. She didn't have time to cry or curse. It would have done no good at that point; plus, it would have interrupted her thought process regarding what they needed to do next. When Sierra tried calling George, she couldn't get a signal and was unable to get through.

They waited and waited. Thirty minutes turned into forty-five, and then an hour passed. Suddenly, a car approached them. Two men got out. They were not police. The men grabbed Sierra and her friends and forced them into the car. All of them began screaming, kicking, and hollering for help, even Jenelle. The man in the passenger seat pulled out a gun and told them to shut the fuck up, or he would kill them. The women quieted down and cried softly, hugging one another. Sierra and her friends had been kidnapped—and it had been planned.

Immediately, the passenger got on his cell phone and dialed someone. Lisa overhead the conversation but could pick up only bits and pieces here and there because the kidnapper was speaking too fast. She heard him say, "It is done. We have them. We're taking them to the caves." Lisa would not let on to them that she knew the language. She had to play dumb. It just might save them if she could collect information, learn the kidnappers' plans, and alert the others, giving them an opportunity to strategize. Her mother often had said, "Don't let the left hand know what the right hand is doing." This was such a time.

They rode for nearly two hours, traveling down a long, dark, and lonely road surrounded by lots of trees and foliage. They were in the jungle. The driver parked the jeep by a cave–like building. There were men standing guard with guns outside the entrance.

"Okay, get out! *¡rápidamente! Vamos!*" said the kidnapper, pushing the women and forcing them through the door to the cave.

Chloe screamed at him, asking, "Why are you doing this? What do you want from us?"

The kidnapper yanked her arm and threw her through the doorway, screaming obscenities Chloe couldn't translate. The women were put in a cell. Was this jail?

Just down the hall, they heard the sounds of other women crying. It was cold, musty, and poorly lit, and it smelled horrible. The floor was hard concrete, and there were puddles of dirty water here and there. Chloe couldn't stop sobbing. Sierra was in a state of shock. She could not believe what was happening to her and her friends.

"My God. I think they are going to sell us for human trafficking. Lisa, what could you gather from what the kidnappers were saying?" asked Jenelle.

Lisa whispered so the bad guys could not hear her. "The kidnapper said while we were in the car, 'It's done. We got them.' He also said, 'He owes us big-time,' whoever *he* is, and they want their money now!"

Jenelle said, "So we're being held for ransom. But why? Who would do this to us? And how in the hell did we get on the wrong plane? I bet our families are worried sick. Listen, right now, while no one is looking, everyone put your passport, credit cards, ID, and cash under your feet inside your socks, so whatever they take from us, if we can escape, we will have money to do it. Just don't take your sneakers off."

"Good idea, Jenelle," said Sierra, and the girls quickly hid their information, money, and credit cards in their socks and hurried to put their sneakers back on.

"And to think I was going to wear my red stilettos!" said Chloe.

"Glad you didn't," said Jenelle.

"Perhaps I could have stabbed one of them with a stiletto," Chloe said.

Huddled together, waiting to see what would happen next, the four friends made a quick vow that no matter what, they would fight for their lives if it came down to a hand-to-hand battle with the men.

"I love you all," said Sierra.

"We love you too, CeCe," her friends said together.

"We're going to survive this. We just have to remain calm. We have to be smart. Do as they say, but stay alert. Remember, only the strong survive. We've been kidnapped, and there's nothing we can do about it right now, but we will do something about it. We will try to escape. We have to, or we will die. Now, let's try to keep warm. Lisa will continue to listen in and keep a low profile. No more crying. We have to be strong. Let's survive, ladies. Okay?" said Jenelle.

"This is horrible, Jenelle," whispered Chloe. "How are we supposed to stay positive when we don't know if they are going to kill us or not? I'm scared!"

"We have to pray and hope and stay calm. Fear will weaken us. Stay strong. Time for our faith to kick in."

An hour passed, and there was no sight of the bad guys. The women were cold and hungry and needed to use the toilet. Sierra called out for help. A guardsman approached their cell. He spoke English.

"Please, I need to use the toilet, sir. Please?" asked Sierra, pleading and crying at the same time.

The guard stared at her for a few seconds and then said, "Follow me." He didn't seem mean but, rather, empathetic. Perhaps he could help them escape.

He unlocked their cell and walked them down the long hallway past other cells. There were women in those cells also. They looked weak, tired, dirty, and exhausted from crying. A few were demanding food and clean clothes, but the guard ignored them. They used the toilet one by one as the guard looked on. It was humiliating.

"What is your name?" asked Sierra carefully.

The guard snapped angrily, "Don't talk to me. You ask me no questions. You understand? Hurry up—get back down to your cell!"

He slammed the gate and walked away, eyeballing Sierra angrily.

"Okay, what was that all about, CeCe? You trying to make friends with these people? Psyche 101 is not going to work with these men. They are terrorists. Got that?" Lisa growled softly in her ear.

"I was testing his patience to see if he had a little heart or sympathy for us," whispered Sierra.

"Did it work?" Lisa quipped.

Sierra turned her head in shame and began to cry.

"Now is not the time to question these men with stupid questions, CeCe. They're not dumb. Evil, yes. Dumb, no," Lisa whispered. As Sierra's eyes filled with tears, Lisa hugged her and told her she loved her and didn't want anything bad to happen to her—to any of them.

"I think we should try to get some sleep, but someone has to stay awake. Sierra and Chloe, why don't you two go to sleep first, and Lisa and I will take the second shift? Sound good?" asked Jenelle.

The women nodded in agreement, and soon Sierra and Chloe had huddled together to fall asleep.

Friday Morning, October 21, 2016

According to Jenelle's wristwatch, it was twelve thirty in the morning. *Thank God I don't rely on a cell phone to tell time,* she thought. *Hardly anyone wears a wristwatch today.* Jenelle was a nurse. She was always looking down at her wrist to take pulses and respiration. She hoped their kidnappers ignored her watch and didn't take it away along with all their other personal belongings they snatched from them.

Time passed slowly during the wee hours of that morning. Jenelle woke Chloe and Sierra at 3:30 a.m., and then Jenelle and Lisa fell asleep, but it was short-lived. Around five o'clock, Julio, one of the guardsmen, summoned for them.

The ladies were taken outside and forced into another jeep. One other woman, who had been in a cell by herself, joined Sierra and her friends. Her name was Ashanti. She was African and spoke little English. It seemed she had been taken care of better than the others. She was young and tall, with an athletic body and long cornrows in her hair. She had a pretty face, but it was broken with sorrow and heartache. Sierra looked at her with sympathy and held her hand. Ashanti managed a tiny smile and then looked away, frightened.

It was damp outside. The trees were dripping with dew. It seemingly had rained like crazy last night.

The driver started the engine and headed toward the entrance. Lisa listened in on their conversation in Spanish.

"Julio, this is crazy. Why don't we keep them here? Alberto is going to be pissed!"

"Listen, Herbieto, the boss said to bring them to Rojo Village, near the bay. Apparently, that's where they will feed them and let them get cleaned up before Raul decides where to transport them to next," replied Julio.

"I'm not staying all day and all night with these bitches! I have things to do!" Herbieto yelled. He had stood guard all night, and he needed to be somewhere else that day.

"Tell that to Raul! We only have twenty-four hours till the boss pays us, and then we can take off to anywhere in the world we want."

"It's just that I've never done anything like this before. I have a wife and children. She thinks I'm cheating on her when I don't come home at night," Herbieto whined.

"Twenty-four hours, *mi hermano*! Quit complaining. One more day, and we are out of here. Shit! Grow some balls, would ya?" Julio yelled.

Oh my God, Lisa thought. *They are going to sell us off for human trafficking just like we thought.*

It was a long drive. Thirty minutes later, they were taken to a warehouse near a body of water. It was a bay where boats docked and checked in and out all day. It was Raul's property—a fishing port used for undercover dirty dealings, including transporting women as sex slaves. Across the water was what looked like a small town of some sort. Behind the warehouse was the entrance to the jungle. Most people who came there had no idea it was used for such evil. At the small neighboring village across the bay, men came to charter fishing boats before heading out to sea. Behind the warehouse, which the public was forbidden to enter, was the building where Sierra and the others would stay before being shipped out. Somewhat of a holding house, it was pretty on the outside, but ugly spirits roamed on the inside.

Julio pulled up alongside the building behind the warehouse and escorted the women inside. It was much cleaner than the caves. There they would be fed, bathed, and dressed for auction. At the front desk sat a beautiful Brazilian woman, who simply smiled as the group passed her by. Sierra thought, *Why in the hell is she smiling? Does she even know why we are here?*

They followed Julio down the hall and entered a large room to their left. It looked like a posh living room complete with a bar and overstuffed furniture. Julio commanded them not to sit their smelly asses down on the furniture.

"Wait here!" he growled.

A few minutes later, a well-dressed man in a designer white linen suit appeared and looked them over. He was Raul, the big boss. He stared at them intensely, pacing back and forth, before giving his approval that they were worthy to be sold to a select group of men.

Afterward, another pretty woman walked in and led them to the bathing suite. She commanded them to remove all their clothes and pick a shower stall. The woman's cell rang, and by the look on her face, she was as happy as a lark to receive the call. She told the women to get cleaned up and pick an outfit from the closet. The woman sat down by the window as Sierra and the rest retrieved clothes from the closet.

"Are you kidding me? They're all jeans and white sweatshirts!" said Chloe.

"I heard that, you!" said the woman, cradling her cell to her ear. "Just get dressed, and shut up!" Based on her demeanor, she was somewhat of a bimbo and not very intelligent. Bimbo had a pretty face and a nice body. That was it. She turned her attention away and continued talking on her cell.

During their showers, Lisa listened in as much as she could to Bimbo's conversation. She learned Bimbo was planning to sneak out with her lover after the men left for a big auction that night. Sierra and her friends were group number four. Group three were already at a hotel in the city. Raul and the rest had scheduled Sierra's group for tomorrow night.

The water felt good coming down all over their bodies as the soft scent of white-lily-and-orchid shower gel emitted a fresh aroma throughout the bathing stalls. They were clean all over, with their hair and bodies completely washed and cleansed. Afterward, the women got dressed in the suite. Bimbo was still on the phone but had walked into the next room for private sex talk with her lover.

"Lisa," whispered Jenelle, "could you get any info from Blondie over there?"

"Yes, I did. Come close. Apparently, we are part of a group who will be sold off tomorrow evening. Also, the men usually leave for the night as the one guard watches the house we're in right now. Get this: the guard is Bimbo's lover!" she whispered.

"Great! You know what this means, don't you? We can try to escape tonight. Hurry up! Let's get our dirty socks over there; pull out our credit cards, IDs, and cash; and stuff them into our clean socks and sneakers right away. Hurry—before she comes back in," said Jenelle.

The women quickly put on their sneakers and tied them tightly. Ashanti had no idea what they were doing, but she knew when she saw them stuff money into the socks that perhaps they were planning to take off. She didn't know how, but she knew that something was going on and that they had a plan.

Sierra looked at Ashanti and whispered to her, "Don't worry. You're coming with us. Just be quiet, and pay attention, okay?"

Ashanti understood and nodded, smiling with tears of hope in her eyes.

"Time for battle," Lisa said.

"I just overheard her telling someone to pick up the dresses today for us. That Raul wants us looking like high-class pros," Sierra whispered to Jenelle.

"I bet he does. Only we are not going to be there for the runway show. Somehow, someway, we must get away before he sells us off; otherwise, by this time tomorrow, we'll be the property of some pervert and his desires. Not going down without a fight," Lisa said.

"I am right there with you, sister," said Jenelle.

Sierra and Chloe were the most afraid and doubtful that an escape could be pulled off. They were in another country, in a place they knew nothing about, not even the language. How were they going to break free from such tight security? Where would they go? How would they survive? The only place to run to was the jungle located just outside the windows. It looked like a big place in which to get lost or killed.

Sierra was angry, scared, and defenseless. Just who in the hell did that man think he was, grabbing all her friends and placing them under submission? Why had Sierra and her friends, out of all the millions of women in the world, been chosen to be kidnapped? Not that she wanted any woman to be abducted. There they all were, changing clothes, taking showers, and being commanded to do this and that. It was as if they were living a nightmare. Someone had disrupted their way of life and forced them into ugly, evil plans by including them in some sort of prostitution ring. Worst of all, they had no defense.

Sierra knew she had to toughen up and grow a backbone. No more whining and crying. Those monsters cared nothing about her emotions. It was time to put on her thinking cap, as Lisa and Jenelle had said, and help come up with a plan to evacuate the premises. But how? She was a zillion miles away from home. Jenelle and Lisa were talking about escaping through the jungle, but then what? There were all kinds of predators in the jungle, animals that could eat them alive. They had no form of communication, because the kidnapping bastards had taken their purses with their cell phones and other personal things. At that moment, she prayed to God in heaven to send down an angel to help save their lives, lead them on a path to freedom, and keep them safe from harm. She prayed in the name of Jesus Christ and said, "Amen."

Sierra realized her faith was being tested. The thought of never returning home and of being someone's slut or used property didn't sit well with her.

Even though Lisa had a tough exterior, she was deathly afraid, as she should have been. She was only human. The monsters who'd grabbed them were not. Sierra was afraid, but if she was going to see her precious George and her parents and siblings again, she needed to put on her poker face and strategize.

After they were clean and dressed, the women patiently waited to find out what was going to happen next. They were quiet yet attentive. There was no way this was going to be the end of their lives. As they sat there waiting for their next command, Sierra began to daydream about her husband and her family. She shed a tear at the thought that she might never see them again. She thought of her sisters and brothers, whom she was close to; her parents, whom she loved deeply; her grandparents, who would be celebrating their seventieth wedding anniversary soon; her darling little nieces and nephews; and, lastly, the baby she might never have with her husband. If her life ended there, what would become of George?

Would he grieve for a long time or remarry soon afterward and start a family? The family she'd been longing for the past eleven years.

"Sierra, baby, you okay?" whispered Jenelle, who sat next to her on the lounge chaise in the parlor room.

"No, Jenelle, I am not okay, but I guess I have to be. I just cannot believe this is happening to us. And why? More importantly, who would want to do this to us?"

"I don't know why or who, but I do know we will get out of here."

"Nelly, you cannot be sure of that. Let's not kid ourselves here. We have been kidnapped and imprisoned against our will. Right now, we are not in control, and we're not winning the battle. I am petrified!" she whispered, sobbing.

"Come on, sweetie. Pull it together. In order to defeat the situation, we must stay sharp, think smart, and fight. We have to fight, and we will as long as we stick together. I love you, my friend, so hang in there with me. With us. You hear?"

Sierra nodded. "Yes, I hear you. I will try to hang on, because I do not want to die here. I promise I will fight."

"That's my girl. We're going to make it. We are. Don't give up on us yet, okay?" said Jenelle with a slight smile.

"Nelly, if we don't make it, this is going to kill my parents, especially my mother. She has a bad heart. What if she has a heart attack?" Sierra cried again.

"If I know your mama well, one thing I know about her is that she is a praying woman. She will immediately give this situation to God. I believe that. Now, it's time for us to trust the Lord, Sierra. We have no one else who can deliver us. Let's have faith."

"Right now, my faith is broken. My mind is racing. How could this have happened, Jenelle? I clearly made reservations for a nonstop flight to Aruba."

"I know you did. We all got a copy of the flight information. Someone has been watching one of us or all of us, wanting to kidnap us and sell us off. I just can't imagine who. I've been thinking all kinds of crazy thoughts, like maybe it was someone I treated at the hospital who was unhappy with my care or my husband's care as an ER physician. Perhaps someone died on my shift, and the family blamed me. I just can't seem to figure it out, CeCe."

"I don't think there is an explanation as to why or who may be responsible. I have seen many programs on television about predators like these people. They lurk about, seeking to find women to sell into the sex slave industry. It's scary, Jenelle. I'd rather die."

"Well, I'm not ready to just roll over, lie down, and die without a fight. I believe in my heart we are going to survive."

"Survive this ordeal tonight or survive years of being some pervert's sex slave? That's not survival. That's hell on earth. Torturous hell too. No, I meant what I said. If there is no way for us to escape, let me die. I can't live like that," said Sierra, staring into Jenelle's eyes.

Just then, the bimbo came marching into the room, yelling at Sierra and Jenelle to shut up and break up their little huddle. She didn't want them sitting so close together. At one point in her life, she had been right where they were right now. She had been only seventeen when she was captured. She was thirty-seven now and more or less had earned her escape-from-death card by being a loyal, trusting assistant to Raul. She was obedient and never caused problems or tried to escape like the rest. Bimbo was Raul's woman, and if anyone tried to do harm to her, that person would suffer like one could even imagine.

Chapter 2

Friday, October 21, 2016
Chicago, Illinois

It was raining, with thunder and lightning, late in the season—no surprise at that time of year. Whenever the start of spring or fall was near, there was always a terrific rainstorm to signal that a new season was approaching. George was a wreck. His hair was unkempt, and he had been drinking scotch all day. It had now been thirty-six hours since Sierra and her friends were reported missing. Where was his beloved wife? He was tired of calling the police department fifty million times a day to ask if there was any news on Sierra and her friends' whereabouts.

His best friend and colleague, Jim Melton, had come to console George and offer moral support by extending a helping hand in locating his wife and her friends, but first, he put on a fresh pot of coffee. George was drunk. During the day, George was fine, but at night, he became depressed and got drunk. Sierra's missing status was a legitimate reason to get wasted.

"It's been almost two days now, Jim. Where the fuck is my wife?" he slurred.

Jim placed a hot cup of coffee in front of him. "Here. Drink this coffee, George. Got to sober up so you can think clearly, my friend. What I don't understand is how come the air traffic controllers haven't been able to locate their flight. What happened to it? Did it just disappear from radar or what?"

"Yeah, or what? Fucking idiots! Trak Airlines is one of the top airlines, if not the top airline, in the world."

"Have you talked to your father about this, George? I mean, surely he can do something. After all, it is his company."

"Jim, my father, the great Samuel McAllister the fucking Third, doesn't give a shit about my black wife. I'm sure that racist

28

bastard is smiling with glee over the fact that her flight mysteriously went missing and—"

"George! What is it? You look like you just saw a ghost!" exclaimed Jim.

"Oh my God. No way. No. Just no. It just can't be. Oh, no fucking way. I think I know," George said, dropping his head down.

"Come on, man. You're scaring me. You know what?"

"He did this. That son of a bitch did this!"

"Who did what, George?"

"My father. He is responsible for my wife's disappearance. I don't know exactly how, but this is his fault. His doing. My God, my father is a monster, Jim. A real live monster. Sweet Jesus." Suddenly, George was no longer drunk, and he hadn't even taken a sip of the coffee yet.

"George, that's a pretty harsh accusation. Watch it, my friend. Your dad may be on the prejudiced side, but I mean, I don't think he—"

George quickly cut him off. "Yes. Yes, he would do such a thing. It all makes sense now. He was so adamant about Sierra flying first class, saying, 'Only the best for my son's wife. Blah, blah, blah.' I mean, he went on and on with the phony bullshit, only I had my guard down. I was just so happy he'd offered to do such a nice thing that I never imagined in my wildest dreams it was a plot to get rid of her. He did this. Somehow, he orchestrated the redirection of Sierra's flight. He is so full of hate that if his evil deed meant her friends possibly would get hurt, then so be it. My darling Sierra, baby, I am so sorry." He walked over to the window, watching the crash of rain hit the ground. It was like a monsoon out there.

"I don't know what to say, George. You really believe your father would go to such great lengths to do this to your wife?" Jim asked sadly.

"Yes, I do," he responded softly, still standing by the window, gazing out.

"So what are you going to do? I mean, how will you approach him?" Jim asked, confused.

"Straight out. Blunt. To the point. Raw—no chaser. Only way to deal with Sam. But then again, maybe I should play dumb. Once Sam knows you have caught on to his shit, he can whip up another plan quicker than you can blink an eye. No, I have to be smooth about it. I have to be the hunter. Set some traps. Lead my prey right to me. Yes, that's it." George smiled.

"I can't believe Sam would do something like this, but when you told me that when you told your family yesterday that your wife has gone missing, he just watched you freak out and stood there with a look on his face like he wasn't surprised. That does raise an eyebrow or two, George. I bet your mom is devastated. She likes Sierra, doesn't she?"

"My mother is a dear, sweet woman. And yes, she loves my wife. How she hooked up with my father is a mystery to me. But you know what they say. Opposites attract. People think Sierra and I are opposites because she is black and I am white, but that's just skin color! Real opposites are my father and mother. That's a whole different definition. Good and evil. It's about character. He's an ugly one. Always has been, really. I forced myself to love him because he was my dad. Not anymore."

"Now, George, remember, this is all speculation on your part. What if this was just some horrible accident? A twisted coincidence of some sort?" Jim said, standing up.

"Not a coincidence, Jim. It was planned. I know what I am feeling. It's all coming back to me. I remember the weeks leading up to Sierra planning this vacation with the ladies. She told my mother she was going away on vacation without me, just her and her friends, and that was when my father intervened and slithered his way in. He had motive and opportunity. His motive was his hatred for my wife because she is black. And he had the perfect opportunity by offering to let her fly with Trak. Yes, Samuel McAllister III is behind this, and, Jim, I will prove it. Listen, I, um, have some phone calls to make. I'll be up late, so don't stay. Go on home to your wife. Hug her. Let her know how much you love her," said George with tears in his eyes.

"It's still early, George. Let me help. I can do whatever you need me to do, but let me help you get your wife and her friends back home safe and sound. You know you can trust me," said Jim.

"I know, Jim. I know, but I need to catch and trap him on my own."

"Be careful, my friend. Call me if you need me. I mean it."

George turned to hug Jim, thanking him for his support. He was grateful to him, but this was something he had to do on his own. It was time to get to work. The first thing George wanted to do was wiretap his father's offices at home and at Trak Industries. Most likely, Sam used his cell to conduct business, so George had to figure out a way to monitor those calls. It was the only way he could catch Sam. Perhaps a private detective was in order. He had to be on point with this and make no mistakes. His father was a clever man not easily fooled. That was why he was so good at manipulation.

★★★

Somewhere in Brazil
6:00 p.m.

After the women were dressed, they sat and waited a long time before their next command. Bimbo escorted Sierra and the rest downstairs to the dining area to eat dinner. An older man in his midseventies, followed by two aides, entered the room, carrying trays of food. He must have been the cook, Sierra thought. He was dressed in a chef's outfit, but he looked depressed and tired. He eyed Sierra with pity and walked away to leave the servants to do the rest. The women were starving. They hadn't eaten a real meal since they were on the airplane. In the cave, the guard had given them only crusty old bread and water. In front of them were rice and beans, baked chicken, empanadas, green beans, and iced tea to wash it all down.

"Eat up, *chicas*," said Bimbo. "This may be the only decent meal you get for a long time."

Chloe eyed her with contempt. *How could she do this to another*

31

woman? Not unless she was brainwashed and trained this way. Who knows how long she has been in this business?

Somehow, Sierra didn't believe she was as evil as the rest. She was just flaky and, yes, trained to do exactly as the men ordered her to do.

They tore into the food like wild vultures. Bimbo, whose real name was Sheila Penney, called out to the cook, telling him to make sure her champagne was chilled for later, as she was preparing to sneak out with Herbieto. It was his turn to guard the transition house while all the others went to the auction. According to the plan, after Raul and his men left for the night and after Sierra and the others were taken to their sleeping quarters, Sheila and Herbieto would sneak away to Raul's private minimansion just a few steps away from the holding house to have a private party alone.

Sheila left the dining area and told the ladies she would be right back. She headed toward the reception area, where another guard would soon be relieved by her lover, Herbieto.

"Sierra, what are you doing?" asked Chloe as she watched her grab about a dozen empanadas in a napkin and stuff them under her shirt.

"I'm stealing food. What does it look like? If we're going to escape, or at least try to, we will need food for our journey. Just mind yourself right now. Go ahead—stuff a few under your shirt," said Sierra, and Chloe followed suit.

After their rushed dinner, with which they were fully satisfied, Sheila returned and led them back upstairs to their suite, where all of them would be locked in for the remainder of the night until tomorrow morning. There were three beds, which meant they would have to share beds. Sierra and Jenelle slept in one bed, Chloe and Lisa slept in one, and Ashanti slept alone. There was no television, radio, or anything that could connect them to the outside world, just a lamp and a Bible on the nightstand. Ashanti picked it up and began to read. She was quiet. She hadn't said a word since they'd been there.

There was a window in the hallway, but the women were on

the third floor. How were they going to escape while locked in and with only one window in the hall?

"Look, Nell. There is a window over here by the toilet and basin," said Chloe.

However, when Jenelle pulled the curtains back, they saw the window was way too small for any of them to fit through. She cracked the window to get some air and sat on the commode, thinking.

"I think we should get some sleep, Jenelle. It's been a long, scary, day," said Chloe.

"Who the hell can sleep, Chloe?" cried Sierra.

"We have to, CeCe. We need our strength to get out of here. Right, Jenelle?" Chloe said.

"Yes, we need to rest," she replied softly, "but I have to think of a way out of here. This is our only chance to try to escape before morning. Lisa, could you translate any more of what Sheila was saying?"

"No, not much. Only earlier about meeting up with her lover later and then coming back to do rounds at midnight. Then something about screwing the life out of him before heading back here."

"Okay, listen. It's almost seven o'clock now. Let's get some sleep. I'll set my alarm for twelve thirty in the morning. After Sheila does her rounds and checks on us at midnight, we'll get up, and I will start working on that door over there. We have to be long gone before the sun rises, which is around five thirty," said Jenelle.

"How are we going to unlock the door without breaking it down? Someone will hear us—the servants, the receptionist downstairs. There's no way to be quiet and skillful at the same time. We don't know how many people in this house are armed and ready to shoot. We don't!" cried Sierra.

"We have to take our chances," said Lisa. "If we want to free ourselves and live, we have to at least try. After tomorrow morning, we're done, baby girl. We don't know if we're going to be sold off, separated, or killed. If I die, it will be because I died trying to save myself. Fuck that! Nobody is going to put a dead stamp on my life unless I give up. Not going down without a fight."

"Lisa is right! We have to try to save ourselves. That door has hinges, meaning it can be dismantled. We just need something sharp to try to unlatch the hinges," Jenelle said, looking around.

Just then, Ashanti pulled two metal sticks from her hair and handed them to Jenelle. She had her braids wrapped up in a bun, and the sticks had been holding it together. Softly, she said, "Will this work, Miss Jenelle?"

Jenelle smiled at her and hugged her tightly. "Yes, I believe it just may work, Ashanti. Thank you, sweetie."

"These were my grandmother's. She made them for me in Africa. I believe her spirit is with us. She would want me to use these if I needed to defend my life."

"And that we shall do," Jenelle said, still smiling at her. The others smiled with hope and gave Ashanti hugs.

Next, as planned, they got in bed and fell asleep. Jenelle had her watch set to beep softly at 12:30 a.m. Sierra was excited and hopeful but also scared to death. They were in a foreign country. They knew nothing about the terrain, the land, the city, or anything else. They didn't know which route to take once they escaped, if in fact they were lucky enough to escape at all. Right now, they had to get rest. They were going to need a lot of energy to pull this off.

By seven thirty, the women were sound asleep. However, Jenelle more or less catnapped. She didn't want to be knocked out, in case Raul and the others happened to change their minds and sneak up on them. She was frightened, but her warrior-like personality wouldn't let her give in to her fears.

The women missed their families. Sierra cried for George, wondering if she would ever see him again. That was all she could dream about. *He must be so afraid and angry*, she thought to herself. But she knew her husband would do all he could to find her and her friends. In the meantime, as Jenelle and Lisa had said, they all had to be strong and smart and get the heck out of Dodge before sunrise. After that, they were done. Perhaps dead.

★★★

Samuel McAllister's mansion, Chicago, Illinois

"Great. Everything is in place, just as I expected it to be. You'll get your money when I get confirmation she and her little posse have arrived safely in Bogotá. I want to hear from you personally, Raul. Not one of your henchmen or concubines. Understood?" Sam said as he leaned back in his chair, tapping a pencil on the mahogany desk.

"Like I said, I will contact you tomorrow evening after the auction. Have a good day, Senor McAllister." Raul smiled with an evil grin.

George's suspicion was right. Sam McAllister had orchestrated the kidnapping. Although Sierra had made reservations at the Dolphin Lagoon Resort in Aruba, Sam had paid his daughter-in-law Bethany to call the hotel to cancel the reservations. Bethany was the wife of his eldest son, John. She was the uppity type and came from wealthy parents who possessed the same mentality Sam did. Just like her father-in-law, Bethany felt Sierra did not belong in the McAllister family, so she was more than happy to help rid Sierra's presence in the McAllister family. However, she had no idea of the horror involved. Sam also had paid the hotel clerk in Aruba $10,000 to act is if no reservations ever had been made to begin with if his son George called to check it out. Sam knew once the women were reported missing, George would call everyone. He had to cover all bases. The tainted poison that George had brought to their family tree had to be eliminated.

Sam's vengeance on Sierra wasn't solely based on her being Black. Sam hated the fact that George was the only son who constantly challenged him on everything. George's brothers never gave Sam such a hard time about business or anything else. George had been defiant ever since he was a child, and his marrying a black woman, whether she was educated and beautiful or not, was just another act of defiance against old man Sam. Well, this time, his defiant son would feel his wrath after years of disrespecting him and his wealth. No jigaboo would ever inherit his billions. That didn't happen where he came from. Sam loved George, but he'd had enough of his oppositional defiance. *Time to pay the piper, Son.* Even if it meant losing his own flesh and blood.

★★★

Raul's holding house, Brazil
12:00 a.m.

Jenelle automatically woke up when she heard Sheila fiddle with the key to the door. Sheila was laughing and giggling while commanding Herbieto to shush. She was drunk. The room was dark. Jenelle pretended to snore.

Sheila hit the light switch. She noticed they were all safe and secure in their beds, knocked out. When she saw that everything was okay, she stumbled out of the room and, in the process, dropped her key, forgetting to lock the door behind her.

Jenelle thought to herself, *Thank you, Bimbo. You just made our lives easier! Stupid bitch.* Jenelle tiptoed to the door, cracked it open, and watched Sheila and Herbieto go down the staircase and out the door. She hurried to the end of the hall, peeked out the window, and saw them disappear behind the trees, walking a short way to Raul's minimansion. She could see one light on in the distance, hiding behind all the green foliage and plants. She snuck past the staircase, pressed herself firmly against the wall, and saw the receptionist dozing off downstairs. It was time to wake the others.

"Sierra, Lisa, Chloe, Ashanti, come on! Get up! Get up now!" she whispered, shaking them hard.

The women rubbed their eyes and gathered their things. Jenelle told them to put on sweaters from the closet. There was one sack in which they could store the empanadas and other necessities for their journey. Lisa volunteered to carry the backpack. Jenelle told them that Sheila had forgotten to lock the door, so now there was no need to break it, but they had to get past the receptionist, who was dozing off and on.

"Is everyone ready?" asked Jenelle.

"Yes," they replied together.

"Okay, first thing I want to do is put the receptionist to sleep."

Chloe laughed and said, "How in the hell are you going to do that? Did you stash some hypodermic needles in your shoe?"

"No, silly," said Jenelle. "There is a way to put someone to sleep with just your fingers. I am going to sneak up behind her and do just that. That'll give us enough time to get out the door."

"Or we could use the side door downstairs next to the dining area," said Sierra.

"How do we know if there are guards outside somewhere?" Lisa said.

"We don't have time to debate, guys. We'll just have to take our chances," said Jenelle, and Sierra and Ashanti agreed.

"Sheila said all the men were in the city at the auction. Only Herbieto was supposed to guard the house tonight. What about the warehouse next to us?" asked Lisa.

"Screw it, Lisa. Let me put the receptionist down first to get us out the door, and we'll talk afterward. Remember 'Kill or be killed'? I'm heading down now. Follow me. Quietly now," said Jenelle as she began her catwalk down the stairwell.

The group following behind her. They stopped as Jenelle tiptoed to the front desk. The receptionist had her back turned, watching television, and the second she nodded off, Jenelle did her sleep-hold technique on her with her fingers somewhere behind her neck. Girlfriend was out like a lamp.

Damn! Sierra thought to herself. *Jenelle got skills. She is a registered nurse, after all.*

"Come on! Hurry!" Jenelle said to them. It was dark and quiet. All the servants slept on the second floor, so everything looked good for their escape, until Jenelle tried to open the door. It was locked. She scrambled at the receptionist desk, trying not to make noise, looking for a key, but there was none.

"I think this door has an electronic code, Nell," Chloe said. "We have the same type of security at the news station. We'll never be able to break the combination! Now what?"

"The dining room side door," Lisa said. Off they trailed to the back of the house, and lo and behold, the dining room door was in plain view; however, it too had a security code.

"Oh my God, we're trapped!" Sierra cried.

"No, stop it, CeCe. Let me think right quick," said Jenelle. She was examining the window next to the door. It was sealed shut.

The next thing they knew, the kitchen light came on. It was the chef. He had walked in on them. They gasped and shook with fear.

"What do you think you are doing?" he asked with a pointed look.

"What does it look like, old man? We're trying to free ourselves," Lisa snapped. She was angry and scared, not knowing what the old man was going to do.

He stared at them for a few moments and then pulled out a small ring of keys. "You'll set the alarm off by trying to jar those windows and doors and get all of us killed. You'll also never make it out alive through the jungle." He entered the code to the dining room door, and the light turned green as he slowly opened it for them. No alarms went off, because the key he had was programmed to the doors in the house.

"Thank you, sir. Thank you!" cried Sierra, giving him a quick hug.

"My daughter was taken by Raul's men years ago when she was only fifteen years old. I never saw her again. He kept me here as a slave to cook for women he brings here to get cleaned and fed before he auctions them off. I haven't seen my beloved Carmelita in over twenty-five years." He shed a tear. "Good luck to you all."

"Why don't you come with us, mister?" Sierra said.

The old man looked up into her eyes with great sadness and

grief. There was a quick spark of interest. Suddenly, he felt perhaps he could be free also. This was his only chance, perhaps his last.

"Come on! I promise if you help us, I will make sure when we get back to America, you live like a king, and perhaps we can help you find your daughter," said Sierra.

"I would only slow you down. I'm seventy-five years old," he said with slight skepticism.

"It's okay. You can direct us on which way to go," Lisa said.

"Look, we have to hurry up here. Make up your mind, sir. Either you're coming or not. I'm sorry. I don't mean to be disrespectful to you. It's just that the longer we stay here chitchatting, the greater the chance we get caught. I mean, look, you caught us trying to get out the door! Let's make it. Now!" Jenelle said.

The old man grabbed an overcoat in the closet and led them out the door. They followed him through a path toward the jungle he obviously knew well. His name was Eduardo. He told them to call him Eddy. It was cold, and the sounds of native animals and birds could be heard throughout the weeded fortress. Eddy told them it would take about four hours to get to the road that led to the neighboring village, but they had to keep walking. According to Jenelle's watch, that meant they would reach the road sometime around three thirty or four o'clock in the morning. Daylight would appear an hour or so thereafter.

"Do you think you are up for this, Eddy? Are you going to be all right?" asked Sierra. She was genuinely concerned for him and his health.

"I'll be fine. Suddenly, I just got a new lease on life and a big burst of energy. No one has ever survived after trying to escape the Rojo House. Tonight is quite different from all the rest. There always is more than one guard watching the house. At least four! But tonight there is an excessively big auction. Women from all over the world will be sold off. I saw Herbieto leave with Sheila, and I knew they wouldn't be back for a couple of hours after they checked on you ladies. However, if Raul finds out they were in his home, he will kill them both. This man is ruthless. That's why it's important we make it to the road before sunlight. I know another path once we cross the road."

"Eddy, how come we can't take one of the boats and go across the bay to the village?" asked Chloe.

"Because the boats have tracking devices on them for when fishermen come to rent them. There is no one in that village across the way but merchants and fishermen. Lots of them. I was a fisherman once. The warehouse is just a big freezer to store fish to be shipped all over Brazil."

They trekked their way through the thick jungle with only the light from the moon to guide them, trying to avoid snakes, bugs, and all other creeping, crawling things. Around one thirty in the morning, they took a quick break and ate an empanada a piece. Sierra had managed to save sixteen of them. Eddy informed the ladies they'd only walked two miles and needed to walk three more in order to make it to the road. Once they reached the main back road, he would direct them to a small remote village far from Raul's compound. Eddy knew the village well, for he and his wife had raised their beloved Carmelita there. The village wasn't terribly big but big enough for them to get lost for a day or two. If they could make it to Pueblo Azul, there was a good chance Eddy could get them transportation. It was a must. Once Raul and his henchmen got wind that Eddy had taken off with Sierra and the rest, all hell would break loose. He would send out trackers. It was imperative they get out of the jungle before daylight so the dogs could lose their scent. Once they crossed the road Eddy spoke of, it would take another half hour or so to get through the river, which was only three feet high. Pueblo Azul was about twenty minutes through the reefs.

Sierra and Chloe were tired but pressed on. They had to. They didn't have a choice. If Eddy could endure the rough walk through the jungle, so could they. They rested for only five minutes at a time before getting back up to walk again.

"Tell me, Eddy. How come you haven't tried to escape before? It seems like it would have been easy. You just punched in a code and led us through the jungle," Lisa said, biting into an empanada.

"I had no hope. No reason to. Plus, it would have been impossible. Like I said before, this is not your typical night. Every guard is with Raul in the city. You girls gave me hope. I knew something was different about your group when you all first walked into the dining room to eat. I felt you all would try to pull something like this. However, you aren't the first. The only difference between you and the others is they never made it past the gates or the guards. Why Raul left you all in the hands of Herbieto is a mystery. The man is careless and has a bad temper. He'll be dead tomorrow. Sheila too. Perhaps Margarita as well." He sighed, taking a deep breath.

"What! He is going to kill them?" asked Chloe, shocked.

"Of course! He's not going to scold them or take them over his knee and spank them. They're dead. They left their post and allowed you all to escape. You women must have rich parents or husbands. Raul only deals with multimillionaires. Trust me. You've been chosen. All of you."

"But, Eddy, you don't understand. We were on our way to Aruba for a girls-only vacation. None of us are filthy, rich as you suggested. I mean, we're not suffering financially, but still. Jenelle is a nurse. Lisa is a principal at a school. I own a small beauty and hair supply company. Chloe is an anchorwoman. Not sure of Ashanti's financial status, but I can assure you we're not filthy-rich women," said Sierra.

"Someone who is awfully close to you must be. I am telling you what I know. Someone paid good money to kidnap one of you or all of you," he said before he took the last bite of his empanada.

"Okay, let's be real, Sierra. We're not poor or broke. We are financially well off, you could say, but no one in my world would do such a thing!" said Lisa.

"Then someone has deeply betrayed you," said Eddy.

Eddy looked weak. Sierra felt bad for him and thought, *I wish we could carry him or something.* He said he was doing all right and just needed to keep moving. He ordered them up onto their feet. Sierra could hear all kinds of hissing sounds and creatures making night calls. It creeped her out. *Four more hours until sunlight.* They had to pick up the pace.

Around three thirty in the morning, it began to rain hard. Buckets of water fell quickly and steadily. There was nowhere to run for cover or shelter. Eddy said the best thing for them to do was keep moving. Then, out of nowhere, something jumped out at them. It was a monkey. It latched on to Chloe's hair, screeching. She screamed. They all tried to get it off her, but it was ripping her hair out of her scalp, until Eddy pulled out his switchblade and stabbed it in the throat. Poor Chloe was bleeding from her head. The monkey had taken a nice chunk from the back of her head. She was shivering and crying and in severe pain.

Jenelle pulled from Lisa's backpack a small towel, poured some peroxide onto Chloe's head, and dabbed it dry as much as she could. The rain was washing it away. Chloe kept complaining that her eyes were burning, and her neck felt as if it were breaking, but Jenelle examined it, and it was not broken, thank God. She couldn't move her neck. Jenelle created a makeshift neck brace using the towel and some short branches and leaves and wrapped it around her, tying it with the leaves and the end of the towel. Chloe couldn't stop crying. Soon she would need medical attention. Sierra hugged her, saying how sorry she was and that she loved her. But the love and kisses were not taking away the pain. The back of her head was exploding with pain.

"It will be okay, Chloe. We're going to get out of here, sweetheart. We're going to make it, okay? Hang in there. We've got you."

"It hurts so bad!" she cried, choking back tears. "I think I should just give up. I don't know if I can stand it, CeCe."

"No! Not going to give up! I know it hurts, sweetie, but we're not leaving you here. Come on. Latch on to me. We've got to keep moving."

The rain continued to fall heavily. They had gained another mile, and according to Eddy, they had roughly two and a half more miles to go before they reached the road. By then, it would be daylight, and their chance of getting caught would be high. If they could make it to Paddle Road before sunrise, they would be fine.

Chloe's head pounded as if someone were beating drums on her head. She needed pain medicine, but Jenelle told her the human body could survive that type of attack. Of course, it would be painful until she could get some medicine, but they had to keep moving in spite of it. They managed to walk half a mile before Chloe had to rest for a moment. Then Ashanti did something nobody expected: she positioned Chloe to carry her on her back. Chloe was petite, no more than a size three and less than five foot two. Ashanti said she had carried jugs of water heavier than Chloe on her head in Africa.

"Queen! Reigning!" Lisa told Ashanti, smiling.

After that, they were in full speed, ripping through the jungle, trying their best to make it to Paddle Road before five thirty. It was closing in on the last hour.

★★★

Chicago, Illinois
Saturday, 7:30 a.m.

George awoke early that morning to someone knocking on the door downstairs. He got out of bed, walked downstairs to the front door, and looked through the peephole. It was his mother. She was on her way to church to pray for Sierra and her friends.

George hugged her and invited her in for breakfast. She declined but did accept a cup of coffee. George's mother was matronly looking. She didn't dress fancy or wear expensive designer things. Her style was simple and plain, yet she was beautiful. She doted on her sons, and she loved all her daughters-in-law. However, George was her favorite child. He was the middle son. Most middle children were ignored or pushed aside and had to fight for position. George surely had to fight for position with his father but not with his mother. She adored him and always seemed to have his back against his father and his brothers, who'd mocked and teased him throughout his life.

43

"Mom, it's early. Mass doesn't start until eleven. Why are you here so early? I'm happy to see you, but is anything wrong at home?" he asked, sipping his coffee slowly.

"Well, yes, Son. I mean, everyone is concerned about your wife. I know you don't believe this, but your father is doing all he can to find out what happened."

George looked at her and saw innocence in her eyes. She had no clue. His father was persuasive and cunning. Ellen McAllister was always easily led by her husband. Sam was so cunning, he could charm the pants off a snake. It was a mystery to George how his darling, sweet mother could have been attracted to his father. It apparently was true that some women went for the bad-boy type, because Sam was rotten to the core.

"I doubt that, Mother. He hates Sierra, and everyone knows it. I just wish everyone would stop pretending like there's no ugliness going on in this family. And I wish you weren't so blind to it."

"Oh, Son. Your father loves you. He does. He's hard on you because, well, he sees a lot of himself in you. You're fearless and a go-getter. You're intelligent, and you're a fighter. Your brothers John and Mike are just skating through life, waiting for money and things to be handed to them. I know your father has some old prejudiced ways, but he means well."

"Means well? Mom, he's a racist! There's no meaning well about that. Listen, Mother. Listen to me. I love you. And I understand your position. You are a dutiful wife who loves her husband no matter what, but the truth is, I despise my father, and I don't want his money or even his twisted love. I don't. I have all the love I need from you and my wife. I used to try to work hard to please him so I could make him proud and inherit my millions but not anymore. It means nothing to me. I learned through hard work that I can do it myself! And I have done just that. Right now, my wife is missing. I don't know where she is or what has happened to her. I'm sad. I'm angry. I'm hurting. I need answers. I need to find the woman I love. Dead or alive. I will get her back. And then, Mother, I am done with Samuel McAllister."

"Son, you act as if this is all your father's fault." She gasped, holding her throat.

It is, Mother. And once it's proven he's behind all this, I hope you will leave him and try to enjoy the rest of your life.

After his mother left, George took a shower, got dressed, and headed out to meet his private detective friend, Jess Livingston, in town at the Log House Grille for lunch. He planned to disclose to Jess that he was convinced his father was responsible for his wife's disappearance. He was ready to hire Jess to do the job of gathering evidence in order to bring Sam down. There would be no more Mr. Nice Guy for George McAllister when it came to his father. He knew the risks involved, and once he was proven right about his father, he knew his brothers would disown him for life. Somehow, he felt his mother would not, but if protecting his wife meant alienating himself from his father and brothers, so be it. He did love John and Mike, but they were definitely on their father's side when it came to not wanting black blood tainting the McAllister name, so if he had to lose them in the process as well, so be it. He would never forgive his father for doing such an evil thing to his wife. Never. It was time to get started.

Jess accepted the job and got right on it after their lunch meeting.

In the meantime, George did a lot praying and a lot of pacing around the house. His company had just landed the biggest deal of the century with Kline Computers, and now tragedy had struck. He was at the top of his career at Drum Technology. Everything was going well. Finally, he had made it big financially without the help of his father's regulated million-dollar stipulation. Before the kidnapping, he'd wanted nothing more than to politely tell his father what he could do with that stipulation. George was finally prepared to give his beautiful princess what she always had wanted: children. Sierra had no idea that at one point, they had been on the brink of bankruptcy and losing their home. George had lost in the worst type of way with several shady investments that had failed. Then Kline

Computers had come along and saved the day. He was back in the saddle, and this time, he was going to do right by his finances.

George had a queen for a wife. She was the strongest and most loving, caring, and confident woman he had ever met, and she was his! He'd planned to finally tell her upon her return from Aruba that he was ready to make the family she always had wanted. This woman had been down for him since their college days and had waited patiently for him to do his career thing, and still, she had his back. If having children was the only gift she sought from him, he would be honored to give Sierra her heart's desire.

He cried day and night for her, continuously praying to God to bring his wife back home to him safe and sound. It was as if someone had reached deep inside his soul, snatched the living love of life out of him, and then taken off full speed ahead, never turning back to give him a chance to try to get it back. Then came the guilt trips. If only he had done this or done that. If only he had gone on vacation with her, as she had suggested from the beginning. *Coulda, woulda, shoulda. Means nothing as this point.* Sierra was missing in action, and he hadn't a clue where to look. But one thing was for certain: George was thoroughly convinced his father knew exactly what had happened to his wife.

In his mind, George wanted to believe that his father would never be that ugly and do such a thing, no matter how much they didn't get along, but his heart was telling him differently, and his heart was winning the race. Sam McAllister was the type of man who set his mind on something and then made damn sure it was completed. In fact, his father had taught his sons to always finish what they started.

George came home after his meeting with Jess and fixed himself a drink. The house was quiet. It was just him and their dog, Bo.

"What are we going to do, Bo?" he asked, petting the dog with sadness. "My father is behind this tragedy that took your mama away from us. But he's going to pay. And once he does, you, Sierra, and I will finally have peace. But take notes, Bo. You're going to be chasing after a couple of kids! Mama and I are going to fill this lonely, big ole house with the sounds of children laughing, crying, and playing—all of that. My dear Sierra, I owe you. Lord, you know I'm not a praying man, but if you can hear me, please, dear God, send my wife and her friends back home to us safe and sound. And make whoever is responsible for this pay dearly."

George held his dog close to his heart and teared up. Time dragged on slowly for him. He started to reminisce about when he first had met Sierra in college nearly thirteen years ago. It had been instant attraction for George. He never had seen such beauty in all his life. He remembered walking back to his dorm from the library, smiling from ear to ear. Being struck by Cupid's arrow for a black woman was new to him. There was something about her that stirred his soul. She was classy, sexy, and obviously beautiful but also intelligent. Sometimes the two didn't go hand in hand, but Sierra seemed to have it all. She was kind and confident, not cocky or arrogant but sure of herself. He liked her strength. He remembered asking her to lunch at Giovanni's Café. She ordered a turkey panini and salad. George had spaghetti. They talked for almost two hours that afternoon. Then, a week later, he asked her out on a real date.

It took three dates before he got his first kiss from Sierra. Once they became a couple, things got a little crazy for them. Some of the guys on campus did not like the interracial couple of George and Sierra. Several of his peers didn't like it. Sierra's friends were okay with it. Regardless of who liked or didn't like their being together, George and Sierra fell in love, and there was no stopping them after that. As a matter of fact, the adversity made their relationship even stronger.

His parents hadn't learned about Sierra until their senior year in college. From the start, George's mother was accepting of his son's choice for a wife. George had no intention of continuing to just date Sierra; she was the woman to be his one and only forever. George's father exhibited resentment from the beginning. He made it clear he did not approve of his son dating, let alone wanting to marry, a black woman. He was cordial with her, but he kept his distance and made sure George knew she would never get his full approval. That bothered George, but his father's disapproval never stopped his love for Sierra or his quest to marry her.

Sierra and George had a nice-sized wedding shortly after graduation. Sierra's parents loved George and went all out for their daughter's wedding day. Sam McAllister did not attend his son's wedding, nor did George's brothers, John and Mike. His mother was the only family member standing in for George. The Jacksons treated Ellen with much love and respect. They even invited her to sit with the family during the reception. Ellen was overwhelmed with joy to know Sierra's family and friends were so accepting of her and her son. From that day on, there was nothing but respect for the Jackson family from Ellen. However, for Sierra and George, it was the beginning of many years and acts of subtle aggression and of hurt and pain caused by his family. Each and every time, George stood up for his wife against his father and his brothers.

George's closest friend back then never had a problem with George's dating and marrying a black woman. A few of his friends had dated women outside their race, and it wasn't about the color of their skin; it was about the nature of their character. There were some differences when it came to dating sistas. Men might have had to work a little harder to come correct with them, but overall, for George and his friends, women were women.

Please, Lord, bring my wife and her friends back home alive and safe. I should have left Chicago after I married Sierra. She kept saying she wanted to live in California, but no, I accepted the position at Drum Technology versus Belt Industries in Los Angeles. I should have listened to her. She's missing because I had a weak moment with my father. I was just so happy he finally showed my wife some love by offering to have Trak fly them to Aruba. He even hugged her and gave her a kiss on the forehead, looking her straight in the eye, smiling, and wishing her fun with her friends. And all the while, he was plotting and scheming to rid the family and me of her. His own son.

48

The phone rang. George jumped up to see if it was Sierra. *Think of the devil, and he appears.* It was his father, Sam. He was acting fake by asking if there was anything Trak could do to help locate Sierra and her friends, as it was his airline. George almost threw up. He was fuming, but he never let on that he knew his father was responsible. He played dumb and said calmly, "No, Father. There's nothing you can do, but thanks." He hung up the phone, cursing.

Chapter 3

Brazil
Saturday, October 22, 2016

The rain had stopped around four thirty in the morning. Sierra and the group had successfully made it to Paddle Road. They rejoiced and hugged one another. Even Chloe, with her head still in horrific pain, was happy to have survived a rough night in the jungle. The sun was slowly starting to rise. They crossed the road and headed toward the river surrounded by trees. Eddy, tired and becoming weaker by the minute, led the women across the long river. When they got to the other side, he said he needed to rest.

Sierra rushed to his side. "Eddy, are you okay?"

He was out of breath. "Yes, sweetheart. Just not used to staying up past my bedtime," he joked. "I am okay. Hungry, though."

"Here. Eat the last of the empanadas," said Lisa.

"He is dehydrated," said Jenelle, checking his pulse, temperature, and respiration. "He needs water. Rest here for a few minutes. Is this pretty much a safe area, Eddy? Just how far away are we from the kidnappers' warehouse?"

Eddy caught his breath. He was starting to look a little better after resting for a few moments. "We're about five or six miles north of Rojo Village. Not far if you have a car but far enough. Right across the lower hills behind us is Pueblo Azul. My home." They all hugged him and cried with Eddy.

Eddy then said, "We cannot stay there, ladies. It will be the first place Raul will look for you and me. Once we get into the village, if my old neighbor is still alive, he can get us transportation to get to Rio."

"'As in Rio de Janeiro?" exclaimed Sierra.

"Yes, my dear. Rio is roughly a three-hour drive. If we get transportation, we'll be home free. We can get to the airport and

50

be on our way to your beloved America. I want to go with you all. Did you mean what you said about helping me find Carmelita?" he asked Sierra.

"Yes, I am serious, Eddy. I will do all I can to find your daughter, no matter what. I will find a way to locate her. Dead or alive," replied Sierra.

"Thank you, my dear. Thank you," said Eddy, trying to swallow some saliva. His throat was bone dry, as were the others', but Eddy's health was most important. Only he could lead them to freedom.

"Eddy, is Rio the city Raul was talking about where they auction the women?" asked Jenelle.

"No. He takes them to a small city across from the fishermen's land. Rio is too open. He would never risk himself there. Listen, we have to get going. Raul will be heading back to his home soon. Bidding closes at six o'clock in the morning. We must get to Pueblo Azul now!" Eddy said as Lisa helped him to his feet.

He wanted his freedom just as much as the women did. If he could get to America, he would be happy. He'd never been anywhere outside Pueblo Azul. Once, he and his wife had gone on vacation to Rio when Carmelita was five, but that was it. Eddy was feeling light-headed and needed his blood-pressure medicine. He didn't want to tell Jenelle. She was a nurse and would worry sick over his blood pressure going up, he thought, so he kept quiet for now. Perhaps when they reached Pueblo Azul and located transportation, he could get to a pharmacy to fill his prescription. Right now, they had to move onward toward Pueblo Azul.

★★★

Raul's compound, Rojo Village
6:30 a.m.

Raul's limo pulled up to the back of the warehouse next to the house where Sierra and the others had been held captive. After a long, successful night at the auction, Raul wanted food and his woman, Sheila. But first, he had to check on the girls.

51

The driver parked the limo alongside the holding house and opened the door for Raul. He stepped out, wearing black shades, a tailored black designer suit, and shiny black shoes. The warehouse was closed, as it was Saturday. He summoned a few of his men to go fetch some fish from the freezer inside and deliver them to Eddy to prepare for him. He wanted fish, rice, and eggs for breakfast.

Seconds later, three black SUVs pulled up and parked behind the limo. Six of Raul's men were laughing and talking about last night. Raul smiled, knowing it had been one of the best auctions yet. "Time to celebrate," he told them as they headed toward Raul's minimansion. Raul punched in the code to the holding house and walked in to find Margarita and the rest of the small staff standing in the hall with tears in their eyes.

"What is going on here? Why are you all standing here looking like sad little puppies?" he asked angrily.

"Senor, there's no easy way to tell you. The women upstairs—"

He cut Margarita off. "What about them? Why are you all standing here twiddling your damn fingers, when there is work to be done? Where is Caterina? She was supposed to relieve you, Margarita! What the hell is all this? Cat got your tongue? Out of my way!"

"Sir, what she is trying to tell you is that the women are missing," said one of the servants.

Raul stopped dead in his tracks. "What did you say?" He lowered his voice to a whisper.

"They're gone, senor. Caterina is here, sir. She went to do rounds, and they're gone!" Margarita said, exhaling.

Angrily, he asked where Sheila and Herbieto were. Margarita told him she hadn't seen them that morning, just once all night, after the first check. Since then, they couldn't be found.

"How did they escape? How did they get past you, Margarita?"

She began to cry. He stared at her for a long time before he slapped her across the face. The servants gasped and put their heads down in tears. He dismissed them all to their quarters, except for Margarita.

"I'll ask you again. How did they get past you?"

"I must have fallen asleep. I am so sorry, boss. I am. Please forgive me!" she cried.

Just then, Herbieto entered the reception area with Sheila. He looked disheveled, as if he had just woken up. His clothes were wrinkled and messy. Sheila looked the same. Guilt was written all over both their faces. Raul knew they had been together. *All night.* He was furious, and they knew it. They also knew they would be dealt with.

"Boss, I checked their room. It's true; they're gone and nowhere to be found," said Domingo, his right-hand man.

"Eduardo is missing as well," added Julio.

"So that's how they escaped. Eduardo must have figured out the security code."

"No, Raul. Our security has not been compromised. He must have used a key," Domingo said. "The only people who have keys are the guards. Julio was with us last night, as were the rest. It must have been—" Domingo stopped to look at Herbieto.

"Hey now, don't look at me. I had my keys on me the entire time I was—"

"The whole time you were what? Screwing this whore standing next to you?" Raul yelled.

"No, boss! The dogs were barking like crazy last night. Come to find out a monkey had found its way to their cage. I went to go see what happened, and I must have dropped them somewhere. I swear!"

The truth was, Eddy had stolen the keys from Herbieto when Herbieto came into the kitchen and demanded he cook a meal for him and Sheila that evening right after Raul left for the auction. The keys were in his jacket, which was hanging up by the kitchen door. When Herbieto wasn't paying attention, Eddy swiped them and placed them under his apron, in his pocket. He took them because he had a funny feeling Sierra and her friends might try to flee, as all the others had tried to do in the past and failed. This time, he was going to help the women escape.

Raul told Domingo to remove Sheila and Herbieto from the

property. Immediately, they began to scream and plead for mercy. No apology or plea could help them. As for Margarita, he spared her life and told her if she fell asleep again, she would be next in line to disappear. He was angry as hellfire. He ripped through the place, banging up things, while everyone watched. Raul was expected to receive a whopping $6 million for Sierra. Her friends would merely be innocent casualties. He didn't know if he would keep them as servants or if they would be sold off as well. Sierra was the hot commodity of the group. What was he going to tell Samuel McAllister now?

Raul marched to his mansion behind the holding house and told Domingo to begin a search with the dogs after he had taken care of Sheila and Herbieto.

Domingo wasn't going to kill them. He was just going to take them deep into the jungle and let them fend for themselves. He was tired of killing people. The jungle was an open grave. If they were going to die, it wasn't going to be by his hand; plus, he always had liked Sheila. She was the house hoe and did him like no other woman had ever done him before. *Goodbye, Sheila and Herbieto.* Domingo hoped they made it out of the jungle alive. Just like Eduardo. Somehow, he believed in his heart that Eddy and the women had escaped to safety. If so, he was happy for them. He hated Raul.

★★★

Village of Pueblo Azul
Saturday morning, 7:30 a.m.

Eddy and the ladies safely made it to Pueblo Azul. It had been a long time since Eddy had seen his hometown. Weekends were usually quiet, and that morning was no different. They walked a short way down the dirt road, passing folks' backyards, where chickens and pigs squawked with the start of a new day. Eddy approached the home he once had lived in with his wife and his daughter, Carmelita.

He began to cry. It was abandoned. He went to touch it and pulled a small piece of bark from one of the shutters for a keepsake. His wife had died many years ago, leaving him to raise his nine-year-old daughter. But he'd had a lot of help from his neighbors. Surely they would help him now if they knew what had happened to him.

About twenty-five years ago, Raul had come through one morning and ransacked the village, kidnapping girls to sell and enslave. He also hunted people to help run his business. Eddy was a chef at a local restaurant in the big city but lived in the village. Raul's men grabbed him and took his daughter for human trafficking—slavery. It was a horrible morning, even though the sun was shining, and the world seemed bright and new. For Eddy and several other families, it was the darkest day of their lives.

Now, twenty-five years later, God had sent him these women to use as a tool to escape to another land. He loved his country and his town, but without his beloved daughter, they meant nothing to him. Eddy never had stolen a thing in his life, but that evening, when Herbieto had been busy frolicking with Sheila, he had taken the opportunity to grab his keys. Unfortunately, none of the keys were to his jeep, or they would have been in Rio and gone a long time ago, but it was okay; they'd made it out regardless.

"What a beautiful, quaint little village, Eddy," said Sierra.

"Yes, it is. It was even more beautiful twenty-five years ago," he said, struggling to walk.

"Where are we going?" asked Chloe, holding her head. She was trying her best to take the pain, which came and went every other minute, it seemed. She kept telling herself she was okay. Everything was going to be all right, and the pain would go away. Ashanti had taken her off her back, and Chloe was able to walk the rest of the way through the river and into Eddy's village.

"Right past that tree with the wooden gate is where my friend once lived. He is about my age—if he is still alive."

They walked up to the side of the house and saw a woman about fifty-five years old hanging up sheets and towels. She turned around and was startled to see Eddy. She covered her mouth and began to cry happy tears. She knew exactly who he was. When he had been captured, she had been only thirty years old. Eddy had been fifty years old then. She placed her basket on a tree stump and raced over to him and the women. Eddy sat down, relieved to have finally found a familiar face. Her name was Teresa. Her father, Elonzo, Eddy's good friend, had died ten years ago, she told him. Her husband, Roberto, had left for work at the crack of dawn. Eddy explained everything that had happened to him and who the women standing next to her were. Teresa expressed her sorrow but rejoiced that they had been lucky enough to escape.

"Come. Come inside. I will fix you all a good meal. *Está bien?* And you can get cleaned up. I have fresh clothes for all of you. There are plenty of towels, soap, and shampoo in the bathroom."

Two by two, the women went into the bathroom to bathe. Teresa had a nice little cottage. It was not extravagant but better than the homes of most of the villagers. She had a tub; a single shower stall; and, next to it, a toilet that flushed with a strong force. Jenelle and Sierra went first, one in the tub and one in the shower. The clean smell of almond soap was sweetly intoxicating as the clear water cleansed their bodies to a heavenly fresh scent. Fifteen minutes later, Ashanti and Lisa took their turn as Teresa tended to Chloe's head injury with special herbs and plants to heal her wound. Once she was done, she took a bath as well. Teresa gave them all button-down dresses to wear. All the village women wore them, so they could blend in with everyone else. She cleaned their sneakers and gave them fresh socks. They felt like brand-new human beings.

Eddy told Teresa they could not stay long. They had to get to Rio but needed a car. After they ate and Eddy cleaned up, Teresa ran across the dirt path to Consuela's house and asked her husband if Eddy could use his car. Manuel walked with Teresa back to her house to verify if she was telling the truth. His '57 Chevy was the only car he owned, and it was in good condition. Because Raul had taken Manuel's sisters years ago, he gladly allowed Eddy and the women to take his car to drive to safety. Eddy didn't even have to worry about gas. Manuel would fill it up with gas, change the oil, wash it, and clean it out.

"Once we get to America, Manuel, I will make sure you are sent a healthy amount of money to purchase another one. I promise you this. We all do, and thank you. God bless you," said Sierra.

"We will never forget any of you for helping us," added Lisa, smiling with tears in her eyes.

"Teresa, I hate to leave, but Raul will be looking for us. Rojo Village is not far away by car. He will come here for sure. It will be the first place he will try to look for us. You must burn those clothes."

"I will, Eddy," said Teresa, and Consuela grabbed the soiled clothes and took them away to burn them. "I will miss you for life, Eddy, but my heart will sing every day, knowing you are free in another place. I love you, my dear old friend. Here—take this. It was Papi's. A leather wallet his father stitched for him when he was a boy. Remember me!" she cried, hugging him tightly.

"Okay, the car is ready," said Manuel, handing him the keys, "but you must get going. Eddy, do not take back roads, as that would draw attention versus blending in with the mainstream drivers. Be safe, and Godspeed to you all."

"Goodbye, my friends. Peace be with you. Goodbye, Pueblo Azul. You will always be my first love," said Eddy, and they all got in the car and took off.

"Are you okay to drive, Eddy?" asked Sierra, who sat up front between him and Lisa. Jenelle, Chloe, and Ashanti sat in the back.

"I am fine, my dear!" He smiled jubilantly.

Eddy made a quick right turn out of the village and headed three miles down the path to get to the main road before finding Route 110, which led to Rio. They were finally on their way. The first thing they needed to do was get to the local authorities, Sierra said, but Eddy was against it.

"You don't know who is working for Raul, my dear. He is an enormously powerful man. He has properties all over the country, and hundreds of people work for him. You cannot trust anyone. We're heading to the airport," he said.

"Eddy, we have American cash on hand and credit cards. Will we be able to use the cash, or do we have to convert it?" asked Lisa.

"No, we take American dollars here. It's worth more if you pay with your money. But I must tell you all something I didn't want to mention before. I need to get to a pharmacy to get my blood-pressure meds. I need them like yesterday. That should be our first stop, and then we can head to the airport. Is that okay?" he asked, starting to sweat from his forehead.

"Absolutely!" exclaimed Jenelle.

"Is there anything else, Eddy? Do you have a passport on you?" asked Sierra.

Eddy frowned and told them he did not. Ashanti then said she did not have one either.

"How do you expect to get on the plane? Oh my God! Ashanti, Eddy, you can't travel without one, and it's too late to—"

"That's the other thing I have to tell you. I know someone who can create one for me and Ashanti, but it will take him at least an hour once we get to him, and then we must hide out somewhere. I am sorry. If you must leave without me to risk not getting caught, I will not be mad at you, for at least I have made it to Rio."

"No! We're not leaving you or Ashanti here. We didn't come all this way to desert either one of you. Don't even think about it," said Jenelle, taking a deep breath.

"Don't worry; Rio is a big city. We will have no problem getting lost there until Jose is done with our passports. It will cost us, though," Eddy said.

"How much, do you think?" asked Lisa.

"I would say roughly five hundred American dollars," he replied slowly.

"We've got it. I have four thousand dollars in my shoe right now," Sierra said.

"What! Why in the hell do you carry so much money around like that?" asked Chloe, shocked.

"I was going to take us on a shopping spree once we got to Aruba," she said softly.

"Oh yes, Aruba," Chloe whispered, looking away.

"Obviously, it came in handy, right?"

Eddy and the women had been driving for more than an hour and a half and were now on the main highway. It was busy but not too bad. Traffic was going at a good speed. In one more hour, they would be in the city. Eddy would drive straight to the pharmacy to get his meds and a painkiller for Chloe's head. Only then would they be able to relax afterward. They were now far from Rojo Village. If all went well in the city, they would be on a plane to America by late afternoon. Sierra took a deep breath and exhaled with joy.

In the meantime, Raul's men had returned from a three-hour manhunt in the jungle. They'd found no trace of the escapees. Raul was so angry he shot one of the men for bringing back the bad news. Domingo looked down at his bleeding friend, whom he had known all his life since childhood, and held back tears. No one was allowed to touch him unless Raul said so. His friend died right in front of him, and he couldn't even hold him in his arms to say goodbye. It was quiet for what seemed like an eternity afterward. Then Raul ordered two men to take the body away. Inside, Domingo was fuming with hatred. It was as that very moment he wanted revenge on the man he'd been working under for more than ten years. He put his chin up as tears rolled down the sides of his face.

Raul smiled at his grief and walked away. "If you don't find these assholes, you will be next. Now, go!" he screamed in Domingo's face.

Domingo grabbed his bag of weapons and headed to Pueblo Azul, Eddy's last known address before he was kidnapped. He was going there not to locate Eddy but to find people he could trust and build an army to come against Raul for destroying their lives and their families' lives a quarter of a century ago. Everyone hated Raul. *I'm sure it won't be hard to get folks, especially the men, to join forces against him.*

However, most were afraid of Raul and would not dare come against him. He was too powerful. When Domingo arrived with two of his colleagues in Pueblo Azul two hours after Eddy had taken off, no one seemed to want to help. The villagers claimed they had not seen Eddy or did not even know of him. The people who lived there now were new villagers. The former residents were either too old or had died. If anything, the residents who lived there now were relatives or children who had grown up and taken over the family homes.

Domingo found Teresa and questioned her intensely. Mingo knew her father and Eddy had been best friends years ago. She remained calm and played dumb.

Manuel was watching from across the way through his screen door. Consuela begged him not to get involved. She didn't understand. Raul had kidnapped Manuel's little sisters. He walked across the yard and introduced himself to Domingo and his colleagues. Manuel did not snitch on Eddy but did say he would join forces to help destroy Raul.

Domingo and his accomplices, Ivan and Carlos, gave him honor and told him they would get in touch with him. They instructed him not to leave his home. Bringing down Raul would take skill. Destroying Raul would take precision and lots of ammunition. He still had many loyal constituents in his circle, and they were just as ruthless. Manuel did not care. His sisters were gone, probably dead by then, and he wanted to kill Raul just as much as Domingo did.

★★★

City of Rio
2:00 p.m.

"We made it, ladies!" Eddy said, and Sierra and her friends smiled and screamed out with joy.

Eddy pulled up to a small pharmacy and gave his script to the doctor. The doctor looked at Eddy suspiciously and asked who all the women were.

"These here are my daughters. This one here," he said, referring to Chloe, "is my daughter-in-law." He smiled widely. Chloe was the only white person in the group. Eddy was a black-looking Brazilian, so naturally, Sierra, Lisa, Jenelle, and Ashanti passed. They all appreciated his quick thinking. The pharmacy filled his prescription as the women purchased a few things, and then they were off to Jose's to get Eddy and Ashanti fake passports.

"I want to call our families to let them know we are all right," said Chloe.

"I wouldn't do that just yet, Chloe," said Eddy. "We should wait until we board the plane. Again, if anyone gets wind of who you are, it could cost you your life. We are almost in the home stretch now. Let's not mess it up by being too hasty."

"But we're basically home free!" she cried.

"No, Chloe. Eddy said no. He knows what he is talking about, and I agree. We are going to see our families soon, but we must get the hell out of here first. Okay?" said Lisa, hugging her. "It's going to be all right. Hold on."

"They must be worried sick! If we at least call to tell them we're okay and—"

"Chloe! No! The answer is no. Let's do this first. We're still in Raul's country. Now, just calm down, and relax," said Lisa.

★★★

Chicago, Illinois
4:00 p.m.

It had been a long day for George. He invited the families of Lisa, Chloe, and Jenelle over to his home to come together to have dinner, pray, strategize, and bond as they tried to figure out a way to locate their loved ones. He told the families he had a detective working on everything and would keep them updated every day or even every hour if need be. The families were devastated. Children missed their mothers, and parents missed their daughters. Nate and George were the only two husbands in the group. Each night they slept away from their wives was torture. Not knowing if they were dead or alive was the worst.

There was a two-hour difference between Chicago and Brazil. While Sierra and the rest waited for Jose to finish the passports, which, unfortunately, would take two hours, they needed to find somewhere to hide out.

Back in Chicago, George was trying to keep it together for everyone. Jess, the detective working on the case, said he might have something significant for George. He wanted to meet him bright and early tomorrow morning at his office if possible. George said he'd rather meet him away from the office, at a restaurant for lunch. They planned to meet at twelve thirty in the afternoon at their usual meeting place, Log House Grille. George was about to receive confirmation of what he already suspected and more.

This couldn't have been all about race, he kept telling himself. There had to be more than simply Sam's hatred of black people. What had George done to him that was so bad in his life that he'd had his wife kidnapped and sent away? George hoped Jess was able to find out where Sierra and the rest of the women were. One thing was for sure: he was never going to forgive his father. In fact, if his suspicions were true, he would do everything in his power to destroy him. George no longer had a father. As a matter of fact, he'd lost him years ago.

★★★

Playa Hotel, Rio

Eddy, Sierra, and the ladies camped out at a nice hotel in the city while Jose worked on the passports. There they rested, grabbed a bite to eat, and waited patiently for Jose to finish. Chloe took a few pain pills and went to sleep for a little while. Lisa followed suit. Sierra turned on the television. It was all in Spanish, but at least it gave her something to occupy her mind and her time while they waited. It seemed as if it had been ages since she'd watched TV. They'd only been missing since Thursday, but it felt longer than that, and if not for Eddy, they likely would have been separated and sold off into the sex-slave industry, lost forever.

Eddy rested on the sofa. He was tired, but for a seventy-five-year-old man, he'd held up well after all they'd been through. Eddy had lived a long life. Half of it had been good, and the second half, spent slaving away for Raul, had been hell. But this day, was heaven. Walking for hours through the jungle at night and in harsh rain had been a struggle for him. Still, they'd made it out alive.

***

Rojo Village

Raul sat in his home office, cradling the phone to his ear while he listened to Sam McAllister spit venom at him for allowing Sierra to escape. Raul was just as angry, if not more so, because a few of his incompetent staff members had allowed Sierra and the others to disappear without a trace.

"They had help, senor! One of my employees helped the women escape. When I find him, he will pay dearly—I promise you. There's nothing I can do at this point. My best men are on the trail as we speak, looking for his whereabouts. He couldn't have gotten that far. They're on foot. Be patient. We'll find them," he said, and he hung up the phone, fuming.

Sierra would have been sold that night. The others he would have kept as servants. No money was offered on their behalf. Raul was especially attracted to Lisa. She had a beautiful Latina glow about her, even though she was a black woman. He liked her style, her body, and her spunk. He had seen the tough-girl attitude in her the moment he laid eyes on her, and that turned him on. Now she was gone. He wanted her back. He wanted all of them back, including old-ass Eduardo. Just who did he think he was anyway—Superman?

***

Playa Hotel, Rio
4:00 p.m.

Jenelle looked out the window of their sixth-floor hotel suite. It was overcast and was getting ready to rain again. At least this time, they would not be in the jungle. She could not believe they had actually trekked through that massive jungle filled with snakes, monkeys, and other animals and survived. It felt good to be away from Raul's slave house. There was a strong sense of relief now that they were safe in a hotel, preparing to head back home. She kept taking deep breaths, trying to remain calm.

Lisa had awoken and was watching television with Sierra. Ashanti and Eddy were still sleep. Chloe was too. She was feeling better with the pain meds Jenelle had administered to her. Jenelle had informed her that once she got back to America, she would need plastic surgery, because that section of hair would never grow back. The monkey had viciously ripped it all away from her scalp, and it would forever be a reminder of the horror they all had gone through.

Around four thirty, there was a knock at the door. Immediately, Eddy woke from his sleep. He looked out the peephole and told the others to go into the bathroom.

"*Quién es?*" he asked in a low voice.

"I have a package from Jose Jimenez for Eduardo Montenegro," a young boy said. He was about fourteen years old and looked scared. He kept looking around.

Eddy invited him in, examined the package, and then opened it up. Inside were his and Ashanti's passports and an invoice for $1,000 American.

"I thought he said five hundred," Eddy said, confused, handing him $500 in cash.

"Two passports, senor. One thousand, *por favor.*"

Just then, Sierra appeared and gave the boy an extra $500. He smiled and grabbed the money. Then he left quickly, thanking Sierra for the cash. The boy raced to the elevator, rode to the first floor, and hopped into a car outside. He was Jose's grandson. Jose, waiting in the car, took the cash and gave his grandson $200, congratulating him on a job well done. Then they took off into the city to have a little fun.

"You can all come out now," said Eddy, smiling. "I've got it. This here is my ticket to freedom. Yours also, Ashanti." She smiled, rubbing the little booklet in her hand. "Now we can make arrangements to fly out of here."

Lisa got on the phone and called American Airlines to see if they could get a flight out that evening. They were so happy that they could not stop laughing and celebrating. Eddy ordered room service and asked for a bottle of wine. A young woman from the restaurant downstairs said dinner would be there in about forty-five minutes.

The Playa Hotel was equal to a three-star hotel. It wasn't luxury, but it was clean and well equipped with a few basic amenities. At first, the others had thought a less-glamorous motel in town would have been better to keep a low profile. "Not a good idea," Eddy had said. "There would be no security, and it would be easier to track." The Playa Hotel was safer, with strong security.

Lisa hung up the phone with a sad face.

"Lisa, what's wrong? What is it? You don't look so happy," Jenelle said nervously.

"The airline said we won't be able to get a flight out until tomorrow morning. The earliest at seven o'clock."

"Why?" exclaimed Sierra.

"Apparently, we are now under a hurricane watch. The airlines are canceling all flights out tonight. The earliest we may get is tomorrow morning, depending on how bad it is. The weather channel is calling it a category four, and unfortunately, it is expected to make landfall sometime around three o'clock in the morning. That's not good. Sorry, guys." Lisa sighed tiredly.

"Not your fault, Lisa. Looks like we have to spend the night here. Well, maybe it won't be so bad. A tropical storm? It could go off its course and ..." Chloe trailed off.

"Doesn't matter, Chloe. American Airlines has shut it down. This sucks! We need to get out of here. What if that monster starts checking airlines and hotels? We need to be gone like yesterday!" Lisa cried out.

"We are all right here. Aren't we, Eddy?" Ashanti asked softly.

"Yes, pretty much so. But Lisa is right. We need to leave. If by tomorrow morning there is damage from the hurricane, we're stuck, and finding us might be hard for emergency folks if this storm is as bad as they are predicting. We could be stranded for hours or even days. However, if the storm is not so bad, finding us would be easier for Raul and his goons. I am concerned as well," Eddy said.

Lisa called every airline except the despicable Trak Airlines, which belonged to Sierra's father-in-law's family. She would never travel with them again. They were incompetent.

Chloe disagreed with Eddy. "Listen, I have covered many hurricanes back home. If we are unable to leave, it will be just as hard for Raul to get to us with flooding, roadblocks, and downed trees and power lines. I mean, I hope it doesn't get that bad, because we do need to get out of here, but it won't be so easy for him either."

"True, Chloe. But like Eddy said, what if the hurricane is not that bad? Raul will have a greater chance of locating us! That is what we're afraid of right now," Jenelle said, shaking her head.

"Any luck, Lisa?" asked Ashanti, worried.

"Well, Brazilian Airlines said they have a flight leaving at nine o'clock tonight; however, it's flying the other direction: Spain."

"Spain?" they said together.

"Oh, that's just great. Farther away from home. We get there, and then what?" Sierra was frustrated.

"If we stay here and the hurricane is as bad as they think it will be, we'll be stuck and in danger far worse than if we travel to Madrid. We can get a flight from there to Philadelphia and then on to Chicago, but we need to decide fast. Personally, I think we should take our chances and get the hell out of Dodge. We don't know how close Raul's people are or where they are searching for us. We also don't know who his people are, like Eddy said. He has many accomplices—police, lawyers, judges, and regular folk we know nothing about. We have no way of knowing who they are," said Lisa.

"And who's to say he doesn't have connections with the airlines? Trust me, it will be the first place he will look for us," said Jenelle.

"Not necessarily, ladies," Eddy said. "Raul thinks we have no money, no resources, and no transportation. As far as he knows, we are on foot. I'm sure he thinks we are hiding out close by in one of the neighboring towns and villages. Hey, he doesn't even know your names." Unfortunately, unbeknownst to them, he knew Sierra's—that was all that mattered. "He knows mine. So I'm the only risk here. Definitely can't make reservations under my name," said Eddy.

"Lisa, will you make the reservations under your name?" asked Sierra.

"Yes, I can do that, but I still need to give him all of our names. Look, what's it gonna be here? Are we staying or leaving?" Lisa asked. She was becoming impatient.

"I honestly think we should take our chances and take that flight to Spain. Once at the airport, we can schedule another flight immediately or the next one leaving Madrid. If we stay here, Lisa is right: our chance of survival is not good. We don't know exactly where Raul is, and we don't know how bad the hurricane is going to be," Jenelle said.

"Okay, is everyone okay with this?" asked Lisa.

They all nodded and said yes. "What else is there to do at this point?" asked Sierra.

Lisa got back on the phone with Brazilian Airlines and made reservations for six to Madrid. Around six thirty, the hotel shuttle drove them to the airport. They arrived thirty minutes later and headed to security with their passports. Sierra said a prayer for everything to go smoothly so they could board the plane with ease. They could not afford to be detained or questioned.

"This is not the same airport we landed at when we first came here, guys," said Sierra, looking around. "This one is much bigger. More modern. The other airport was lonely and isolated." That observation led her to wonder if their kidnapping had been planned, as Eddy had suggested. The thought was savage. She and her beloved friends had been roughed up, thrown about, and held hostage. But why, and by whom? Who would have wanted to do something like that to her and her friends? They kept asking themselves. The women had no enemies to the best of her knowledge. They were simply plain folks trying to live every day to the best of their ability. There was nothing special about any of them. Yes, they were educated and had great careers and businesses, but to single them out to be kidnapped and taken to another country was crazy in Sierra's mind.

"This is the main airport, senora," Eddy said. "The other one was a private landing strip, more or less. Usually, planes that land there are carrying important people who don't wish to be seen."

"Okay, it's not like we're special dignitaries, the president of the United States, or something. Why—oh, never mind. That's over with. Don't want to think about it. We're here now. I'm ready to leave this place once and for all," Sierra said, shaking her head.

They got through customs with no problems. Eddy's and Ashanti's passports worked with no questions asked. Besides, TSA was hurrying them through because an altercation had broken out with some people on the other side, and most of the security personnel's attention was drawn to them. *Thank God for small favors.* The distraction helped them breeze through customs.

Everyone headed toward gate fifteen. They found seats and waited patiently for their flight to Madrid. In one hour, Sierra and her friends were leaving Brazil. Another plane arrived and emptied the passengers from that flight. There were not many, perhaps thirty or forty. Then the flight attendants walked out smiling and talking to one another. Suddenly, Sierra recognized one of the flight attendants from Trak Airlines. She was tall and blonde, with green eyes and full lips. It was her! The zombie who'd acted as if Sierra were crazy when she told her something was wrong with their flight information. Sierra alerted Jenelle.

"Oh my God, it's her!" she whispered to Jenelle.

"Who, CeCe?"

"The stewardess from Chicago!"

She was moving fast, as if she were walking the runway of some fashion show.

"I didn't know flight attendants could work multiple airlines," said Jenelle, shocked to see her after their horrible ordeal.

"It's not illegal. I mean, people work two jobs all the time. It's just ironic to see her—that's all. Should we approach her?"

"I don't know. Why do I have this ill feeling she may work for Raul?" Jenelle said with conviction.

"Please let her not be the flight attendant for our trip to Spain."

"I doubt it, CeCe. They usually go home after a long flight. There go our attendants now."

The familiar flight attendant's name was Madeline Benson. She was originally from Chicago but lived abroad in Rio de Janeiro. She was also Sam McAllister's mistress. He'd been having an affair with her for the past four years. Sam had hired her to help with the disposal of Sierra. He also had paid off the pilots to make sure his plan went through smoothly. Each one had gotten paid $250,000 to help make Sierra disappear. Madeline worked for both Trak and Brazilian Airlines. After receiving word that Sierra was missing in Brazil, Madeline had been ordered to fly there and contact Raul to help locate Sierra and her friends, but she wanted no part of someone like Raul, so she'd ignored Sam's request and gone on about her life. She had taken her $250,000 and kept on moving.

Madeline entered the ladies' room down the hall with the other attendants. At that time, flight 700 to Madrid was boarding. Jenelle alerted Chloe and Lisa that they had spotted the flight attendant from Trak. They were confused too, and they all agreed to hide their faces while boarding, because in their gut, they believed she might be an employee of Raul's, based on the way she'd acted that day toward them. Blondie could not be trusted.

Seniors and women with children boarded the plane first, and then it was their turn to board. Madeline was in the ladies' room, scrambling through her purse, and realized she'd left her wallet on the plane. She exited the bathroom quickly and raced back toward gate fifteen. Sierra and the others found their seats midway down the aircraft and buckled themselves in. There were lots of passengers on the flight. Madeline approached the breezeway and was stopped by another flight attendant named Maria.

"Whoa, whoa. What are you doing, senorita?" Maria smiled. "Slow down, Maddie."

Madeline was out of breath. "Thank goodness I got you in time. Maria, I left my wallet in the galley by the drinks. I need to get it."

"Okay, hold on. It's crowded; let me retrieve it for you. What color is your wallet?"

"It's mint green. Leather," she said, catching her breath as she waited in the entrance to the plane.

Maria found it and quickly handed it to her. Madeline opened it and checked to see if everything was there.

"All good?" asked Maria.

"Yes!" she replied, smiling. "Thank you, Maria. Have a good flight."

"Yes, and good luck to you. Stay safe. Hurricane watch, you know."

"Oh, I'll be fine. We're staying up in the hills, the girls and I," said Madeline, smiling.

"As in Salita Hills?" Maria smiled widely.

"Yes, as a matter of fact. My lover only reserves the best for me, darling." She winked. "Listen, I must be on my way. I have a limo waiting for me."

Just as she hugged Maria goodbye, Madeline spotted the back of Chloe's head and had a flashback. She remembered a redhead who'd been traveling with Sierra's group. This woman's hair was much longer than she remembered, though, and it looked as if she'd had some sort of surgery. Her head was bandaged up. Madeline shook it off as a coincidence. Sam had said the women were missing, but there was no way they had the resources to find their way to a busy airport, such as Brazil International. Besides, she couldn't even remember their names, only Sierra's. She stretched her neck to see if Sierra was close by, but there were too many people in the way, with kids crying and passengers looking for their seats. *No way*, she thought, and she threw it out of her mind that the redhead was one of the missing girls. Madeline left and hurried through the airport to catch her limo.

Sierra was nervous. She was having major anxiety. First, they were flying to yet another country and didn't know what was going to happen once they got there. Second, she was missing her husband and family something awful. Third, the fact that she was on another plane scared her to death. Eddy and the others were comfortable and seemed at ease. She was a nervous wreck. Again, she sat next to Jenelle. Eddy sat with Lisa, and Chloe and Ashanti sat together. Thirty minutes later, they were told to buckle their seat belts as the plane prepared for takeoff. Minutes later, they were flying high, only this time, it was dark out.

Goodbye, Brazil. At another time and place, you may have been one of the places on my bucket list, Sierra thought to herself. *I would have loved to see the Amazon rain forest, but I'm sorry to say I never want to see you again!*

She leaned back in her seat and exhaled. They had done it. They had escaped from their captors. Once she got to Spain, she would call her husband, George.

The attendant passed by, checking for seat belts.

"Excuse me. How long before we land in Madrid?" Sierra asked.

"Madrid is five hours ahead of Rio. We should be landing there at seven o'clock in the morning." She smiled.

"Thank you. This is a nonstop flight, correct?" she asked. She wanted to be sure after what had happened with Trak.

"Yes, it is. Don't worry; we'll be there in no time. Just sit back and relax, and once we are airborne, I will be serving snacks and drinks." Maria smiled and kept counting seats.

★★★

Rojo Village
11:30 p.m.

"Where have you been, Domingo?" barked Raul. He was lounging in his bedroom with one of his lady friends, holding a glass of cognac.

"I've been all over these streets, ripping and running night and day. Nothing! Either they're hiding out in a really good place, or they're dead. Ever think of that? Nobody survives a night in the jungle; besides, there's a hurricane brewing. Perhaps they'll wash up to shore, but wherever they are, they're nowhere to be found."

"You'd better hope the jungle won or the hurricane buries them. If I find out otherwise—well, you already know," snapped Raul.

"You're going to kill me just because your boy Herbieto left his post to go screw your bitch? You've taken care of the problem. Why do you want to get rid of all of us, Raul? I've been loyal to you for over ten years!"

"Watch it, *mi hermano*. You are getting a little too big for your britches! When I ask for a job to be done, I mean to do it well! If not, you are no longer good to me. You have a week to find out what happened to them. Now, go!"

Raul was angry about losing $6 million over Sierra. If he was going to lose, so was everyone else, even if he had to kill everyone off. *Fuck that!* Reality was staring him in the face. He feared he might never get that $6 million for Sierra.

Domingo stormed out of Raul's bedroom and down the stairs. Offing Raul was going to be pleasurable. Perhaps not easy, but in the end, he and Raul would battle the angel of death. Raul had killed his childhood friend. The gloves were off. It was time to exterminate Brazil's biggest pest.

Ivan and Carlos, Domingo's right-hand men, waited for him outside in the SUV. Hurricane Thelma was starting to kick up her heels. They could feel the wind ripping through the leaves on the trees. A light rain fell as the three men drove away. One of the safest places to be was Salita Hills. It was a posh, high-class community high above the city. Domingo knew folks up there, and that was where he and his boys planned to hide out until Hurricane Thelma had done her shit and left. While there, he also could strategize in peace with Ivan and Carlos about taking out Raul.

"Why don't we make a quick stop in the city to pick up some things to ride out the storm, Mingo?" asked Ivan.

"Sounds good, man. Plus, I heard my boy back there," he said, gesturing to Carlos in the backseat, "has got us some ladies lined up!"

"Yeah, one of them is a flight attendant," said Carlos. "Can't wait to take off on that!" He laughed, and the others joined in.

"You think it's going to be a bad one?" asked Ivan.

"I don't know, but at least we'll be away from Raul's ass for a few days. He is giving me a week to find Eddy and them girls. I ain't finding shit! I hope Eddy got so far away he will never be found. The girls too. I've always hated that man. He destroyed my childhood, forcing me to join his regime when I was only thirteen years old. Marco and I both. Hell, Ivan, you were only eleven, and, Carlos, you were seventeen, a young man on his way to college. Fuck him! He's a dead son of a bitch. I'm using this week to bring him down!" barked Domingo as he got on the main road, heading toward the city.

"We could always bring law enforcement into this, Domingo," said Carlos.

"How stupid does that sound, Carlos? We're hardened criminals. We've done shit under Raul's orders. Murdered. Stabbed. Held people hostage. We've witnessed rapes and all kinds of torture. We're no better than him. We're damaged goods, my man. Law enforcement is not going to help us. Hell, they'll kill us for even being associated with him. Got to think, Carlos. Think! If I'm going to leave this world, I'm not leaving it alone. That piece of shit is coming with me. And his entire entourage."

"He doesn't have that many people left," Ivan said, lighting a cigarette. "He either killed them off, or they were killed during that big showdown in São Paulo three years ago. Give him enough rope, Mingo, and he'll hang himself. You may not have to off him."

"I want to. I want to kill him. What he's doing to our young girls and women is despicable. Kidnapping them and selling them off! His time is up. I've been thinking about the perfect opportunity. By the end of this week, Raul will be food for the sharks. Done!" Domingo smiled as the others laughed.

73

Carlos and Ivan hated Raul as well but were not as fierce with their thinking as Domingo, nor were they as passionate. They were desensitized after living life under Raul. As Domingo had said, they'd been kids when Raul snatched them up. That life was all they knew. Now in their thirties, they felt there was no other life to live.

★★★

Miranda Mansion Hotel and Suites, Salita Hills
11:30 p.m.

Flight attendant Madeline Benson and four of her friends had rented the Opa Penthouse on the tenth floor of the Miranda. They were getting themselves ready for their company. Carlos and Madeline had met a year ago at the airport lounge over drinks. He had been waiting for a flight to London. Raul had been looking specifically for British women to fill his inventory. He turned to find a seat at the bar, when Madeline strolled past him, wearing a well-fitted flight attendant uniform. She was beautiful and bubbly, so he invited her over for a drink with him, and lo and behold, she was also heading to London. Carlos, tall, dark, and handsome, was the type of debonair man any woman would have been attracted to. He spoke sexily, and he looked sexy, with a well-sculpted body. Domingo and Ivan were handsome men, but Carlos was eye candy for all women, no matter who they were, and he loved them all too. Black, white, Latina, Asian—it didn't matter. He gave a new definition to the term *ladies' man*.

When he'd found out recently that Madeline had a layover in Rio for a couple of days, especially with the hurricane coming, he had taken the opportunity to arrange to meet up with her. Since Raul had ordered them on a weeklong hunt for Eddy and the women, it was the perfect time to kick back with real women instead of the ones who were worn and used by Raul.

When they arrived in the city, it was raining—not heavily yet, but the storm was about to hit. Everyone was prepping for

Hurricane Thelma. Windows had already been boarded up, and most of the merchants had closed shop. Domingo pulled into a small shopping plaza, and Ivan went into a liquor store to purchase alcohol. Raul called him on his cell to check in. Domingo was going to give him the rat race of his effin' life.

"Yeah, I think we may have a lead," lied Domingo.

"Really! That's good news, Domingo! This pleases me. What have you learned, my friend?"

Domingo cringed at the word *friend*. *Not your friend, you monster from hell*, he thought. "According to someone who spotted them outside Pueblo Azul, they were picked up by someone heading to Buenos Aires. Don't know why or who lives there, but that's the latest."

"Ah, excellent. Very good. I know people in Buenos Aires. Knowing Eddy, he is probably heading toward the low village where many of his father's people once lived. However, I thought they were all gone."

"They are, Raul. Perhaps he wants you to think since there's nobody left there, he wouldn't go there."

"Exactly. Good thinking, Domingo. Very good. Okay, after this hurricane passes, I want you all to head to Buenos Aires tomorrow evening. Got that?"

"Got it. I'll check in tomorrow after the storm passes." He closed his cell.

Raul got on the phone and called Chicago. It was nine thirty at night there. Sam was getting ready for bed. He had a long day ahead of him tomorrow with meetings and the training of new employees at Trak. Raul informed Sam that they had a lead on Sierra and the others and that his best men were on it. It was only a matter of time before Sierra was back in his possession. Sam smiled and told him the $6 million was still good, but he wasn't going to wait forever. If she was not found within the next forty-eight hours, there would be hell to pay for sure.

"Darling, who was that you were yelling at?" asked Sam's wife, Ellen.

"Oh, no one, dear. One of my employees messed up at work,

and I have to find new people to train the new employees come Monday. You know how I am. I'm a perfectionist, and I can't stand it when things aren't in order." He smiled and climbed into bed next to her.

"Well, don't get so upset, Sam. Tomorrow is Sunday! Can't you take one Sunday off to go to church with me?" she asked.

"I don't think so."

"Well, calm down. Don't need to raise your blood pressure right before bed. Take it easy, okay?"

"I will, my dear. Good night."

"Sam, there's something that's been bothering me."

"What is it, Ellen?" he said, turning over.

"George."

"What about our son George?" He sighed restlessly.

"I'm concerned about the two of you and the relationship you have with each other. I don't like all this animosity and strife the two of you have been putting out. The spats and arguments and degrading each other. When is this going to end? My heart breaks every time you two are together, which is not that much lately. Why cant you two bury this ugliness between you both, whatever it is?"

"Ellen, George is a grown man. He has always been belligerent and offensive toward me. I have busted my tail for all our sons to have a good life, and what thanks do I get from him? None!"

"Your definition of a good life is about money, Sam. George doesn't want your money; he wants your love and acceptance and to be treated well like his brothers. He's a middle child, Sam. He's always had to fight for position. You and I both know you've favored John and Mike, the eldest and the youngest."

"And you babied and favored George!"

"I had to. I saw the way you shunned him for most of his life. He's bitter and angry. Can you blame him, Sam?"

"He's an adult! Get over it! I never denounced him. I told him I loved him many times, but he argued and fought me on that, so I stopped saying it."

"Saying it is one thing. Showing it is what matters. And

what's even more heartbreaking is that you show his wife the same ugliness, because I know you don't like the fact that your son is married to a black woman."

"He did that to get back at me. I never said I hated her or black people. Hell, I have top-notch engineers working at Trak who are black. I respect them and treat them wonderfully. My good friend Lemar is black! So what the hell?"

"Yes, as long as your sons don't marry one. I remember when George first brought Sierra home to us. You pulled him aside in the library and asked him, 'How dare you bring darkness to this family?' That hurt him. He loves this woman. They've been married over ten years now, Sam. She's not going anywhere, and neither is he. They are going to have children one day soon. Please, for the love of God, end this hatred with your son now before it's too late."

"Already is, Ellen. And I'm not fighting a ghost anymore. I'm through having this conversation with you, okay? The subject is not only closed but dead. I don't want to hear any more talk of George or his wife or any of this mess. Good night!" he stammered, and he pulled the covers over his shoulders.

"You are so wrong, Sam."

"Good night, Ellen."

Ellen turned away with tears in her eyes. It was no use. Her husband was not going to change, and she was going to have to either live with it or start living a separate life apart from her husband. One thing was for sure: she was not going to neglect her grandchildren from George and Sierra once they'd made a family. She would love her grandbabies the moment they arrived in the world.

Ellen had a great relationship with Sierra. They often went shopping together, and every now and then, they had lunch. Sometimes the two of them even attended church together. Ellen would visit Sierra's church and vice versa. Sierra adored Ellen. She was different from Sam.

George's brothers were cordial with Sierra but not overly nice to her. They tolerated her because they loved their brother George. However, they were more or less like their father; they just expressed it differently. John's and Mike's wives were uppity and standoffish toward Sierra, not the kind of sisters-in-law one would have cared to be close with, especially John's wife, Bethany. She was a pure driven bitch. Mike's wife, Linda, was from the Hamptons. She too had an uppity way about her, but she wasn't as bitchy as John's wife. Sierra couldn't have cared less. She had a black-girl attitude as if to say, "So you don't like me? I don't give a fuck. Kiss my ass, bitches, because I am not kissing yours." Sierra was an expert at ignoring people in her presence. She was incredibly good at treating people as if they didn't exist, even if they were standing right next to her.

At family events, which she was rarely invited to, Sierra often stood alone in a crowded room, whether the gathering was inside or outside. Typically, George would mingle with everyone while Sierra stood back and simply observed the bullshit until George nicely demanded she be by his side and not hide from everyone. The only person who would keep her company was George's mother.

In the beginning, before she got to know her, Sierra thought Ellen felt sorry for her. Sierra wanted no one's sympathy. She was a strong woman who could hold her own and didn't want anyone to be fake. However, in reality, Ellen loved Sierra from the first day George brought her home to meet the family.

Mike's wife had tried to get along with Sierra at one time, but she was a fake. She only talked to Sierra in private, when no one was around. As soon as the entire family were together, she would ignore Sierra as if she were dirt under her feet or as if she were invisible. Not her dear mother-in-law. Ellen genuinely loved her daughter-in-law and couldn't wait to have beautiful biracial grandchildren running around at her feet. As a matter of fact, Ellen was more comfortable with Sierra than with her other sons' wives. If they hadn't been so busy hating on Sierra, they could actually have enjoyed being around a beautiful human being. Well, it was their loss, because Ellen Jane McAllister was never going to turn her back on Sierra. She was not going to allow even her own flesh and blood to break her heart. Perhaps that was why the other wives didn't like Sierra—because Ellen paid so much attention to her and because George was her favorite son, even though she would never have admitted it to John and Mike. Sam had his picks. Ellen had hers, yet she loved all three of her sons just the same.

Now, almost eleven years later, the squabbling continued between George and Sam. The situation with Sierra had divided the family; however, what really hurt George was that neither of his brothers had come to him to express sorrow for the disappearance of his wife. Now George was ready to turn his back on them as well. How could they have been so evasive toward the situation? If he hadn't had the love of his mother, he would surely have been all alone in the world.

★★★

Chicago, Illinois
10:30 p.m.

Once again, George was unable to sleep. He spent most of his nights awake, watching the news to see if there was any mention of the disappearance of his wife and her friends. His thoughts always reverted back to his despicable father. That night, the tears fell. He shed tears for his wife, of course, but also because of Sam. *How in God's name could one man have so much animosity and hatred for a person just because she is of a different race?* George knew, as the rest of his siblings did, that Sam McAllister had always been a somewhat racist individual. But never had he imagined his own father would be cold and calculating enough to have his own son's wife kidnapped to be taken off the face of the earth. Yes, he cried, for he knew now that his father did not have one ounce of love or concern for his son's life or well-being.

Around ten thirty, he got a call from his mother. Sam had fallen fast asleep. Ellen had walked downstairs to make a cup of warm milk. She couldn't sleep.

"Mother, are you okay?" George asked.

"Yes, Son, I'm fine. It's just I've been upset with your

father and how he's been treating you lately. Especially with Sierra missing. He acts like he doesn't care, but I do, Son. I just want you to know that. Whatever I can do to help, please let me know. I love you, Son."

"I love you also, Mother. And don't worry about Dad and me. I'm no longer affected by his ugliness toward me. Now, try to get some sleep. We'll talk tomorrow."

Chapter 4

Sunday, 8:00 a.m.
Madrid, Spain

It had been four days since their disappearance. Sierra and the others landed safely in Spain early the next morning. She felt relieved, and she felt free. They all did. It was a beautiful morning in Madrid. The airport was busy, as expected. They walked to the ticketing area to see if they could get a flight to America. The clerk told Sierra the next available flight was not until Ten o'clock that night. Every other flight to America, from the East to Central, was booked. Ten o'clock it was. They would fly into Philadelphia International Airport, change planes, and from there head to Chicago O'Hare, where they would arrive around noon. Sierra booked the flight with her credit card as the others rejoiced, hugging and smiling. Soon they would be home free.

Tears flowed down Sierra's face. They had done it. They had survived a horrible kidnapping. Although Eddy and Ashanti were from different countries and didn't know what lay ahead in the United States, they were happy, knowing they were also free from Raul's torturous reign. Eddy sat down, thinking about his beautiful daughter, Carmelita. Twenty-five years she'd been gone. She was probably dead by then, he knew. He started to cry. Lisa hugged him and said it was going to be all right.

"Okay, guys, it's done. I'll hold on to our tickets. We just need to be here two hours before check-in, and then we'll be on our way! So what can we do for the next twelve hours? Surely we don't want to sit here in the airport all day and half the night, do we?" asked Sierra.

"I don't know. I'm afraid to leave the gate, fearing something might happen," said Chloe.

"Me too," Ashanti said, wrapping her arms around herself.

"I think—no, I know—we are all right now. Why don't we enjoy this beautiful city, go have brunch somewhere, and do a little shopping? Look, we survived a horrifying nightmare. By rights, we should not even be free or alive. Yesterday we could have all been separated and sold into slavery! That was Raul's goal. God was with us. We prayed for deliverance, and we got it. We're in another country, true, but we're not in Brazil, where Raul is. We're going to make it back home.

God would not bring us this far to let us fall now. Trust him. Have faith," Sierra said.

"She's right," said Eddy. "Let's catch a cab and find a nice place to eat, and you ladies can go shopping. I'll tag along and just watch you all shop until you drop!" he teased.

"Okay, that will at least give us four hours. Then what?" asked Chloe.

"How about a hotel room close by? We can rest up and call our families! Actually, I think that's the first thing we should do: phone home. But all our cell phones were taken when those men snatched us in Brazil," said Jenelle.

"Use the hotel telephone, silly!" Lisa laughed.

It was settled. They caught a cab into town, had brunch, and went shopping, and around three thirty in the afternoon, they checked into a five-star hotel. Madrid was a beautiful city, and they were glad they had an opportunity to explore and have a little fun. After all the hell they'd been through, it was the first and only day they could actually call a vacation. They came back to the hotel with mountains of bags, including, of course, gifts for Eddy and Ashanti. They took showers and rested up. For the first time since they'd left Chicago, everyone was feeling hopeful, thankful, and incredibly happy. Freedom never had felt so good. The past few days seemed like a bad nightmare, and now they had awakened from that nightmare.

Sierra picked up the phone to dial home, but the hotel was experiencing connection problems. Frustrated, she gave up. No one was able to phone home. The front desk clerks said telephone technicians were working on the issue as they spoke and would be done by nine o'clock that night. They had to leave for the airport by seven thirty, and Sierra needed to contact her husband, so the clerk said Sierra could use her cell phone but only for an emergency. *Calling my husband to tell him I'm alive is an emergency, woman!* Sierra thought. The clerk was hesitant because of the extra charges on her phone—big charges—but she allowed Sierra to use her cell phone. She dialed George's cell and then the house phone. Both were busy. George's voice mail was full. *Damn!* she thought. *Clear that shit, honey! It's your wife calling.* But it was no use. The calls just kept going to voice mail.

★★★

Meanwhile, back in Brazil, Hurricane Thelma was in full force. The wind was ripping through Rojo Village and Pueblo Azul like an angry lion. There were downed power lines and trees and some flooding. It was looking pretty bad. Everyone, including the servants from the holding house behind the fish plant, had taken cover in Raul's minimansion.

Up in Salita Hills, the hurricane was creating mayhem but not as much as down in the city. The women were drinking with Domingo and his friends, laughing, having sex, and just living it up. Madeline sat by the massive window, staring out into the wet, harsh darkness. The rain pounded against the windows. She could not get the redhead from the airport out of her mind. The thought that she might have been the woman from Sierra's group kept eating at her soul. The woman had looked exactly like the chick from Chicago who'd been with Sierra.

Madeline picked up the phone and called her coworker Maria Jaramillo. They had worked a few flights together and were friendly acquaintances. They even had hung out a couple of times in between flights. Unbeknownst to anyone, Maria happened to be staying at the same hotel as Sierra, on a layover until tomorrow evening. She had just come out of the shower and was preparing to go downstairs to the lounge to meet a male friend for cocktails and dinner.

"*Hola?*"

"Maria? Hello. It's Madeline."

"Who?"

"Maddie from last night. You found my mint-green leather wallet I left behind. Yes! Remember me?" She laughed.

"Oh, hi, Maddie. What's going on?" Maria asked with slight suspicion. "Did you lose something else?"

"No." Madeline giggled. "I'm just really battling over something—or someone, I should say. Someone I thought I saw. I swore I saw my friend Sierra on that plane, and I'm like, *What the heck is she doing going to Spain?* We were supposed to meet up next week, and I told her if I wasn't working, we could hook up. It's the craziest thing. Do you remember if a Sierra was on board that plane?"

"Seriously, Maddie? I don't know all the names, nor can I remember names of passengers. What does she look like?"

"Real pretty black girl with long, wavy hair; striking gray eyes; and brown skin. Incredibly unique looking. You would have noticed her for sure. Trust me."

"Oh my, there were quite a few black women who boarded that flight, Maddie. I mean, come on—we're talking Brazilian women. Half of Brazilian women look like that. I am sorry. I can't remember her."

"Well, I do know she was traveling with one of her best friends. I recognized her, and I'm like, oh, she must have asked Sarah to go with her. You must have seen this one. She was a white girl with copper-penny-red hair. Sierra and I had talked about going to Spain, and then she said if I couldn't make it, she would go on ahead with her friend, and I would meet her there next week. Not this week. I just can't believe she left without calling me!"

"Hmm. Well, I do remember a redhead. She had some sort of bandage on the back of her head. Petite. Extremely nervous-acting. Perhaps that's her friend, but I don't remember a black woman with long, wavy hair and gray eyes. Sorry, Maddie. Listen, I have someone waiting for me downstairs. Hope you find your friend."

"Yeah, sure. I'm sorry for disturbing you. Have a good time. Probably just some strange coincidence." Madeline giggled again.

"Probably. Good night," said Maria, and she closed her cell.

Maria caught the elevator down to the lobby to meet up

with her friend before heading to the lounge bar area, when out of nowhere, she spotted the redhead Madeline had been speaking about. The woman walked past carrying soft drinks from the vending machine with a black woman but not the one Madeline had described. This one was light-skinned, with a short haircut. Maria nearly dropped her drink.

"Ha! I don't believe it! Oh my goodness, how weird is that?" Maria exclaimed. Her male friend asked her what was wrong. She told him she needed to make a quick call, so she stepped aside for a minute and stood near a potted plant while she dialed Madeline.

Madeline was laughing it up with Domingo, watching the others salsa to some hot Latin music. They were having a ball, when she felt her phone vibrate. She picked it up and was surprised to hear Maria tell her about spotting Chloe in Madrid with a black woman but not the same person Madeline had described. It didn't matter, Madeline was overwhelmed with joy. She had to notify Sam McAllister right away. She just hoped she was able to get a connection, because Maria's voice had faded in and out during their conversation. The hurricane was affecting their signal. She smiled at Domingo, told him she would be right back, and hauled ass to the kitchen to call Sam, who was at the country club, having dinner with some friends. Domingo noticed Madeline's jumpy, erratic behavior, so he followed her and stood behind the wall, listening to the entire conversation. He almost shit bricks when he found out this Madeline chick was in on the kidnapping of Sierra and her friends. His eyes nearly popped out of his head. He covered his mouth in shock. What the hell did Carlos do when he hooked up with this bitch? Was he in on it also?

Domingo walked back to the living room and pulled Carlos aside. He told him all about Madeline and her connection with Raul. Carlos was shocked. He saw how angry Domingo was. He accused Carlos of turning on him, but Carlos stood his ground. He said Madeline had no idea who he was. Madeline thought Carlos was just some big-time builder for a large excavation company. Carlos even pulled out a fake employee card to prove it. At that point, Domingo knew he was telling the truth. He quickly hugged him and asked for forgiveness. Carlos forgave him, but now they had to deal with Madeline. They had to get rid of her somehow. The other women were innocent, but unfortunately, they likely would have to perish as well. Madeline knew of Sierra's whereabouts. Both Madeline and Raul were working for Sam, yet neither one knew it. Once Raul found out Sierra and her friends had successfully made it out of Rio, all hell would break lose. He'd call his men, have them locate her and bring her back and sell her off quickly. He wanted his damn $6 million.

★★★

Horse Trail Country Club, Chicago, Illinois

"Sam, I think I may know where Sierra has escaped to," said Madeline.

"Where, God damn it?" he growled in a low voice.

"Madrid. I don't know how. All I know is that a flight attendant I worked with on a few occasions happened to spot Sierra's friend. They are all at the same hotel as Maria. Do you know her friend's name, Sam?"

"Hell no! I don't know their names!"

"Okay, but I am almost one hundred percent sure she is the same woman who was with Sierra."

"Find out whose name the reservation is under. You'd best make sure this is in fact the same woman who runs with Sierra, or I'll have your ass. I paid you and those damn pilots a healthy amount of cash to redirect their flight to Brazil, and now they're missing from there! All of you are working my last nerve. Get this shit done and over with already. I'm running out of time. I need to get Sierra's ass sold off and out of my family! I have someone there in Brazil who can help me. Just don't you worry your pretty little head about it, toots. I want you to report back to me within an hour with the name of the hotel and who reserved their rooms. One hour, Madeline!" screamed Sam, and he closed his cell and rejoined his buddies at the bar.

"Hey, mami, what're you doing? You going to stay on the phone all night?" asked Domingo, being sly.

Smiling, she replied, "No, hot stuff. I was just checking in on my mother. She lives alone, and I was making sure her nurse was there on time. Now, where were we?" She grabbed him by the collar and kissed him passionately on the lips.

"Now the party has really begun." Domingo smiled.

★★★

Suite 404, Seven Columns Hotel, Madrid, Spain
5:30 p.m.

Chloe and Lisa arrived back at the suite with sodas and fruit juice from the vending machine. They were excited because in two hours, they would be heading back to the airport to go home.

Meanwhile, downstairs, Maria and her beau were enjoying each other's company over a nice steak dinner. Later, she would invite him back to her room to seal the night with a bubble bath, champagne, and lots of hot sex. She turned off her cell for the remainder of the night, an act that would save Sierra and the rest from being captured again.

Every chance Madeline got to pry herself away from Domingo, she went into the bathroom and dialed Maria, but her phone had been turned off. She cursed every time. Her hour was up! Sam had told her she was done. Madeline knew she was stuck in a trap she might never be able to get out of. Sam knew she was in Rio but not her exact whereabouts. Her heart began to break. What had she done to herself when she got involved with Sam McAllister four years ago? She'd had an affair. She'd become his mistress. He'd lavished her with expensive trips, gifts, and even a brand-new home for her and her ill mother. How had she gotten herself tangled up in the kidnapping of his daughter-in-law? She loved him, but it was not like her to do something criminal like this. Apparently, $250,000 was not a bad price for slipping mickeys into the women's drinks so they missed their connecting flight to Aruba. She felt regretful—and scared. Now she was the one looking to escape, but where to? There was a hurricane going on, and nobody would know the extent of the damage until tomorrow morning, when it had passed. She had a funny feeling it would be too late by then. She sat on the edge of the tub and cried softly. She whispered to her mother in her heart that she was sorry.

Raul had learned from Sam that he believed Sierra might be in Madrid, but it was mere speculation. He spoke of a redhead, and immediately, Raul confirmed that a woman in Sierra's group had long strawberry-blonde hair and green eyes and was on the petite side. Sam told Raul he had no idea what Sierra's friends looked like, but he felt it was too much of a coincidence to let slip by.

"I have a connection in Madrid, senor. I will have Fernando check out every hotel and get back to you," said Raul. He felt like a king at that point; he was back in business. He called his buyers in Bogotá and told them the auction might still be on. He told them to hold tight.

There were more than a hundred hotels and motels listed in Madrid. Fernando was a geek. He knew how to hack too well to sit back and dial every hotel in the city. He needed only Sierra's first and last names, but it would have helped if Sam had had the name of the hotel. After he got the call from Raul, Fernando went to work. He only had an hour to track them down, because Sierra and the rest were preparing to head back to the airport.

★★★

Jenelle summoned the shuttle van to come pick them up. The driver said he would be there soon. The airport was twenty minutes away.

Sierra made sure she had all their tickets in order. The travelers were clean and fresh and ready to go. She tried to call George one last time, but again, his voice mail answered, which she found strange. All kinds of thoughts raced through her mind. One of them was *What if he is having an affair?* That would have hurt her deeply. Or what if he was involved in her kidnapping? George was always obsessed with money and blowing her off about having children. It was a thought that scared the life out of her and made her sweat. She quickly threw that notion out of her head. She knew George loved her and would never in ten lifetimes have done something so cruel and ugly.

★★★

Chicago, Illinois
Sunday afternoon

George and his detective friend, Jess, met for a late lunch at Jewels Restaurant in the city. Jess informed George that his father was in fact responsible for his wife's kidnapping; however, his racist heart was not the only reason. George was so angry he could have spit fire. He calmed himself down and listened to what Jess had to say.

"It's pretty deep, George," said Jess, shaking his head. He tapped his finger on a manila folder before handing it over to George to open and examine. He dictated everything inside the folder as George read along.

"I knew it. I knew my father was responsible!"

"Your father may be a racist bastard, George, but that wasn't the entire reason for his kidnapping Sierra. Years ago, Sierra's father, Benjamin Jackson, worked at a steel mill owned by your uncle Ryan. Ben apparently was head of the union or part of it and led a revolt, so to speak, for higher wages, health care, and better working conditions for employees. He fought long and hard, and surprisingly, he won. The union won. The steel mill employees got their higher wages, health-care benefits, and better work conditions, with renovated bathrooms and an eating area, but it nearly caused Ryan McAllister to go belly up. He lost millions. It affected him so much that he had a heart attack and died six days later. Sam blamed Ben and vowed to get him back, thus using Sierra as the perfect subject for revenge. So there you have it!"

"You've got to be kidding me!" George gasped.

"I kid you not," said Jess.

89

"Does Ben know this?" asked George, in shock.

"No. He was never aware of your father's vendetta. Totally oblivious to this. We did some wiretapping and surveillance, and you were right. Sam orchestrated the entire operation. His plan was to sell Sierra off to the sex-slave industry in Bogotá. I am sorry, George. However, the good news is that we've learned Sierra and the others have escaped from some drug lord and human trafficker by the name of Raul Serranos in Brazil. They managed to get to an airport and were redirected to Spain—Madrid, to be exact. So far, that's all we've got. My hunch is that they had to go there because, from what I understand, there were no flights leaving Rio because of the hurricane that was approaching, and the only airline leaving that evening was Brazilian Airlines, going to Spain. None to the United States."

"Sierra probably said, 'Let's get out of here, go to Spain, and get a flight to the United States from there!' So my baby is alive?" George was near tears.

"Looks like it, yes. However, your father had a conversation with a Madeline somebody. She was part of the whole Trak thing, along with two pilots. They were each paid a quarter of a million dollars to redirect the plane to Brazil. Do you know of a Madeline Benson?"

"Never heard of her, but I will have them fired and have charges brought up on all of them! Including my father."

Jess looked up into George's eyes, shocked. "You want to press charges against your father?"

"Damn straight! Are you serious, Jess? Of course! He's evil. My wife could have been killed! And her friends!"

"I understand, George. I just want to make sure you realize what you are saying and how it's going to affect your relationship with your father."

"Fuck him! We have no relationship. What kind of father does this to his own son's wife? Black or white or whatever the reasons were. As far as I am concerned, he is dead to me. Listen, we've got to find out where they are in Madrid."

"My men are on it. Try not to worry. At least we know they are alive. Has Sierra tried to call you?"

"I don't know. I don't think so. I've had so many calls, and I—oh no! I need to clear my phone!" said George. He pulled out his cell and began deleting messages as he listened. He had more than sixty messages, and twenty of them were unheard. By the time he got to the fifth one, he was livid. Sierra had called him twice. He began to cry at the sound of her lovely voice.

"What is it, George? Did she call?"

"Yes, Jess. She did. Here is the number she called from twice!"

Jess took down the number and immediately transferred it over to his IT team. They were instructed to track it and see where it came from.

"This is good! If we can trace where the call came from in Madrid, we can try to get to them before Raul's people," said Jess.

"Please tell your men to hurry."

★★★

Salita Hills, Rio
5:00 a.m.

Hurricane Thelma was pummeling Rio and neighboring cities and communities. It was rare for Rio to experience such raging waters from Mother Nature. No one had thought Thelma would come their way; they'd expected her to follow a different path. She had not. She was there, and she was angry. Madeline continued to try to reach Maria on her cell to ask which hotel she was staying at, hoping to do some investigation for Sam, but it was no use. Maria was busy, wrapped up in her man's arms. She'd receive no more phone calls until tomorrow morning.

Madeline exited the bathroom and entered the living room, where Domingo, Carlos, and Ivan had been laughing it up and fooling around with the other girls. Domingo shot her a suspicious look. She gave him a half-assed, phony smile and said she was tired and ready for bed. She wanted to hop into her SUV with the girls and leave. There was something sinister and disturbing about Domingo she didn't like. He was giving her the creeps. It was as if he had read her mind and knew what she was up to.

"Gentlemen, I'm sorry, but I think the girls and I should call it a night. We have a busy day tomorrow."

"Are you kidding? Have you looked outside, mami? There's a hurricane brewing! You want us to leave?" asked Carlos.

"I'm sorry, but yes, you'll need to go. Besides, don't you have a room here at the hotel, Carlos?"

"Maddie, loosen up! You've been trippin' all night. Things are just beginning to get interesting." Her friend Geneva smiled, wrapped up in Ivan's arms.

Domingo sat quietly, giving her a deadly, piercing stare. "Why don't you come sit next to me and relax, Maddie?" he said, patting the white leather sofa next to him. She hesitated because she felt Domingo's spirit. It was cold and chilling.

Slowly, she walked over to him and sat down. He could feel her fear, for she was shaking. He whispered in her ear, "What's wrong, beautiful lady? Scared I might ravish you to death?"

The word *death* sent a jolt of fright throughout her body. Then he escorted her to the enclosed glass balcony and slid the door shut behind him. He forced a kiss on her and grabbed her butt. She resisted, but it only made him want her more.

"No! I can't. I'm sorry if I misled you, but I just can't, Domingo."

"Misled? You've misled many people, haven't you? Who is Sam?" he asked, jerking her closer to him and holding her tightly so she could not break free.

Her eyes lit up like fireflies in the night. He had been listening to her secret conversations. She was afraid. She had no choice but to tell him who she was and what her connection to the Sierra McAllister kidnapping was, but why was this stranger interested? She'd thought they were just a few gigolos from the city looking to have a good time and then get out of there.

"So you know Raul?" Domingo asked.

"Raul? I have no idea who he is. Sam never mentioned any of his Brazilian connections to me. I swear. He just told me to do what I could to find his daughter-in-law, because he was planning to have her exiled, I believe."

"And you were part of that? What a good woman you are. Hmph! Who abused you when you were young?" Domingo asked, disgusted by the blonde femme fatale.

She didn't respond. She was too afraid. "What are you going to do with me?"

"What would you do to someone like you? Obviously, you can't be trusted. You're a scheming, conniving little bitch, aren't you? Are you a snitch as well?" Domingo asked as she shivered in his arms.

"No!" she cried. "Please. I am sorry. I didn't know you work for this Raul character. I didn't realize she had escaped until I saw someone who was part of her traveling group, and I called a fellow flight attendant and asked if Sierra was in Madrid with this woman who looked like her friend."

"Madrid, eh? Wow! So you went on a scavenger hunt for this Sam and called him over a hunch perhaps? No wonder he wants to fuck you up! I would too. Now, tell me what you know! Tell me—what are Raul's plans next?"

"I am telling you the truth! I don't know! Honestly, if I did, I would tell you."

"And disobey your Sam? So you are a snitch." He laughed raucously. "Okay, snitch bitch, I'll let you live. You and your little friends. But under one condition."

"What's that? I promise I will do whatever you want," she said.

"I want you to get a message to Sam. Tell him that you ran into his Brazilian connection in Rio and that he was found dead."

"Okay. When shall I make this call?"

"Tomorrow afternoon. Raul will be dead by morning. But if you call this Sam a day or moment sooner, I will come back for you and deliver your obituary on a silver platter to your beloved mother. And just so you won't skip out on me, your boy Carlos will be babysitting you until then. After that, get your Goldilocks ass out of my country, and never come back! You understand?" he said into her ear. Actually, he was trying to save her life.

"Yes, I understand!" she cried.

Although it was storming severely outside, Ivan and Domingo were able to make it down from Salita Hills into the city. There was slight flooding, but roads were passible, and that was all that mattered. There were some windows blown out and a few downed wires, but the damage was not as bad as everyone had expected. Carlos stayed and entertained the women. He even enjoyed himself further by having a threesome with Madeline's friends Geneva and Pauletta right in front of her face. She ran to the kitchen and stayed there until they were done.

When Ivan and Domingo pulled up to the warehouse in Rojo Village, they could see that Raul's lights were on and that the holding house had been locked up. Domingo texted two of his accomplices inside the mansion to tell them he was there.

Poppo texted, "Hey, Domingo. Where exactly are you outside?"

Domingo replied, "By the drawbridge. I'm approaching the front door."

Poppo said, "No! Why do you want to do that? Raul is not expecting you until midweek. This has to be a sneak attack. Don't risk it, man."

"Fuck it! I will tell him I found Eddy and the girls. I want you, Ricardo, Enrique, and Calderon to be in their places when I walk through the door."

"You packing?"

"Hell yeah! Behind my back, tucked inside my belt. Ivan will cover the back entrance in case Raul tries to bail. I want to take him right there in the living room. I want him to see my face when I empty my Glock on his snake ass. What about Juan? Is he going to be a problem?"

"Juan has Raul's back until the end. He knows nothing about this. We did not disclose anything to him, because he is, after all,

Raul's blood. Good luck, my friend. Freedom to the people of Rojo Village! I have to go. See you in a few."

Both men erased their texts and prepared for the final showdown with the man who had oppressed them for more than twenty-five years. It was time for retribution.

★★★

Madrid, Spain

The driver was a little late in picking Sierra and the others up from the hotel; however, they managed to get to the airport on time. They had one hour until boarding.

"Aren't you going to call George, sweetie?" asked Jenelle happily.

"No, I, um, just want to make it to Philadelphia, and then I will call him," said Sierra, fiddling with her fingers.

"It's okay, CeCe; we're almost home. Not too much longer now. I still can't believe what happened to us. It seems like a bad dream."

"It was a bad dream, only we were awake. Jenelle, I just don't understand why or how this could have happened to us. Those bad men kept talking about wanting their money from someone, and even Eddy said someone paid big money for us to be taken. Who? Who in God's name would want to do this to us? We've never hurt anyone or committed any crime against anyone!" cried Sierra.

"This shit happens a lot more today than we realize. Human trafficking. Doesn't matter what color you are or how young or old. I'm shocked because most of the time, they capture people who travel alone or walk alone. I don't know. Maybe I've watched too many thriller movies. I just know it's over with, and now we can live our lives again."

"It's never going to be the same again, Jenelle. We are constantly going to be looking over our shoulders and will be fearful of every stranger we pass on the street. And I don't want to even breathe the word *vacation* again. Scares me too much."

"But that's when the enemy wins. We can't let this destroy our peace of mind. We escaped! We did it. C'mon. They're boarding. Let's go home," said Jenelle, and the two friends hugged and then boarded the plane back to America. By nine thirty, they were airborne.

The flight attendants came down the aisle, and as they were checking seats, Sierra and the others became a bit anxious and nervous. Even Jenelle twitched in her seat. Eddy reached over from his seat to Sierra and grabbed her hand, telling her, "It's going to be okay. You're free now." Still, the fear was there. The attendants were friendly and smiled at them. Drinks and snacks were served, and before long, Sierra fell fast asleep. Eddy was the last one to fall asleep around three o'clock in the morning. At that time, Sierra was awakened by turbulence, and she stayed awake for the next four hours until they were in Philadelphia.

"CeCe, what's the matter? You can't sleep?" asked Jenelle, who sat next to her.

"I did for a little while, but I think I'm going to stay up for the duration of the flight until I see we've landed in Philadelphia. I'm good."

"Okay, just checking. You know, I could use a bottled water. How about you?"

"I have one. Thanks."

The flight attendant brought Jenelle a bottled water as she adjusted her headrest. "You know, I've been thinking a lot about all this too, and I feel the same way as you. I do believe we were set up somehow. I do. What bothers me more than anything is that we don't know who it was and why."

"It's so mind-boggling. We're just ordinary women. Yes, we're financially stable somewhat, but this is the kind of shit people do to people who are their enemies. Whose enemy am I? Or you, Lisa, or Chloe? What did we do that was so bad that someone wanted to have us kidnapped and taken to another country to be sold off into the sex-slave industry? That's evil, Jenelle. Pure evil. I've been thanking God every moment since we broke free from that holding house. I have never felt so afraid in all my life. I mean, we're coping right now, but I know we all are going to need therapy. There are going to be nightmares. I had one the other night. God, just get us home."

"He will, my sister. We are on our way. Everything's going to be all right. God was with us the entire time. We were in a battle, and we won. From this point on, let's concentrate on getting back to our lives, and yes, I agree we should all attend some type of group therapy when we get back to Chicago."

"Look out over there, Jenelle." Sierra smiled. "It's almost daylight. What time is it?"

"Five twenty-five in the morning. We're scheduled to arrive in Philadelphia in about an hour. There is a thirty-minute layover, and then we head to Chicago O'Hare. We'll be in Chi-town by lunch." Jenelle smiled, looking over her ticket information. "Won't be long now."

"I can't wait to see my husband," said Sierra softly. "I've missed him, and I can only imagine what he's been going through. Do you want to know something funny?"

"What?"

"It's Monday, correct?"

"Yes. Why, Sierra?"

"Monday, Jenelle! Today would have been the end of our vacation in Aruba and the day we returned home! Ha! Talk about irony."

"Amazing. Funny how things happen like that. We sure have stories to tell when we're old and gray!"

"I can't say this is something I'll want to tell my grandchildren when I'm old and gray—if I ever become a mother first."

"You will, CeCe. You will," said Jenelle, holding her hand.

Just then, the flight attendant announced they would begin serving breakfast in about thirty minutes. At that moment, the others woke up, stretching and yawning.

Sierra said to them, smiling, "Did you have a good sleep, everyone?"

"I know I did. Felt like Sleeping Beauty," replied Lisa.

Eddy smiled and agreed he also had had a good sleep. Chloe's head was starting to hurt again. Jenelle told her it was okay to take another pain pill.

"Ashanti, good morning. How are you? You've been so quiet," Sierra said.

"I'm good." She smiled. "Just nervous about America, but please believe I am extremely happy and grateful to be free. I was in Raul's holding house for eight months. I guess I'm in shock, but I am very happy and thankful to you all. I have a mother and father and sisters and brothers, and I miss them. I want to be with them, and I don't even know if they are alive or not." She began to cry softly.

"We are going to help both you and Eddy, Ashanti. Please trust and believe we will. I can't even imagine what you have been through, and I am so sorry, but yes, you are free now. I will not let anything happen to you once we get to America. I promise. Don't worry about a place to stay or any of that. And that goes for you too, Eddy. You will be welcome in my home until we find your family," Sierra said.

"Thank you," they replied together.

"What a kind and generous woman you are, Sierra. I can't imagine who could have done this to you all. I hope they pay dearly for what they did to you and your friends," said Eddy.

★★★

Rojo Village, Brazil
Midmorning

Hurricane Thelma had gone on about her way, leaving most of Rio and the neighboring villages and towns destitute. The locals had little power, with quite a few blackouts. The damage was pretty bad. Merchants and villagers began doing all they could to rid their homes and businesses of debris and looters. Police were plentiful in the city, patrolling and assessing the damages.

Up in Rojo Village, the jungle, Domingo had successfully penetrated Raul's mansion and was holding him and his cousin Juan hostage. Raul was furious, of course, and even more so because Domingo had betrayed him and turned on him in the worst type of way after managing to get most of Raul's men to side with him. As for the servants and women, Domingo had happily let them go. He'd let them take Raul's money and told them to get the hell out of the village. He even had let them take Raul's expensive cars and SUVs. They'd cried and rejoiced at the same time. Most of the servants were not a threat. They had been used and abused for many years. All they ever had wanted was to be free again, and it was their blessed, lucky day. He wasn't worried they'd go to the authorities or set up their own revolt. They were in their glory, knowing they had permission to flee.

Raul had been beaten up and tied to a heavy iron-cast chair. Domingo did not want him to go out quickly. He wanted him to suffer. Raul and Juan had been tied up for hours.

"You will not get away with this, Mingo!" shouted Raul with blood dripping from his nose and mouth.

Domingo whacked him across the face again with the back of his gun. "I will, you son of a bitch! I will get away with it. You murdered my best friend. Marco was loyal to you, and you killed him in cold blood right in front of my face. You knew he was the closest person to me, the only person who was like family, and you took that away. You wouldn't even let me hold him. I hate you. Always hated you. You've destroyed many lives. Took innocent children from their parents and families and friends." Domingo paced back and forth as Raul held his deadly stare on him.

"I killed Marco because he was weak and incompetent. He wasn't a fighter like you. You I could depend on. You had guts, and you were fearless." Raul struggled to speak while spitting out more blood. He was weak and broken.

"Just as I am now. Fearless. You are the lowest life-form, Raul. Your presence on this earth is no longer valid." Domingo pointed the gun at Raul's face as he watched him beg for mercy.

Boom! He fired one shot to the forehead and then another one to verify Raul was in fact deceased.

His cousin Juan cried out his name, and then Domingo shot him point-blank. It was over. The monster who'd dwelled deep in the jungles of Rojo Village was gone. Domingo watched the smoke from his gun dissipate into the air. The others stood around silently, but inside, they were celebrating. Domingo ordered his men to burn the mansion and the holding house. Soon the flames and smoke would alert emergency personnel to come extinguish the fire. Remaining were Domingo, Ivan, Carlos, Julio, Calderon, and Manuel from Pueblo Azul, the neighbor who'd helped Eddy escape.

The hurricane had damaged the fish warehouse, so it would have been safe for the authorities to assume the fire had started because of the storm, but they were smarter than that. They knew who Raul was. Everyone knew that Raul owned the fish warehouse. Either way, the local police wanted him dead or alive, and if he was dead, that was just one less job they had to do. Raul had outsmarted everyone with the fish factory, using it as a legitimate cover for many years, so Domingo decided to set it ablaze too. The small town across the bay would have to find another way to market their goods. Too many ugly things had occurred in that warehouse. It had to be destroyed.

Domingo split the $8 million secretly stashed inside the warehouse six ways, and of course, Domingo received a tad more. After all, he was the mastermind behind the whole operation. No one objected. Then, around noon, the men went their separate ways. What they did with their cut of the money was their business.

Domingo headed to Costa Rica, where his parents had been born and buried. He had an older sister there, whom he never had met. It was time to reunite with his only blood left. Ivan and Carlos headed back to São Paulo. Julio, Calderon, and Manuel returned to Pueblo Azul but had no intention of staying. Manuel gathered his wife and family and headed north. At last, the evil reign of Raul Serranos was no more. Soon law enforcement would get wind of the situation, and by then, the posse would be long gone.

Ivan gave Madeline permission to call Sam McAllister to tell him Raul had been killed during the storm. Whether Sam believed it or not, his scheme to rid the world of Sierra was a closed chapter. He didn't care, because now that Sierra was missing, he saw no reason to feel defeated. She was missing, and he believed she would never be found again. That would suit Sam just fine. He could go back to his regularly scheduled life.

Little did he know, his son was about to bring the shock of his life: evidence of what he had tried to do to his beloved wife. His plot had failed. It was time for Sam to face the music. His guilt-ridden brain was about to blow up once Sierra stepped off that plane in Chicago.

★★★

Above Philadelphia International Airport
Monday morning, October 24, 2016

After breakfast was served, the flight attendant made her final announcement, preparing the passengers for landing. They arrived safely at Philadelphia International Airport at 7:05 a.m. amid a lot of hand clapping, happy tears, and jubilation from Sierra and the rest. They walked through the airport after kissing the floor, thankful to be on American soil. They headed to their next gate for the connecting flight to Chicago. Then, finally, the women found a phone to call their loved ones. Eddy and Ashanti waited patiently as the women broke the news to their families that they were home.

"Hello?" said George. He was getting ready for work.

"Honey?"

He hesitated and nearly dropped the phone. His heart began to pound out of control. "Sierra! Honey, is that you?"

Sierra began to cry happy tears, laughing at the same time. "Yes, my darling! It's me! Your wife! Honey, I'm in Philadelphia!"

"Sierra!" he cried, dropping to the floor. "Baby, I am so glad you are safe. Oh my God, I've been worried sick! How are your friends?"

"They're fine. We all survived. Honey, we were kidnapped!"

George held his tongue for a moment. He didn't want to disclose to his wife that he already knew what had happened to them. Instead, he sounded shocked and continued to try to calm her down. "Baby, it's okay now. All is fine. Listen, get home. I will have the girls' families come to our house to greet you all. What time does your flight leave for Chicago?"

"In about an hour and a half. We are at the gate now. I'm on a pay phone. Honey, they took our purses and clothes and everything! It was horrible! I cried for you day and night. How are my parents and my sisters and brothers?"

"They're heartbroken and sad, but I will call them right after we hang up to tell them you've been found alive. So your plane will get to Chicago at what time, baby?"

"Um, let me see," she said, fiddling inside her purse to find her ticket. "Noon, my love."

"I will be there. I'll be in a twenty-passenger limo, waiting for you and the others at the pickup zone."

"Honey? There's something else I need to tell you."

"What, baby?" He was so happy to hear her voice live.

"There are two other people who escaped with us. As a matter of fact, one of them actually helped us. If it weren't for him, we'd be dead or sold. His name is Eddy. He's seventy-five years old and very frail, even though he won't admit he's not well. And there is another girl, Ashanti from Cameroon, who also was abducted. They are both with us. They have no place to stay and—"

"No problem, love. Our home is their home. Everything is okay. Just get home. I'll be waiting for you at the airport."

"Thank you, George. I love you, honey."

"Love you more. See you soon, baby."

As promised, George got on the phone, happy as a lark, and told the families to meet him at his home around one o'clock. Next, he called Jim at the office, told him the good news, and asked him to cover him for the next few days, as he was taking off from work. He told Jim to keep quiet about his wife's return. He didn't want pandemonium in the workplace. He couldn't wait to see the look on his father's pathetic face when he told him that Sierra was alive and that he was going to be charged with her kidnapping. He figured he would save the best for last. Lastly, George called his detective friend, Jess.

That day was going to be the best day of George's life and the first day of a new beginning. It was a beautiful, crisp autumn afternoon when George pulled up to the airport in a white stretch limo to pick up Sierra and her friends. The moment Sierra saw George, she dropped everything and ran into his arms. The others stood around happily, ready to go home. All the families were waiting at George's home when they pulled up. Jess had promised George there would be no news media waiting for them, because George wanted to break the news to all the families first before any calls were made to the news stations.

Madeline, along with the rest of the world, learned of the death of Raul Serranos, whose men were being sought by the authorities. Domingo was one of them, along with Carlos, Ivan, Julio, and Calderon. All had left the country without a trace. Although Manuel was not on the wanted list, he still felt it necessary to take his family and leave in case there was any evidence or suspicion he had been involved in the execution of Raul. He had a million dollars to his name. He could live anywhere he chose. He even offered to take Teresa, Eddy's old neighbor, who lived next door to him, but she declined, saying her husband and children loved their home, and now that Raul was gone, Pueblo Azul was a lot safer. There was no need to run. She wished him well, and that was that. They left in a whirlwind, vowing never to return to the village again.

Standing by his car, Manuel said his final goodbyes as his wife and kids waited patiently inside the car. Before taking off, he offered Teresa one last time to leave Pueblo Azul. "Are you sure, Teresa?"

"*Si*, Manuel. I am sure. But please be safe, and take good care. I will miss you all." She softly cried on his shoulder.

Manuel pulled from his pocket $50,000 and stuffed it into her hands. "I want you to have this. You and Roberto."

"No, no, Manuel! I can't. This belongs to you. I can't!"

"Stop it, Teresa! Roberto works way too hard as it is. At least put it away for your two kids' college educations. *Te amo*, my friend. I have to go. Don't forget me. Goodbye, Teresa."

"Goodbye, everyone," she replied softly as she watched them drive off into the distance, giving one final wave.

She was going to miss Consuela. She was her best friend and the only person she had daily interactions with. They had hung up clothes together, driven to the store together, and more, and their kids had hung out with one another. Their favorite place to sit had been under the lemon tree they shared between properties. They would sit under the tree, sipping cool drinks and gossiping about everyone in the village. Consuela always had been there for Teresa. Now who was she going to turn to when she needed a friend? She ran into the house and cried.

★★★

George and Sierra McAllister's home, Glen Hills, Illinois
1:00 p.m.

There was no way to describe the joy and relief felt by the families when they walked through the door to George and Sierra's home. A lot of crying, hugging, and kissing on the cheek ensued. Most of all, they praised God that their loved ones were safe and sound and back home where they belonged. It was kind of awkward for Eddy and Ashanti at first, but then everyone gave them love and showed them kindness. George had quickly put together a little welcome-home party by hiring a caterer at the last minute. At one point, Sierra gathered everyone together as her friends stood beside her and announced that their return wouldn't have been possible if not for God first but also Eddy. Everyone clapped and cheered. Eddy put his head down, smiling. He wasn't used to being praised for such things. Then they ate.

During dinner, George thanked Eddy in private and told him that he and Ashanti would stay at their home until George could get them stable there in America. Ashanti wanted to go back home. George promised to send her home. But for however long it took, George and Sierra's home was their home, and they were free to be free there.

Outside, the leaves were falling off the trees, and the smell of Bob's Apple Orchard nearby intoxicated the air. Sierra sat outside in the backyard, wrapped in a sweater, sipping on hot cider and eating apple cider doughnuts with Eddy, Ashanti, and George. Everyone was happy to be home. Still, the tears fell. She couldn't believe what had happened to them. But they had been blessed to escape and make it home. It didn't seem real, but it was, because there they all were, celebrating at her home.

It had been a long day and a long flight, and everyone wanted to go home to be with family. Eddy and Ashanti expressed how tired they were, so Sierra showed them to their rooms and the bathroom to get fresh and clean before their naps. George and Sierra had a beautiful four-bedroom home with three bathrooms, a den, a spacious living and family room, a large kitchen, a dining area, and a library and office that had a view of the backyard and their modest in-ground pool situated on three acres of land.

Chapter 5

Chicago, Illinois
4:30 p.m.

"Sierra, I love you, my friend," said Chloe as she prepared to go home to her mother's house with her sister, Megan. "It's time for me to go now."

"Okay, my dear. Rest well, and I will call you in the morning. Welcome home, my friend." She hugged Chloe goodbye.

Then came Jenelle and her husband, Nate, to say their goodbyes, followed by Lisa and her ex-husband, the famous NFL player Marquise Brown.

"Thank you, Sierra, for bringing my friend, the mother of my children, back home safe and sound," said Marquise as he gave Sierra a quick kiss on the cheek.

"It was all or none for us, Marquise. Lisa, love you, sweetie. I'll call you tomorrow, okay?"

"Absolutely. Enjoy your husband, and we'll meet up later this week. Love you." Lisa left arm in arm with Marquise and her children.

Sierra smiled, praying that perhaps the situation would bring Lisa and Marquise back together once and for all.

Now that everyone was gone and Eddy and Ashanti were napping, George decided to tell his wife why she had been kidnapped and who was responsible. He cuddled up to her on the sofa in the living room.

"Babe, I am so happy to see you. When I found out you were missing, I panicked like it was the end of the world. I was so afraid. I thought about you every second of the day. I couldn't function at work, so I took some time off after the first day just to get myself together. I admit that alcohol became a great comfort. I couldn't sleep or eat most of the time. I kept asking, 'How could this happen? What in God's name happened to my wife and her friends?' I cried for you, Sierra. But mostly, I prayed for you day and night. You taught me that—how to pray and believe in God. To have faith. Your parents, sisters, and brothers were devastated. Especially your parents. Your mother called me at least four times a day. I felt horrible! Your sister Tamia was the strong one who kept everyone together. She held it down for your family."

"Yes, that's Tamia. The strong one. The survivor." Sierra smiled.

"Actually, Sierra, you are the true survivor."

"George, it was just all so crazy and strange! I mean, one minute we all were so happy and excited, and then we took a nap, and when we woke up, all hell broke loose! I knew something was terribly wrong. We had been in the air for hours, and it was dark. The flight attendant was nowhere to be seen. She hadn't checked on us in a while. The other strange thing was that most of the passengers were gone when we woke up. I was like, *Where did they go?* I would say only about twenty of us were left on the entire plane. There was some crazy shit happening at an extremely fast pace. The flight attendant said we had a connecting flight, when I knew I'd booked a nonstop flight. Then, once we landed, we were told, 'Welcome to Aruba,' only it was Brazil! It was then that I felt somebody somewhere had somehow messed up our flight. I was scared, and I panicked.

"Thank God Lisa was fluent in Spanish. As soon as we got there, which was around ten o'clock at night, I think, we tried to get a flight back to America or to Aruba, but the airport was closed. We were told to wait for a police officer to help us outside, and that was when some men pulled up, grabbed us, and took us away to cave-like holding cells deep in the jungle. It was nasty, cold, dark, and wet. Puddles of muddy water were everywhere, and there were other women there too, crying and hollering. A few of them were sick. Extremely sick. Near death. At that point, we figured that not only had we been kidnapped, but we were being prepped to be sold into the sex-slave industry!"

"Human trafficking," whispered George as a tear fell from his eye.

Sierra wiped it away with her finger and leaned in to kiss him. "It's all good now, my darling. I'm here. Never leaving your side again."

"Did any of them rape you or your friends, babe?"

"No. No, darling. They never touched us sexually. We did get roughed up a bit and thrown about, but I guess we were off-limits until we were sold. This Raul character made that clear. He was the head honcho. His compound was the second location they took us to. It was some sort of holding house or transition house where they took the women to be showered and fed before being sent to some kind of auction. It was there where we escaped, but, honey, if it weren't for Eddy, we would be dead, and that's a fact. We owe him our lives."

"Eddy will be taken care of for life too. And we will get Ashanti back home to her people. But, babe, there is something I need to tell you," he said, lowering his head in shame. He reached for her hands and held them in his, caressing them slowly.

Sierra looked at him strangely. "What's the matter? What is it, darling?"

He was quiet for a few moments.

Sierra had to play the guessing game with him. "George?"

He looked up at her with guilty eyes because he knew what he was about to reveal to her would destroy her heart.

"Babe, I ..."

"George, did you cheat on me while I was gone?" Her eyes filled with tears.

He took a long, deep breath and said, "No. No, babe, I did not cheat on you. Listen, sweetheart. I found out who did this to you and why."

"What! What are you talking about? George, you know who did this to me and my friends?"

"Yes."

"Who?"

There was silence again. He took so long to answer that she was ready to beat it out of him.

"George Adam McAllister, who did this to us?" she yelled.

"Babe, it was my father. My father is responsible for your kidnapping."

Sierra's eyes grew wide with fear. Her skin turned as white as snow. George explained everything to her. He told her that years ago, her father, Ben, had organized a rally at the steel mill for better wages, conditions, benefits, and so on, and Sam was angry because the strike had led his brother, Ryan, to go bankrupt; have a heart attack; and die. In a nutshell, Sam blamed Sierra's father for his brother's untimely death; thus, he'd sought revenge by having Sierra kidnapped and sold off into human trafficking.

She was numb after hearing her husband explain to her why she had been taken. Sierra always had known Sam McAllister didn't like that his son had married a black woman, but finding out that the ordeal was all about her father's quest for better wages for the steel mill employees twenty years ago sent her into a state of unbelievable shock. She looked into her husband's eyes and cried. He held her tightly and promised her that his father was not going to get away with it and that his lawyer and the private detective were preparing to have a warrant issued for his arrest.

"I nearly died, George! And so did my friends! Oh my God, does my father know?"

"No, he doesn't have a clue, but he will find out soon enough. My father doesn't even know you are alive. Won't he be shocked when he sees your face? He doesn't know you are home, so it will be quite a scene, I'm sure. I told Jess to be here tomorrow with law enforcement, because I am officially pressing charges against him."

"I can't believe it. Your father hates me that much? I mean, he used my father as his reason to get rid of me?"

"I want nothing more to do with him, Sierra. I love you, my darling. Love you more than life itself. You are a beautiful, loving woman inside and out. I would die for you. I once loved my father, but at this point in my life, after what he did to you, he is dead to me.

Babe, you look awfully tired. Why don't you go upstairs and rest? I will have dinner ready for you when you get up."

Tuesday, October 25, 2016

The next day, George planned the reveal. For that day it felt like the 4th of July! For it was Independence Day in Glen Hills, Illinois.

"Sierra, I've invited my parents to dinner this evening. I want to see the reaction on my father's face when he sees that you're alive!"

While Sierra was on the phone with the girls, George got things ready for this evening's event. He only felt bad about how his mother would take Sam's arrest. They'd never spent a night apart in more than thirty-five years. Of course, once bail was set, Sam McAllister would be released shortly thereafter. Most likely, he would go right back home to his wife, Ellen. Jess had told George he had all the evidence they needed to give to George's attorney to prepare for a trial should Sam turn down a plea bargain. George took no pleasure in doing this to his father, but it was the right thing to do. And why shouldn't he have pressed charges? His own father had tried to have his wife sold off and possibly killed. How could he expect George to have any loving feelings for him after that?

When the time came for his parents' separation, he would take care of his mother and offer to let her live with him and Sierra. The other issue would be dealing with his brothers. For sure, his older brother, John, was going to hate him for the rest of his life, because even though John showed cordialness to Sierra with a handshake and a smile, he despised her and was just as ruthless as Sam. Mike, the youngest of the brothers, didn't show hatred toward Sierra but always had been sweetly standoffish. George didn't know how he was going to react. Mike wasn't as hateful as John and Sam. He just went along with his father and his big brother because he assumed everything they did was right no matter what. However, Mike knew right from wrong. He knew it was wrong to treat Sierra unkindly.

He knew his father and brother were hateful. Still, even though Mike never talked badly about black people, he still was part of his father and older brother's prejudiced bond.

George had had no idea Sierra's father was an advocate for the union at the steel mill. From what George had learned, Ben Jackson had been a loyal, hardworking employee for McAllister Steel Company for more than twenty-five years, and from what Jess had gathered, the working conditions and wages had been horrible back then. Because the employees had been primarily men and women of African and Latino descent, the steel mill had not felt obliged to make their lives at the mill safe and clean. Ben had retired from the steel mill with a healthy severance pay and retirement package, as he should have. Sam McAllister didn't feel he deserved any of those accolades. He blamed Ben for his brother's heart attack and death.

Ryan McAllister had been far from broke or destitute even after the strike. He'd had a healthy bank account with more than $10 million. But for someone who once had kept $40 million in his personal account, it seemed $10 million was a poor man's salary according to Ryan McAllister. He would have made the money back tenfold within the following five years if he'd just held on and been patient. McAllister Steel had supplied to merchants and buyers all over the United States and Canada. Sales had never slacked off the entire time it was in operation. However, greed was a genetic code that ran through the majority of the McAllister men. Six years after Ryan McAllister's death, the mill had closed. A company in Pennsylvania had bought McAllister Steel and moved its base of operations outside Philadelphia.

Those were the reasons for Sierra McAllister's kidnapping. Sam almost had succeeded; however, there had been too many people in Sierra's family praying for her. Her parents were devout Christians, as were her aunties and uncles. It was nothing for them to tarry and pray for days at a time. Their faith in God was strong. Nobody could break it. Sierra's mother, Tina, never had given up hope. Once the world found out her son-in-law's father was responsible for it all, it would take an army of prayer warriors to prevent her family from wanting to knock his lights out. It wasn't the Christian way, but sometimes even the best of humanity could go left when it came to someone harming their kin. Sierra was the youngest, but she was the motivator of the family, the breadwinner, and the one who typically brought the family together. Sam surely was going to pay.

***

Sam McAllister's home, Chicago, Illinois
5:30 p.m.

"I think it's nice our son is inviting us over for dinner. He's been sad ever since his wife went missing," said Ellen.

"Yeah, well, these things happen, Ellen. You hear about this kind of stuff all the time in the newspaper and on television. I'm afraid she may be lost for good."

"How can you think so negatively, Sam? Sierra is our daughter-in-law! Don't you have any feelings at all for her? This is a bad thing that has happened to her and her friends. She's lost!"

"Of course, I feel bad for our son. You think I enjoy seeing him suffer over his woman?"

"Not his woman, Sam. His wife! Say it. Say her name: Sierra McAllister. Oh, what's the use? Just don't be so cold tonight at dinner with our son. Show some compassion for once in your life with him. Now, zip me up, please. We're running late as it is. It's a thirty-minute drive to Glen Hills, and I want to use this time with our son to relax and be free from negativity," said Ellen, annoyed.

Sam didn't care one bit about his wife's attitude. He didn't care that Sierra was missing. But for that night, he would fake empathy for his son and the whole ordeal. However, the fact that Raul was dead and his henchmen were missing left Sam wondering where in the hell Sierra and her friends had escaped to.

Sam and Ellen hopped into their brand-new Cadillac and headed toward Glen Hills to have dinner with their son. Everything was in place. The police were waiting for Sam, along with Jess,

George's detective friend, who'd proven that George's father was responsible for the nightmare. George had one request of law enforcement: right before Sam was handcuffed, he wanted Sam to see Sierra's face—and Eddy's, Ashanti's, Lisa's, Jenelle's, and Chloe's faces. Oh, there was going to be a dinner all right but only after his father was whisked away in a patrol car. Again, his heart was heavy only for his mother. He knew the revelation was going to shock the hell out of her and break her heart into a million pieces. Sam McAllister was not above the damn law! Who was he to have another human kidnapped and perhaps murdered?

★★★

George and Sierra McAllister's home, Glen Hills, Illinois
6:45 p.m.

The doorbell rang twice. George went to answer, and the first thing he did was hug and kiss his mother. He looked at his father and turned away, inviting them in.

"Smells good in here, Son," said Ellen.

"Pot roast, Mother. Your favorite." He smiled.

She kissed him on the cheek.

Sam looked around for a place to sit. "Not going to offer me a drink, George?" he asked.

"Sure. I think you deserve that much, especially with the night you're going to have," he said, handing his father a scotch on the rocks.

"Now, what in the hell is that supposed to mean?" Sam snapped, jerking the glass of scotch from his son's hand.

"Oh, nothing much. You'll see." He smiled.

"Are we going to have an evening or not?" Sam said.

"Yes, we are going to have an evening, Father. Just you wait and see how exciting it's going to be. But first, let me present you with a surprise I've been holding on to all day."

George opened the French doors to the dining room, and

there stood Sierra. Ellen gasped with joy as she ran to her daughter-in-law, crying happy tears.

"Sierra! You're alive. You're home!" cried Ellen, full of joy.

Sam almost dropped his drink. His mouth gaped wide open. His face was as red as a beet. He felt his heart sink damn near to the floor. George hoped that Sam, just like his brother, Ryan, was having a heart attack.

"Father, look! My wife has been found safe and sound! Isn't that great? Isn't it a miracle?" George smiled. He was in his glory, watching his father's reaction to Sierra's presence.

Sam forced himself to smile. He was shaking all over. Sierra gave him the deadliest stare imaginable. Sam realized his daughter-in-law knew he had been responsible for her disappearance. He could feel the fire of hatred burning from the top of her head to the soles of her feet.

"Sierra. You made it home. That's great," he said nonchalantly. He was fuming with anger.

"Yes, I have made it home, and so have my friends." She summoned them to show their faces. All wore strong looks of dissatisfaction. They were angry but didn't say a word. "Oh, by the way, thank you for the flight to Brazil."

After that, it was all over. Sam looked to his right and saw the look of glee on his son's face. Sam realized his son also knew he was responsible for the kidnapping. Sam slammed his drink down on the table and proceeded to leave, but he was stopped by the local police.

"Samuel McAllister? You are under arrest for the kidnapping and human trafficking of Sierra McAllister, Lisa Hamilton, Jenelle Collins, and Chloe O'Connell. Please turn around and place your hands behind your back," said Officer Romano, and he placed the cuffs firmly around Sam's wrists and read him his Miranda rights.

"What the hell is this? I don't have any idea what you are talking about! I will sue the entire police force. You'll be sorry. Do you know who I am?" he barked, but the officers paid him no mind and walked him out the door.

Sam turned to his son and said, "George! How could you do this to me?"

"The same way you allowed my wife to be kidnapped and sold off to murderers—that's how! Goodbye, Father."

His mother stood in a state of shock, sobbing, not fully understanding what was going on. She cried hard in George's arms.

"I'm sorry, Mother, but it's true. Your husband, my father, was behind the entire ordeal. So sorry for you, Mother. So sorry I am. I love you."

"George," she sobbed, "tell me you are wrong! This has to be some horrible mistake. Your father would not do such a thing, no matter how much you two don't get along!"

"Ma'am, I'm afraid your son is telling the truth. We have proof and evidence," said Jess Livingston. "He will be charged and booked and seen before a judge, who will most likely set bail. Whether they release him or not will be up to the judge. George, I am sorry for all of this. I will be in contact with you." Jess left with the officers.

Everyone gathered in the living room. It was quiet for a few moments. George, still consoling his mother, made a speech to everyone.

"Listen, everyone. First, I want to apologize for what my father did to all of you. I wanted to believe he had nothing to do with your kidnapping, but unfortunately, the hate and vengeance he carried for my wife and her father were too great for him to resist doing what he does best: evil. I am ashamed. I am appalled. I am sad. This was the man who raised me. Now here stands my mother. Take a seat next to Sierra, Mother. Her entire world has been turned upside down because of what my father has done. I can't tell her everything is going to be all right, because it's not going to be. My father is going to face criminal charges."

Ellen let out a loud cry, and Sierra tried to console her to the best of her ability.

George continued. "Mother, I am here for you. Sierra and I love you. We are not going to desert you. The last thing I want to say is that I pray all of you can try to begin to live normal lives again.

Eddy, Ashanti, I am going to do the best I can to help you. Eddy, we will find out what happened to your daughter. Ashanti, I will send you back to your family if that's what you desire, which I know you do. Just know our home is your home. I don't want you to worry anymore. Well, I know no one is probably hungry, but there is food in the dining room. Please help yourself."

"Excuse me. George?" Chloe said.

"Yes, Chloe?"

"I heard that our captor was killed. Do you know if that is true?"

"My private detective got intel from the Brazilian authorities, and they have confirmed that Raul was killed in a fire that burned down his house along with the warehouse and the holding house. So yes, looks like he is deceased."

"I'd be lying if I said I was totally at ease, because a few of his men escaped, I heard," Chloe said.

"Yes, they did, but from what I could gather from Jess, they have fled to other parts of the country or left Brazil altogether. I don't think they will be coming to America to hunt you all down. The man who killed Raul was his own right-hand man. Again, I know this is going to be hard for all of you, including my wife, but I am here for everyone if you need me. I mean that."

Just then, Marquise pulled his ex-wife close to him. Sierra watched as he looked into Lisa's eyes with sympathy and love. Yes, it looked like Marquise was trying to come back into his ex-wife's life. Later, while everyone was nibbling on food, Marquise told George it was time for him to stop the madness and protect his wife from there on out. It was time to reunite. The question was, would Lisa take him back in spite of what had happened?

The next morning, Sierra woke up extra early. She was having problems sleeping. Nightmares were constant. George had to go into the office but said he would cut his days short until his father's trial started. He didn't want to leave Sierra, Eddy, and Ashanti alone for too long, but Sierra claimed she was fine during the day. Still, George was home by one o'clock every day.

George tried to contact Ashanti's relatives by phone but had no luck. He hired his detective friend, Jess Livingston, to try to locate Eddy's missing daughter, Carmelita. They sat down for coffee one afternoon in George's home to discuss the search.

"First, you've got to realize, Eddy, this is not going to be an easy task. Your daughter has been missing for over a quarter of a century. It could take weeks or months, or we may never find out, and then it becomes a dead file. But I will try my best. I know you don't have the resources, so we will try to work something out," said Jess.

George interrupted. "Jess, don't worry about money. Whatever it takes, I will cover the costs. After all, if it weren't for this man right here, Sierra and her friends would be dead."

"Thank you, Mr. McAllister," said Eddy, smiling.

"Please call me George." He smiled back, reassuring Eddy that everything was going to be all right.

After about an hour or so of getting some vital information from Eddy regarding his daughter, such as her physical description, a photo, her date of birth, and more, Jess closed his notepad. He also informed George that the judge had not released his father on bail. Sam was presently in the county jail downtown.

"I know your mother is suffering, and I am very sorry, but I have no control over the law," said Jess, looking at George with empathy.

"No, I understand. Mother is coming along okay. Her doctor prescribed her some sort of sedatives, and she's been staying here with us. She and Sierra took Ashanti to have lunch with one of the girls. They should be coming back soon."

"No matter what, I'm sure this has to be difficult for you also, my friend. I mean, he is your father, you know?"

"Honestly, Jess, I feel no hurt or pain for him. He meticulously planned to have my wife—my heart, my vessel, my partner in life, whom I love more than life itself—kidnapped. She could have died. All of them could have. He's dead to me."

"Well, I can tell you this, George: your father has hired an exceptionally good attorney. Tops in the country. Just be aware of the fact that he may win his case. I've seen defendants who have actually murdered get away with it."

"Jess, please. Don't say that to me. I will kill him myself!"

"No, George, don't talk like that. I just want you to be prepared. But believe in your attorney as well and that the jurors will do the right thing. Listen, you and Sierra have one of the best prosecutors in the state. If you win, which I am hoping you do, my friend, well, your father is facing at least thirty years. At the age of sixty-five, that's basically life for him."

"Good. I hope that will be the verdict when it's all over with," replied George.

"Gotta run. Have another client to meet with this afternoon. Tell Sierra I said hello, and keep the faith. Eddy, I will be talking to you soon. Stay strong, everyone."

"Will do, Jess, and thank you for everything," George said as he walked him to the front door.

There is no way Sam McAllister is going free after what he did. Jess was right; George had to trust the judicial system to do the right thing.

***

November 10, 2016

It had been nearly three weeks since Sam McAllister was arrested and jailed. A preliminary trial had been set for right before the Thanksgiving holiday. The fall season was in full effect. Crisp, clean air and the smells of apple orchards and burned leaves tickled the nose. Colors of orange, red, brown, and yellow were in full bloom throughout Glen Hills, Illinois, and the season of giving was upon everyone. Life was slowly returning to normal for Sierra. Still, the nightmare of being abducted and chained inside a dirty, smelly, dark, muddy, wet cave cell was frequently in her dreams. She could still feel the cold concrete floor upon which they all had sat before being transferred to Raul's transition house. And their daring escape, although liberating, had been fierce, including traveling through a jungle at night. Thoughts of Chloe being attacked by the monkey sent chills up and down her spine. They talked to each other daily, and Eddy and Ashanti, living in Sierra and George's home, had become more than friends; they were family. Sierra enjoyed their presence in her home. Eddy was like an overbearing uncle. Plus, he was a chef and insisted he do all the cooking. George and Sierra didn't argue about that. As for Ashanti, she was like a little sister, but she was always quiet.

"I believe Ashanti is depressed, George. I can't blame her after all she's been through," said Sierra, gripping a hot cup of apple cider, as she watched Ashanti through the kitchen window. Ashanti was slowly swinging back and forth in the gazebo.

"I have to tell you, babe, Jess is having a hard time locating her folks. It's not looking good. He did find her brother, but—"

"But what, darling? That's great news!"

"No, actually, it isn't. He wants nothing to do with her. Says she's been tainted or spoiled by her kidnappers, and he feels it's best if she doesn't come back to their country."

"Are you effin' kidding me right now? It's her fault she was kidnapped and raped? Wow. Some family," she said, shaking her head in disgust.

"Tell me about it," said George. "Just ask Sam McAllister. He's got all kinds of family love running through his blood."

Sierra lowered her eyes and said, "He must really hate me and my father."

"He hates himself, CeCe. Look, babe, after the trial is over, what do you say you and I, along with Mother and your parents, take a trip up to the mountains?"

"I don't know, darling. I am not so excited about traveling anymore, at least not right now, and—"

"It's okay. I won't let anything happen to you ever again. I just don't want you to lock yourself away from the world. You had a horrible experience last month. Just horrific! I just think the sooner you get back out the better. Don't let a dead man's reign rule you. You have successfully escaped from another country, babe. You could be a positive force in the life of someone else who went through the same thing."

"I've researched the percentages regarding human trafficking, and most do not come back, my darling, dead or alive. Plus, I am in no position to mentor anyone, George. I have yet to try to begin to heal myself. This whole ordeal with the kidnapping, especially with your father being the one who set everything up, has taken a toll on me. I mean, reality has set in more so now than when we were held captive. Honey, we were in a foreign country with no direction. I thank God every day for Eddy. I really do. How are you coming along with finding his daughter, by the way?"

Eddy was in the kitchen, preparing dinner for everyone. Ashanti was still sitting quietly outside, enjoying the autumn weather.

"Nothing yet. Jess says he needs to find someone who had a connection to Raul. Perhaps the men who managed to escape. Jess believes one of them is Raul's killer. Can you remember any of those men's names, Sierra?"

Sierra thought long and hard and said, "Yes. I do remember at least two. A Carlos and a, um, Meego? Ming? Domingo! That's it! There were quite a few, but I remember hearing Raul call out their names at one point. Perhaps we can find them."

"If they're alive. Jess believes they may have left the country after they killed this Raul character. It's a long shot, babe. Would be damn near impossible to get any info or locate them."

"Wait! Eddy has a friend in his village. Her name is Teresa. And there was a man who lent us his car—Manuel. Perhaps he could help somehow. It's worth a try."

"We will ask Eddy during dinner."

Indeed, during dinner, George asked about the men Sierra had named as people who might be able to help with locating his daughter.

Eddy was a great chef. For dinner, he made them Moroccan salmon and garlic string beans with lemon couscous. They could tell he had years of training in culinary arts, for the meal was delicious. They felt as if they were dining at a five-star restaurant.

George poured everyone a glass of white wine, except for

Ashanti. She didn't drink; plus, she was only nineteen years old. She had lemonade.

"If we can get Jess to get in contact with any of those men, perhaps they can shed some light on what may have happened to Carmelita, but I'm going to be honest: these are criminals and murderers, and contacting them may open up a whole new can of worms, Eddy," said George, sipping his wine.

"I know all of them. I worked in that transition house for over twenty-five years. Domingo and Carlos were very young men when Raul recruited them. Manuel is older, but he didn't live in the village when I lived there with my daughter. I will contact Teresa. She left me a number to reach her should I ever need her."

"I will give this to Jess. We have a meeting with him on Wednesday. Try to remember as much as you can." George then turned his attention to Ashanti. "Ashanti, I am sorry about your brother. Is there anyone else from your country we could try to reach out to?"

She shook her head. "The only other people are my mother and father and my sister, Talani. The last I heard before I was kidnapped, she transferred to a university here in America."

"That's great! What state? Do you know?" exclaimed George.

"No, I do not know the name of the state. Her name is Talani Faharte. She married a doctor, and they moved here to America five years ago."

Sierra interrupted. "That should not be hard to do, George! We could google the last name Faharte and see what we come up with!"

"Yes, my love, you are absolutely right." He quickly grabbed his laptop from the kitchen counter.

Ashanti smiled widely. "You can find my sister?"

"I think so. How do you spell the last name?" asked Sierra.

"F-a-h-a-r-t-e. Her husband's first name is Bakmuhl," Ashanti said, and she gave the spelling of his first name too.

Sierra's fingers flew like lightning across the tiny keyboard. Everyone stopped eating dinner for a moment, holding his or her breath with great anticipation. "Thank goodness for the internet and the information highway," Sierra said.

Seventeen Fahartes appeared in the search. Three had the first name Bakmuhl. They found photos for two of them. Ashanti looked at the photos. Her eyes began to water, for the second one was her brother-in-law, a Dr. Bakmuhl Faharte located in Los Angeles, California. He was an MD, and his business contact information was listed right there on the screen. Ashanti cried happy tears.

"Let's call him! Now!" cried Sierra.

Eddy clapped his hands, smiling, and reached over to hug Ashanti. He was happy she'd found her family and sad he had not found his daughter. But he had faith. He believed in Sierra and George. He knew they would stop at nothing, so he let Ashanti have her shine time and celebration. His day would come, even if he found out Carmelita was dead.

"What time is it in California?" asked Ashanti with tears rolling down her cheeks.

"It's about five o'clock. Hurry—dial his number, George. He might still be at his office."

"Okay, okay." He smiled as he dialed Dr. Faharte's number.

"Good afternoon. Dr. Faharte's office," the receptionist said.

"Hello. My name is George McAllister, and I would like to speak to Dr. Faharte if possible."

"Are you a patient of his?"

"No, ma'am, I am a friend of his sister-in-law and—"

She quickly cut him off. "Sir, we don't take personal calls here at the center. You'll need to contact him at—"

Then George cut her off. "No, please. Please listen. His sister-in-law, Ashanti Nahali, has been missing, and we've found her. She is here with me right now. It's very urgent we speak with him as soon as possible. Please help us out here. Please, miss."

"I'm, um, sorry, but Dr. Faharte has left for the day. I was just about to turn on our answering service."

George pleaded in desperation. Then Ashanti grabbed the

phone and told the receptionist who she was, begging her to have him call George's house number as soon as he got the message.

"If you can get a hold of him, perhaps on his cell or something! My family needs to know I am alive. I need to see my sister, Talani."

"Wait. You know Talani?" asked the receptionist. She was slowly starting to thaw out from the ice treatment.

"Yes, of course I do. She is my older sister! Bakmuhl is my brother-in-law. We are originally from Cameroon."

"Oh dear. Oh my. Listen, sweetheart, I'll tell you what I am going to do. I will call Dr. Faharte and leave a message with him with the number where you can be reached. I can't promise you anything, but if he doesn't call back tonight, call tomorrow morning. He is here by nine o'clock. Okay?"

"Yes, thank you," she replied softly, and she hung up the phone.

The receptionist immediately called Bakmuhl. He was on the freeway, heading to his home in Rancho Bernardo. The Fahartes lived an amazingly comfortable life in a five-bedroom luxury home with all the amenities one could have thought of, including an outdoor Jacuzzi and swimming pool. He drove a black Benz, and his wife, Talani, drove a white BMW. They had a four-year-old son and a two-year-old daughter, and they did not want any more kids. They were both educated and doing well, living the American dream. In addition, Ashanti's mother, Veeta, and father, Sahar, lived with her sister and brother-in-law. Bakmuhl had sent for them two years ago.

"Yes, Gwendolyn? What can I do for you?"

"Doctor, sorry to disturb you, but I just got a very strange call from a young lady claiming she was kidnapped but now is free. She said you are her brother-in-law."

Immediately, Bakmuhl's face turned from glee to shock. "What? What did you say?"

"A young lady called and left you a number to call her where she is. I see the area code is Chicago."

"I don't know anyone in Chicago. What did she say her name was?"

"Ashanti Nahali."

Bakmuhl nearly ran off the freeway in shock. He thanked his receptionist and immediately punched in George's house number. Minutes later, George picked up the phone.

"Hello?"

"Hello, sir. My name is Dr. Bakmuhl Faharte. I got a message from my receptionist that my sister-in-law may be at this number."

"Yes! Yes, sir, she is. Here—I will let you talk to her!" exclaimed George. Everyone got excited as Ashanti grabbed the phone.

"Bakmuhl? It is me—Ashanti!" she cried. From there, they talked for nearly an hour on the phone as Sierra, George, and Eddy gave her privacy.

Sierra and Eddy were in the living room, seated in front of the fireplace, watching the flames crackle. It was November in Chi-town, and it was cold outside. Temperatures dropped rapidly during that time of year in the Big C. Eddy said he never had experienced weather like that before; he'd only read about it and seen it on television. He was amazed and delighted at the same time.

Eddy loved being with George and Sierra. They were taking great care of him and made him feel like part of the family. It was hard to believe he had been a slave for many years, living in turmoil and pain, serving a ruthless, heartless, evil man. He would always look at Sierra and her friends as messengers from God, for without them, he would have never attempted to escape. Plus, it had always been impossible to do such a thing anyhow, because Raul always had kept tight security. He'd only dreamed about his freedom, until Sierra and three other brave women had shown up in his life. It was meant to be. Never before had the holding house been left unattended with only one guard to watch over it. Herbieto's lust for Sheila had been their ticket to freedom. Now Eddy was living in peace. Freedom never had felt so good. If Eddy died today or tomorrow, at least he would die a free man. But hoped he would not die without finding out what had happened to his precious daughter.

"Wait until the snow comes. In Chicago, it will come very soon, my friend," said George, entering the room with two cups of steaming coffee for himself and Eddy.

"I am so happy for Ashanti. I hope they're having a good conversation, especially after getting negative feedback from her brother," said Sierra.

"He sounded happy when I answered the phone," George said. "Anxious but happy."

"She will be fine. I just feel it." Sierra smiled.

Ashanti walked into the room, wearing a huge smile, and said, "Everyone? In two days, I will see my family! My brother-in-law is flying out here with my sister and my parents! I'm going to live with them in Los Angeles."

"Ashanti, that is wonderful!" cried Sierra, and they all took turns giving her a hug. "How do you feel?" Sierra asked.

"I am so excited! I haven't seen them in over a year. They thought I was dead. You have to understand. I was kidnapped in Africa. I was attending school, and on my way home, I was snatched along with two other girls. They were sold off about a month after we were kidnapped. Raul said there were no orders for dark-skinned girls yet—that's why I was in the transition house for so long."

"Wait—were you in high school?" asked Sierra.

"Yes and no. I had just graduated high school and was on my way to attend college that summer. I only made it the first week."

"So where were your parents?"

"They had already left to live with Talani. My brother and I were next to come to America. At the time, we were living with my aunt and uncle, when I was taken. Worst day of my life. But because of you, George; you, Eddy; and you, Sierra, I have been given a second chance at life. I am going to be with my family, except I am sad because my brother refuses to be in my presence. I don't understand how he could feel this way. I love him."

"It's not your fault, Ashanti! Your brother doesn't realize that what happened to you was a criminal act against you. You didn't run away with those monsters! They kidnapped you! You did not willingly go with those men. They snatched you! It wasn't your fault you were violated. Does he not understand that? Why can't your brother accept truth?" Sierra was on fire.

"I honestly don't know, but my family will be here on Thursday to take me home with them. I am free, Sierra. Free!" She smiled.

Eddy turned his head away as she spoke about family, freedom, and happiness, thinking of his daughter. She had been abducted by Raul's men, but she never had had the chance to escape, as he had. Every other thought was of Carmelita. Ashanti was lucky to have found her family—and she'd only had to google a name. If her brother-in-law had not been a doctor there in America, things would not have been as easy for her. But her success gave Eddy hope that maybe Sierra and George knew what they were doing, and soon he would be reunited with his daughter. However, his situation was a lot more complicated—so much so that a private detective had been hired. Still, he was going to hold on to his last bit of hope right until the end, even if that end meant his life.

The next morning, Sierra called the girls to tell them the good news about Ashanti. They came together for lunch at Bayside, a well-known five-star restaurant in downtown Chicago. Plus, she wanted to catch up and see how the other women were thriving and surviving. If they were feeling anything like she was, they were not doing so well, for Sierra was not yet free from the nightmare of the kidnapping. Every day she was scared—frightened that it might happen again.

***

Bayside Restaurant, downtown Chicago
November 11, 1:00 p.m.

It was a beautiful yet cold afternoon. Temperatures were in the forties. It was beyond sweater weather. Hats, coats, and gloves were the necessary attire to wear, unless one loved the cold weather and found that a sweater or cardigan was all he or she needed to withstand such temperatures. Sierra and the girls came out wrapped in wool jackets, scarves, and earmuffs—the whole nine. While Ashanti was enjoying perhaps a final lunch with the women, Eddy and George were meeting with Jess at his office regarding finding Eddy's daughter.

Seated at a table for five with elegant dinnerware, fresh winter flowers, and lit candles as the centerpiece, the women made a toast to Ashanti, wishing her love, peace, happiness, and a prosperous life. Tomorrow her family was coming to take her to a new home in California.

"I must admit I'm feeling a little sentimental here," said Chloe with tears in her eyes. "I mean, we've been forever bonded by our ordeal in Brazil, and now I feel like part of my flesh has been ripped apart. My scalp was enough! That damn monkey!" Everyone laughed, including Chloe.

Ashanti leaned over and kissed her on the head. "I will miss you all, and I will never forget you or lose contact with you, but I need to be with my parents and my sister. I just wish my brother would join us. He's the only brother I have, and we're all we've got. Plus, he is the only one left in Cameroon aside from my auntie and uncle."

"Perhaps one day he will join you, Ashanti. Have faith. Anything is possible. Escaping from our captors has taught us that. Pray for him, and I will do the same. We are happy for you," said Sierra, smiling.

"Thank you, Sierra. I am feeling bad for Eddy, though. I truly pray he finds out what happened to his daughter. You do know his health is failing, right?" said Ashanti.

"I felt he wasn't doing so well. I convinced him he needs to get a checkup, so we've scheduled an appointment for him the day after tomorrow. He was coughing a lot last night. If it gets worse, we will take him to the hospital," Sierra said with concern.

Lunch was served, and the women began to eat.

"It's the weather. He's old, and he's not used to the cold

climate. I don't know, CeCe. I think you should take him today. He could catch pneumonia. That's instant death at his age. I can take a look at him after his meeting today," said Jenelle.

"Could you, Nelly?"

"Hey, I am a registered nurse, you know. Of course I'll take a look at him! I'll follow you home after lunch. I have my bag in the car."

"Thanks, Nelly."

The friends were doing well since Brazil. Lisa said Marquise had asked to be reunited with her and their children. She was hesitant but had told him, "Let's take it one day at a time." Lisa did not want to get hurt again. After all, Marquise had left her for a young woman during the height of their marriage and his career. He'd failed her and bailed on her. She was careful nowadays. Just because she'd almost died in Brazil didn't mean he had an automatic pass back into her life. Marquise thought he could just pick up where he had left off and dance his way back into Lisa's life as if nothing had ever happened before the kidnapping. Plus, Lisa just didn't trust him.

As they exited the restaurant, Lisa said she was having a dinner party next week before Thanksgiving and invited the girls over for drinks. "Just the ladies. Bring the kids if you must."

They hugged Ashanti, told her to be happy, and wished her good luck in California, and then they all left and went their separate ways until next time.

Later, Jess and Eddy arrived home. Jenelle did a brief examination of Eddy. She took his temperature, pulse, respiration, and blood pressure and listened to his chest. It didn't sound good—either bronchitis or worse. She demanded they take him to the ER immediately. Jenelle alerted her husband, Nate, the ER physician, that she was on her way to the hospital with Eddy and Sierra. Eddy didn't want to go at first, but Sierra begged him to go and told him that if something happened to him, he would never get the chance to find Carmelita. He wanted to be healthy for whatever might come, so he went.

Sierra waited in the ER for almost four hours before Nate

confirmed that Eddy had pneumonia. He was admitted with no questions asked. He was frail and weak, but Nate gave him a good recovery prognosis. They'd gotten to him just in the nick of time.

"Thank God!" Sierra and George rejoiced.

They stayed until Eddy fell asleep and left the hospital late that evening. Ashanti was waiting for them at home. She had been talking on the phone to her parents. She was excited. Bakmuhl was bringing her mother. Talani and Ashanti's father had decided to stay in California to get things ready for her to come live with them. She couldn't wait to see her mother. It had been a long time. How they must have worried about her after she was abducted. She couldn't imagine the pain and grief they had suffered. Ashanti cried at the thought that if not for Sierra and Eddy, she would still have been there or, worse, sold off or dead. She would never forget Sierra and her friends, for they were her friends now. For life.

It was sad to watch Ashanti leave that afternoon. Sierra cried happy tears, for when Ashanti saw her mother, she fell into her arms like a baby. It was a reunion that would have made anyone's heart blossom with great joy. Her mother kept crying out, "My baby! My baby!" They stayed for a few hours, and then just like a strong wind, Ashanti was gone.

There was an emptiness with Ashanti gone. Sierra had gotten used to her being in her home, but now Ashanti had a home to go to with her family. With Eddy in the hospital and George's mother returning to her own home, the house felt lonely and empty.

George went back to work full-time afterward, and Sierra found herself alone most of the day, so she started going back into her store just to keep busy. She did not like being in her big ole house all day by herself. Honestly, she was scared most of the time.

Her siblings were the best. They called every day and stopped in to see her twice a week. She had two sisters and three brothers, all of whom helped to run her beauty supply business. Until Eddy was back home, she planned to spend time at the store with her sisters. Besides, she needed to check on the business and see how things were progressing. She missed her sisters. Her brothers were doing a bang-up job at the factory with production. Her brother Benny said they were getting lots of orders for the holiday season, which was typical that time of year, especially right before Thanksgiving.

That Thanksgiving, everyone in her family was coming to Sierra's, including George's mother, Ellen. George's brothers and their wives had been invited as well, but of course, they'd turned down the invitation. John and Mike had stopped speaking to George after Sam was arrested. Sam's trial was set for January 15, and both John and Mike blamed George for the breakup of their family. They did not believe their father was responsible for what had happened to Sierra, even though George had basically proven to them otherwise.

That evening, George and Sierra decided to go out for dinner to a trendy little bar and restaurant in Glen Hills. The crowd was always cool, calm, and collected, and the food was excellent. It was not for the young folks; the patrons were mostly over-forty businesspeople just getting off work and going out for happy hour.

"I went to see Eddy today at the hospital. The doctor said he's improving, but it doesn't look like he'll be home for Thanksgiving, honey," said Sierra, cutting into her well-seasoned steak.

"I sort of figured that. Better if he stays in as long as he can until he is completely healed. You know, I've gotten pretty attached to Eddy. He is like a father figure to me. The kind I always wanted. He's loving and stern, loves to talk sports, listens to my corny jokes, and fake laughs just to make me feel good. And he gives good advice. He's highly intelligent. I especially love listening to his life stories. Very intriguing man."

"Sounds like you're in love—just like me." She smiled, touching his hand. "What do you think? Keep him for as long as we can?"

"That would be a yes." George chuckled warmly. "Oh, before I forget: Mother said she wants to prepare the turkey for Thanksgiving and her special stuffing."

"Great! My mother says she will bring her famous homemade cranberry sauce and green beans. I'll do the mashed potatoes, and my sister—oh my God, George, she makes the best candied yams! Ah! I can hardly wait. Speaking of your mother, how is she doing?"

"She smiles and carries on, but she hides her grief well. She loves my father. This situation is killing her. She misses him an ungodly amount. But I think she is beginning to come to terms with the fact that my father committed a horrible crime against you, and that hurts her even more. She was angry the other day, and from what John said, after I left, she was using profanity, which none of us has ever heard from her mouth. I don't know how she is going to hold up at the trial."

"Maybe she shouldn't be there. Might be too much for her."

"Do you plan on attending, babe?" asked George.

"Yeah. I want to see his face and hear his reasoning for why he did this to me. My father did not kill your uncle Ryan. He had a heart attack. I remember Dad saying something when I was a kid about the owner of the mill blaming his employees and the union for his going bankrupt."

"But he didn't go bankrupt. He just lost a few millions. Uncle Ryan was not a poor man after the union won. He wasn't. Listen, babe, I am at a good place financially with Drum Technology. I've made my five million dollars without the inheritance from my grandfather's will. I told my father I didn't want anything to do with Grandfather's will or his money. I told him to give my inheritance to John and Mike."

"Really, darling? You turned down your inheritance? Why?"

"Don't you see, Sierra? My father is evil. I don't want that evil money. I earned my millions by working my way to where I am right now as CEO of Drum Technology. My decision to seek out Kline Computers was what put the company in the position it is in right now, and that's a highly secure position, and I'm proud of myself. The difference between myself and my father and Uncle Ryan is that I am not greedy. I've shared that fortune with my employees and colleagues. We're not poor, babe. Your beauty supply company has been bringing in steady revenue for the past six years. And now ..." He paused.

"Now what, darling?" Sierra was smiling, for she felt George was about to tell her they could start the family she always had wanted.

He smiled and held her hand after he put down his fork. "And now, my love, I want to give you babies."

"Oh, honey!" Sierra smiled with tears in her eyes. "You mean it?"

"Um, yes! We're not getting any younger," he teased. "And besides, we're going to have a hell of a lot of fun making them." He winked.

"You'd better know it, handsome," she replied, and she gave him a passionate kiss on the lips.

After dinner, George and Sierra visited Eddy in the hospital one last time for the evening before heading home. He was sitting up in bed, eating, which was a good sign he was getting better. Before, he'd only been able to drink his nutrition; now he was chewing his food. He smiled widely when George and Sierra walked into his room. A nurse had just finished taking his blood.

"Late dinner, Eddy?" Sierra smiled as she leaned over to give him a kiss on the cheek.

"I suppose so, my dear. Suddenly, I was very hungry. How are you both?" he asked in a soft voice.

"We're fine! How are you doing? That is the more important question," George said as he pulled up a chair next to Eddy's bed for Sierra to sit in.

"I'm feeling a lot better, but they won't let me go home. I want to go home. I am sorry I won't be home for Thanksgiving next week."

"It's okay, Eddy. We would rather you be in tip-top shape before you come home to us. Pneumonia is nothing to play with. We'll come visit you on Turkey Day, okay?"

"Listen, Teresa from my village has gotten a hold of Consuela, Manuel's wife. He wasn't living in the village when Carmelita was taken, but Domingo and Carlos were. They were young boys at the time. They might know who took Carmelita. The man who lived next door to them, a man by the name of Benito Segarro, had a daughter around Carmelita's age who was taken also. I've forgotten her name. Paola, I believe it was. But anyhow, Domingo knew her brother; they were friends. Geraldo, Domingo, and a boy named Marco—but Marco was killed, I heard. Yes, Geraldo Segarro. That's his name, but nobody knows where he is. He is the only person who might know what happened to his sister and my daughter," said Eddy, sipping his soup.

"Jess tried to locate this Domingo, but apparently, he has left the country, and no one knows where he is. We'll see if we can locate this Geraldo and see what we can come up with. Hang in there, Eddy," said George.

"I will, my friend. I will do just that. Before I die, I need to find out what happened to Carmelita."

"After you get over this, Eddy, you'll be as healthy as a horse. Don't give up, okay?" Sierra said.

"I can't give up now! I've come too far to give up hope. After all, look what God has delivered me from. For twenty-five years, I lived hell on earth. And now I'm free. Still alive and given another chance and opportunity to find out what happened to Carmelita and if she is still alive."

★★★

Thanksgiving Day, November 25

Ellen McAllister had spent the night at George and Sierra's home so she could be up early to start the turkey and stuffing. The house was smelling good by the time George and Sierra rolled out of bed late that morning. The family weren't coming over until later, so they had time to relax and hang out in their nightclothes for a while. George did not reach out to John and Mike because he knew they would be spending Turkey Day with their wives' families. Besides, they would never have broken bread with him and Sierra.

Seated at the kitchen counter, Ellen, George, and Sierra had coffee, eggs, and toast. They were saving their belly room for the main course later.

"George, I want you to do me a favor today. This morning, actually," said Ellen.

"What's that, Mother?"

"I want you to take me to the county jail to visit your father."

"You sure, Mother?"

"Yes, very sure. He's still my husband. I want to see him. There are some things I need to say to him. Don't ask questions either, George. Turkey is in the oven. The stuffing has already been prepped. It's in the refrigerator. I'm going to get dressed. I'll be ready in an hour."

"Okay, whatever you want, Mother." He turned to Sierra. "I sure hope she rips him apart for what he did to us. It's time my mother fought back."

"She still loves him, George, regardless. Give her time. She can't just let go overnight. They've been married for thirty-five years. That's a long time, regardless of what he's done to me. I love your mom. She's been all the way good to me since I first met her."

Sierra looked at George, and both felt that maybe Ellen was going there to finally confront Sam about what he had done to their daughter-in-law. At any rate, she looked strong, as if she were ready to give him a piece of her mind and perhaps her ass to kiss.

George got dressed and took his mother to the county jail. They didn't say much to each other, but George could feel his mother's anguish. She looked fed up, tired, and defeated. *Lord, please give her the strength to end it with her evil husband once and for all.*

★★★

County jail, downtown Chicago
11:30 a.m.

Sam McAllister was in his cell with his cellmate, a man by the name of Harold Spinster, who was in for a Ponzi scheme. Sam knocked on the cell bars with his fork, signaling that he was still hungry. The guard came and told him to shut up. That was all he was getting until dinner. Sam was angry about being locked up but more so was depressed that his sons had not come to see him once since he'd been there, though he was not expecting George to visit him. His eldest son, John, had at least accepted Sam's collect calls, but he refused to visit his father. Mike could not take the sight of his father behind bars. It made him feel sick, scared, and hurt. Sam had been his strong, proud, successful businessman father, and now he was nothing more than a lowlife criminal chained up and locked behind bars. Who was going to run things now that he had been put away? How long would he be locked up?

John immediately took over the business to keep it from going under. At times, George believed John was greedier and more selfish than his father. He was highly intelligent and a sharp businessman, but he was full of greed. There was no way he was going to let Trak Airlines or any of Sam McAllister's other businesses fall. No way. John forced Mike to get it together so they could act like the vicious, cutthroat businessmen Sam had raised them to be. Michael Raymond McAllister was acting like a wimp, according to his big brother John. John already knew George was out of the picture and had been for years, even before he'd declined their father's inheritance. John knew of all his father's transactions and documents, including wills and other estate-planning papers. Deep down inside, John did love George, and he really did not hate Sierra simply because she was black. In fact, at one point, he'd had the hots for her himself, until George had up and married the ebony princess before he could get a chance with her. John never had been interested in having a real relationship with her; he'd just wanted a piece of her body. That was it. She was a vision of sexiness, with a big butt and big boobs, all natural; full lips; brown skin; unusual gray eyes; and jet-black curls down her back that bounced just like her ass. John had many visions of Sierra on top of him and imagined doing her so nastily it was criminal. He had never been with a black woman before but always had been curious. He had never gotten the opportunity to make love to a woman with so much to offer physically. Sierra was the opposite of the women John dated. Sierra was well endowed. Most of John's women were pencil thin, with bodies not far from that of a supermodel.

In order to kill his lust for his brother's black wife, John had had to develop a reason to resent her. That was where Daddy Sam had come in. Once John had learned that Sierra's father, Ben, had been the main cause of his uncle's business going belly up after the union win, he'd joined forces with his father to take every opportunity to despise her and make her feel it. However, he'd known nothing about the kidnapping, airplane diversion, and trickery. If only his father had come to him first, he would have found another way to oust her from the McAllister family. Now it was too late. Sam McAllister was scheduled for trial after the first of the year.

Ellen clicked her heels down the long hallway, following the guard to the visitors' room divided by windows and phone handsets. Sam appeared before her. She immediately began to cry. He looked old, tired, frumpy, and just like a criminal in his orange jumpsuit. The guard released the shackles around his wrists so he could talk with Ellen on the phone.

There were tears of shame in his eyes. "Ellen, my dearest wife, I am so sorry."

"Sorry? What exactly are you sorry for, Sam? It's Thanksgiving. You're in jail. It's the first time in over thirty-five years we've been separated, excluding all those business trips. Those were nothing compared to this. What are you sorry for? Tell me, Sam. Tell me the truth. Is it true? Did you conjure up a plan to have Sierra kidnapped?"

He looked her dead in the eyes and then dropped his gaze. He didn't confess to it, but he didn't have to; just by the look in his eyes, she knew he was guilty. Sam didn't want to confess right there in the jail with all ears on him and their conversation. Of course, it was true, he said to himself. Ellen shook her head at him in shame.

"I knew you had your ways about certain types of people in this world, and maybe I was blind or just didn't want to see it. Maybe I did all I could to convince myself over the years that you were not this monster that some people, especially your son, kept accusing of you of being, because I loved you so much. I didn't want to see it or accept it. So I swept my fears and all those little darts and remarks of ugliness under a rug. Ben Jackson, Sierra's father, was a faithful employee at McAllister Steel. He had a right to fight for what he believed in, Sam. He had a right to demand a safe work environment, higher wages, medical insurance, and clean and sanitary bathrooms and kitchens. That was his legal right to bring awareness for a company he loved."

"Loved? Are you kidding me? Ben Jackson was a troublemaker! An overly sensitive individual who was ungrateful. A whiner," Sam said angrily.

"Ungrateful? He melted steel bars for your brother for over twenty-five years! He was never late to work. Worked overtime, even though he didn't get paid for it, just to complete his work on time, Sam! I read all the transcripts. I found them in our attic the other day. Everyone loved him. He was a leader. He was kind and humble. Strong. A fighter. And he was black! And you and Ryan didn't like that. There goes another black person fighting for equality, stirring up trouble, as you say. A whiner? That's funny because four hundred employees had his back and fought with him. That's a lot of compatible whiners, Sam. I am ashamed of you. Ashamed! You were my king, Sam. I trusted you to always do the right thing in life and in business. Maybe I don't understand business or the corporate world, but I know righteousness when I see it, and righteous you were not. Our daughter-in-law suffered because of what you did. She could have been killed! And her friends! Our son, your own flesh and blood, suffered! I feel like I don't know who you are. I feel like I married an imposter!" she cried.

"I love you, Ellen. Please forgive me. I never meant to hurt you, and I surely never meant to be separated from you. You think I'm not in here thinking about all that has happened? Our son sold me out and pressed charges against me!"

"He did what he thought and believed to be true. You tried to kill off his wife. What did you expect him to do? I will never forgive you for that, Sam. I pray that God sends you peace and that you repent and ask for forgiveness from our Father in heaven. Only he can save you now. As for you and me, I am filing for divorce from you, Samuel Jacobson McAllister III. I will not live with a man who seeks to murder his own. Yes, that's right. Sierra became part of you and me the day she married our son."

"How can you turn your back on me after thirty-five years, Ellen? Look at me! Look where I am at! You're just going to leave this marriage? What about 'For better or for worse,' huh? What about that?" he yelled as the guard started walking toward him.

"I didn't do this to you, old man! You did this to us! You! You did this to yourself. I will not be there for your trial. Whether they find you guilty or not, I am no longer your wife!" she cried.

Sam looked at her and placed a hand against the window, pleading for her forgiveness. He said he loved her and asked her not to throw away thirty-five years, but Ellen's mind was made up. The guard grabbed the phone away and told him his time was up. He was taken away yelling and screaming. Ellen turned her head away. She was deeply heartbroken. Never in a million years had she thought she and Sam would be separated by divorce at the age of sixty, especially through incarceration. Now it was time to move on.

It was a Thanksgiving she would never forget. She left the county jail with George, who had been waiting outside the entire time. She fell into her son's arms. On the way home, she shared with George that come Monday, she was filing for divorce.

"You were right, Son. He did do it."

"He confessed, Mother?"

"No. He didn't have to. His eyes said it all. I'm sorry for doubting you. I love you, George."

"Oh, Mother, don't apologize. I am sorry for you!" he cried. "It's going to be all right. I promise you. Let's go home now."

Sierra had showered while they were gone and dressed in a brown velvet peasant-girl dress. She was in the kitchen, peeling potatoes to soak in cold water, when George entered the back door with his mother. George complimented how beautiful she looked.

"Hi, Mom Ellen. How did things go?" Sierra asked, giving her a hug.

"Not good, my dear. Not good at all. I told him I was filing for divorce come Monday. That's how it went." She was tired and felt as if she had carried a ton of bricks on her back for the past several weeks.

"Oh, Mom Ellen, I am so sorry." Sierra reached out to hug her again.

"Listen, it's Thanksgiving, and I just want to concentrate on family today, even though not all my family are here. I may have lost my husband to the judicial system, but I still have you and George, and let's have a good day. When are your parents and siblings coming over?"

"They will be here around three thirty. I started basting the turkey. Is that all right with you, Chef?"

Ellen laughed and said, "That's great. Now, scoot! You and George leave me be. Why don't you two go practice making my grandbaby?"

"Mother!" exclaimed George, laughing.

"Oh, I have no problem with that." Sierra smiled, hugging George around the waist.

Thanksgiving was celebrated the traditional way with family and friends and lots of turkey eating. At one point, George and Ellen sat back and just watched Sierra and her family interact. Sierra's family were the only guests who had come to dinner, but it was okay. They were enough. Her brother Benny, the eldest, had twin boys—twins ran in the family—who'd just turned twenty-four and would be graduating from college that spring. They had plans to continue to work with the family business, Sierra's Beauty Supply. Tamia, the eldest girl, had a twenty-year-old son and a sixteen-year-old daughter. The twins, David, and Darryl, at the age of thirty-nine, did not have children yet, but both were married—to sisters. Kiana, who was a few years older than Sierra at thirty-five, had the most children. She had two boys and two girls, whose ages ranged from five to fifteen. Now it was Sierra's turn.

Ellen watched how they all got along with one another, laughing, joking, and reminiscing about old times and previous holidays. It made her smile. They were a big family, but they were close. George and Ellen felt like outsiders on the outside looking in. One thing was for sure: the Jackson children loved their parents and worshipped the ground they walked on. They also loved George something awful, which made Ellen smile with happy tears. She thought about her own family. The fact that John and Mike had turned down George's invitation to spend Thanksgiving with them made him feel bad. Separated—they had been that way for a long time. It wasn't any surprise to either family; in fact, Sierra remembered spending only a few holidays with the McAllisters, early in her marriage to George. After that, they'd made it somewhat clear they did not want Sierra to be part of their life, and that's when George separated himself from his family. Now the family would be separated even more with Sam in jail and with their mother preparing to divorce their father. Once the divorce news hit John and Mike, George knew in his heart that would be the end of their family unit. John would have full reign of their father's business, and Mike would be his puppet. One thing was for sure: George would make sure his mother was not left without anything. He would hire the best attorney and have him fight like hell for his mother.

Everyone was stuffed, and by six o'clock, they all settled down with the kids to watch a holiday movie. Afterward, everyone went home. It was late when Ellen insisted George drive her home.

"Mother, I really don't like the idea of you being in that big ole house all by yourself now that Father is in jail."

"Oh, it's okay, George. You need to stop worrying so much over me. I'm fine. I'm sixty, not six hundred. I'll be fine. You know, I joined a fitness club last week with two of my neighbors. We go four times per week and are taking a self-defense class."

"Really? Wow, Mother. That's great!" George laughed.

It was unlike Ellen to do such a thing. She was extremely matronly and methodical. Her routine hardly ever changed. But she was now going to a gym. It amazed the hell out of George, and he loved it. It meant she was beginning to come out of her shell and was no longer going to center her entire life on house, husband, and kids.

Snow fell days later, and around the first week in December, Eddy was well enough to come home. As a matter of fact, he was in great condition. He'd gotten over the pneumonia and felt brand new.

It was a busy week. George had been working late and coming home close to dinnertime. However, a lot of positive things were happening at Drum Technology. Contracts were being offered by several feasible big moneymakers, so he signed more contracts and made more millions, which was why he was coming home later those days. Sierra always cut her days short at the store and made sure she was home by midafternoon.

Ellen had started divorce proceedings, and by that time, John and Mike had learned their mother was calling it quits with Sam. John was angry. Mike was sad. George was happy, of course. John had stormed into Drum Technology one day, accusing George of tearing their parents apart. Boy, had he caused an ugly scene. George had grabbed him by the collar and thrown him into his office, ripping into him, first for having the nerve to come to his business and cause a disruption with his employees and second because their father was a crazed, racist, hateful, and vengeful individual. To plan and calculate to have his own son's wife kidnapped and murdered was the epitome of hate. Sam wore it well. George had told John he was just like Sam. They'd argued for what seemed like an eternity, until George had told him to get out and never set foot in his company again. He wished he had the kind of loving, close-knit family his wife, Sierra, had with her siblings. Right now, the only people he wanted to protect were his mother and his wife.

In the second week of December, Jess Livingston, George's private detective friend, made a visit to George's home regarding Eddy and the search for his daughter. It was early afternoon on a Saturday. There was about six inches of snow on the ground. Folks were beginning to decorate for Christmas. Eddy was helping Sierra decorate their home, and tomorrow after church, they were going to decorate the tree. Kiana, Sierra's sister, planned to come over to help.

"Come on in, Jess. This is a surprise to see you on a Saturday. Let me take your coat. Have a seat in the family room. Got a nice fire going. Can I get you some coffee?" asked George.

"That would be great," replied Jess, rubbing his hands together.

George came back with the coffee and then summoned Eddy and Sierra to join them. They all sat down as Jess began to give Eddy the full results of his search. Eddy was nervous, scared, and, for some reason, not feeling hopeful. He said he would try not to get upset if his daughter could not be found. He would accept whatever defeat came his way.

"Well, Eddy, I do have some news for you."

"Okay, I'm ready," he said softly.

"We found your daughter, Carmelita."

"Oh my God! You did? Please tell me she is alive. Please!" he cried with his face buried in his hands.

"Yes, she is alive. Let me start from the beginning, okay? It wasn't easy. It was extremely difficult because our men had to go into some harsh terrains to try to locate her. We spoke with Teresa, and she gave us information on Geraldo, who used to run with Domingo. We found him. Geraldo's sister, Paola, was captured with your Carmelita. We found Paola in Argentina. Our men flew to Argentina to meet with her, and she remembers Carmelita. As a matter of fact, they are good friends, apparently. She told us she and your daughter were both sold to a man from Germany by the name of Clopton Klantz. They were twenty years old at the time. They were transported to Germany, enslaved for five years, and then sold off to a man by the name of Martino Jimenez from San Rafael, a city in Argentina.

"Paola and Carmelita escaped from San Rafael and fled to Buenos Aires. The girls lived together for ten years. Paola met a rich man and married him and had a son. Carmelita left Buenos Aires shortly thereafter. Paola's husband gave her fifty thousand dollars to start over. From what I learned, she went back to Brazil to try to find you. She went undercover but was unsuccessful. She didn't want to stay there forever, so she left, thinking perhaps you may have died. That's when, according to Paola, she fled to—are you ready for this, Eddy?"

"Yes, yes!" he cried. Sierra was holding him tightly.

"Your daughter, Carmelita, has been living in Miami, Florida, for over fifteen years. She is forty years old, with two sons—Miguel, fourteen, and Eduardo, ten—and a daughter named after your wife, Margarita, who is eight. She is married. Her husband is an African American engineer by the name of Jerron Daniels. So there you have it! It's all here in this folder, including her contact info and a photo of what she looks like now. Everything you need to get in touch with her." Jess smiled.

Eddy let out a loud wail. He fell to his knees, crying and thanking God. It was a touching moment for everyone present. He was so happy that he could have died. He had grandchildren, and two of them were named after him and his wife. It was the best. Jess confirmed Eddy's case was one of the best cases he had ever worked on.

Eddy stared at his daughter's photograph for a long time, studying every line and inch of her face. She had been very young when she was taken from him. But her wide smile with a dimple on either side was still there.

"There's more, Eddy. Carmelita is being told about you as we speak. One of my guys in Miami just texted me, confirming Carmelita has been notified. And *happy* is an understatement, I presume." Jess laughed.

"How can I ever in this life repay you for what you all have done for me?" he asked, holding his daughter's photo close to his heart.

"Be happy. Be free," said George.

"Yes, Eddy. Again, if it weren't for you, I'd be dead right

now. Now, why don't you pick up that phone over there and call your daughter?" Sierra smiled.

His hands shook like leaves as he dialed her number.

"Hello?" Carmelita said softly.

"Carmelita, my beautiful baby girl. It is me—Papi."

"Papi? Papi!" she cried. "I thought I'd lost you forever!"

"So did I, but I am here, my darling daughter. I am here. Free!"

"And I am free as well. I am coming for you, Papi. I will see you tomorrow."

"Tomorrow?" he asked excitedly.

"Yes, I found out earlier today that you were alive, and my husband, your grandchildren, and I are flying to Chicago tomorrow morning. I missed you, Papi. I can't believe I'm actually talking to you. I cannot wait to see you and hug you. I've thought about you every day since I was captured. Every day and night. Some days I felt I couldn't go on, and at times, I didn't want to. But the love you had for me and the love I had for you kept me still here. God kept me so that we would see each other again someday, and that day is here. *Te amo*, Papi. I will see you tomorrow morning."

"I love you, my angel. Tomorrow morning."

"Eddy, I can't believe it! You found your baby girl, and she's coming here tomorrow?" Sierra exclaimed.

"Yes! She is coming with her husband and my grandchildren! I am a grandfather! Oh my, this just seems too unreal for me!" he cried, smiling and laughing.

George and Sierra were so happy for Eddy they could have burst. Sierra admitted she was going to miss Eddy something awful after he left. She had gotten used to his being in their home. George didn't want him to go either. First Ashanti's family had been found, and now, finally, after months of investigation, Carmelita had been found—and she had been in America all that time, for almost fifteen years.

"I am going to take a nap, you two. I need my rest. Tomorrow is Christmas, New Year's, and my birthday all rolled into one.

Carmelita, my baby. She and I were set free," said Eddy as he slowly ascended the stairs to his room.

"Okay, Eddy, enjoy your nap. We'll wake you for dinner. Tonight Sierra is cooking. Right, babe?" George smiled.

"If you say so, hun. Eat at your own risk!" she teased. However, Sierra was a great cook. During their first year of marriage, George had seen just how good of a cook she was and had gained forty-six pounds. Now, George hits the gym every day after work.

The next morning, Carmelita arrived with her husband and children. It was midmorning. Eddy had been up since the crack of dawn, waiting by a window in the sitting room, near the front door. He looked dapper in dark brown dress pants, alligator shoes, a cream-colored shirt, and a chocolate-brown plaid sweater. Carmelita's limo pulled up to the front entrance. Eddy power-walked his way to the front door to open it before Carmelita even had a chance to get out of the car. Then the miracle occurred.

"Papi?"

"Carmelita?"

"Papi!" She ran over and hugged him tightly, kissing him all over his face, crying.

"Please, everyone come in. It's cold outside," Sierra said happily.

Eddy didn't care what the temperature was outside, for his beloved baby girl and only child was in his arms again after twenty-five years. Minutes later, they all sat in the living room as George served food and drinks. The kids were tired and fell asleep in front of the fireplace. The little girl was wrapped snugly in Eddy's arms, staring up into his eyes, before she dozed off.

"Eddy, George and I are going to take off for a bit and leave you and your family to enjoy one another. We'll be back in a few hours or so. Okay?"

"Okay, my dear. Thank you. Thank you both." He smiled with tears still in his eyes.

He was so happy Sierra thought he would burst. Carmelita was beautiful. She and her family spent the night at George and

Sierra's home, and she and Eddy stayed up late, talking some more. Sierra felt happy for everyone. Her heart was missing Eddy already, and he hadn't even left yet. The day after tomorrow, Eddy would go home with his daughter.

Sierra met with the ladies for lunch that day. Soon the trial would begin for her husband's father. She was sure they would have to take the stand during the trial, and she was ready for that. She just wanted to make sure the others were.

★★★

Bells Bistro, downtown Chicago
1:00 p.m.

It was the week before Christmas, and the restaurants downtown were packed with people. Lots of office parties and luncheons were happening. Thankfully, Bells Bistro was not crowded with people. Chloe, Jenelle, Lisa, and Sierra met up for lunch to discuss the trial coming up in four weeks.

"Are we ready for this? I mean, we'll have to relive every single detail of our nightmare," said Sierra, biting into her gyro.

"I am very ready to nail that son of a bitch for what he did to us!" Lisa said. She was angry. "We all could have been killed! That asshole felt he had the right to take us, exploit us, and then have us sold off as sex slaves! Hell, my descendants were slaves. I ain't trying to repeat history."

"My mother said my daughter still has nightmares because she overhead my husband talking about Mommy being missing," said Jenelle.

"Chloe, what are your thoughts?" asked Sierra.

"I'm with everyone. It's just …"

"Just what, Chloe? You're not going to testify?" asked Jenelle.

"It's what I've been going through with the network at Channel 7. I may lose my job, guys. I'm a reporter, and according to Blake, the head honcho in charge, I will put Channel 7 in a biased state. I'm head anchorperson airing at eight o'clock at night. That's prime time. He's already demoted me and taken me off the schedule. I'm really, really upset about it, ladies!" she cried.

"Oh no, Chloe. I am so sorry. I had no idea," said Lisa.

"I have worked extremely hard to make the anchor team, and now I'm off-screen and working at my desk, chasing stories, including my own. I can't do that! I'm so scared."

"You know what would have been scarier? You dead in Brazil. It's going to be okay, Chloe. You're smart. You must fight for what you want, and you can always go elsewhere. I know Channel 7 is a mighty big and powerful network and is seen throughout the world, but there are others. Cheer up, mama. One hurdle at a time," said Jenelle.

"I guess you're right. Thanks, Nelly," said Chloe, smiling.

"Well, I have a little bit of news for everyone. Marquise and I are back together. We're getting remarried." Lisa smiled.

Everyone dropped her mouth open. Sierra was happy for her, and Chloe was too, but Jenelle was not overwhelmed with joy. She knew Marquise was a jackass of a person, based on the way he'd dogged Lisa during their marriage the first time. Jenelle wasn't going to be phony with the congratulations, but she wasn't going to be rude either. She simply said to her, "I hope you'll be happy and that he will do right by you this time, Lisa." That was it. She wasn't saying any more.

Lunch ended on a good note, and then it was time to prepare for Christmas. That year, George's mother was spending the holiday with George and Sierra. George's brother John had hoped their mother would spend it with him and his family. Mike and his wife had been invited to John's home for Christmas dinner as well. However, Ellen did not want to. She was upset with John and Mike because they had disowned George. Ellen was appalled and shocked that her eldest and youngest sons basically had their father's back, despite knowing what he had done to George and Sierra. She was angry but mostly hurt. These were her children she had given birth to, and she felt as if she didn't know them at all.

Two days before Christmas, George drove to his mother's home and picked her up. John had just pulled up in the driveway with his little girl. Susana ran to her grandmother, smiling, and received big hugs. It was cold outside, and about three inches of snow covered the ground.

"Mother, glad Susana and I caught you before you left. We wanted to give you your Christmas gifts," said John as he looked over at George.

"Grandma! I made this plant holder for you myself at school!" shouted the little six-year-old.

"Sweetheart, you're not supposed to tell Grandma what's inside. That will spoil the surprise." John chuckled.

"Sorry, Grandma." She frowned.

"Oh, it's all right! I am still going to be surprised because I haven't seen it yet. I bet it's beautiful. Thank you, my darling baby girl."

"Well, we'd best get going, Mother," George said. "Sierra is making Christmas cookies and needs me to get to the store. John, have a good one."

"Yeah, you too, George. Mother, merry Christmas," said John, hugging Ellen.

"You also, Son. I love you," she replied, and she got into George's SUV. Susana hopped into her dad's car as John turned to face George.

"Listen, George, you and I need to talk," John said.

"About what?" asked George, irritated. "We have nothing to talk about."

"We do. Our father. The company."

"I don't give a fuck about his company or him, for that matter. You deal with whatever it is you need to do when it comes to that man. *Your* father."

"He's still your father too, George! Look, our family can't go on like this. We need to get past all this mess and start over."

"I moved on a long time ago, John. You and Mike have always disregarded me all my life, and when it came to Father, I was lower than dust. After what he did to my wife and her friends, I will hate him for the rest of my life. He tried to sell Sierra! How can any decent human being stick up for that? Tell me—how? You and Mike are worse, because you were all for it. Starting over? I already started over a long time ago. I could never side with Sam or with you for condoning what he did to my beloved wife! Never!" snapped George.

"That's where you are wrong, my brother. I had no idea, and I had nothing to do with it. I am sorry about what happened to Sierra. I am. I just want us to be brothers again."

"Again? When did you ever treat me like your brother, John? You have always ignored me and shut me out of your life. I'm sorry, but I have to go," said George as he opened the car door and hopped inside.

Ellen waved to John as they pulled off. "What were you and your brother arguing about?" she asked, turning up the heat in the car.

"I'll give you one guess, Mother."

"Sam?"

"Yep! You got it!"

"Does he not care about what his father did to Sierra?" Ellen asked with a confused look on her face.

"He doesn't care at all, and I'm not trying to hear any more crap when it comes to the way my wife's been treated by the family. I just want to have a nice Christmas. Eddy is leaving tomorrow to go live with his daughter in Miami. I want this to be a nice send-off for him."

"Are they having dinner with us tonight?"

"Yes, Sierra said Carmelita will be here around five o'clock, and after that, Eddy is gone. I'm going to miss him but am so glad his daughter was found. Perhaps he can live the rest of his life in peace and love," said George as he approached the on ramp, heading toward Glen Hills.

"I believe he will. I pray for them all."

"Good, because Sierra has nightmares often, and it's starting to affect her."

"What about counseling, Son? She should really go see a therapist."

"We talked about that, and after the holidays, she has an appointment with a psychologist. What scares me is that those thugs who killed the kidnapper are still out there in the world somewhere."

"You don't think they will come looking for Sierra and the girls, do you?" asked Ellen. She was frightened.

"Jess said probably not. They're wanted themselves. The authorities are not even sure exactly who they are, except one. A Domingo somebody, and the word is that he's the one who offed the big guy. Looks like his own man turned on him. I don't think they will come seeking to kill the girls."

"Every day, I think about the reason why my husband is gone. I cannot believe the man I married over thirty-five years ago would conjure up a scheme to have his son's wife abducted and possibly killed. Hurts my heart."

"Mine too, Mother, believe it or not. I feel like I lost my father the moment I grew up and became a man. When I was a child, he was good to me. As soon as I turned about thirteen, he became ugly toward me. Just harsh. I don't want to relive those days, but as a teenager, I was miserable because of it, and I didn't understand why he treated me differently than John and Mike. I hated him then, and I do now."

Ellen began to cry over her son's statements. "I'm so sorry, Son. I had no real idea that was how you felt. Your father was hard on you because, I feel, he saw a lot of himself in you."

"I take that as an insult. I am nothing like him. Let's stop talking about him. You've filed for divorce. You're still young enough, Mother, to have a good life ahead of you. Sixty is the new forty, you know!"

Ellen laughed. "Oh, I don't know about that! However, I'm looking for a new life without Sam. Going to be hard. Whether he is convicted or not, I won't be there with him."

★★★

Christmas Eve, 7:30 p.m.

Sierra had visited her parents and siblings that evening to wish them a Merry Christmas, even though her parents were coming over tomorrow for dinner. Next year, she prayed she would be pregnant or have given birth to her first child. After all she'd been through, a child would replace all the hurt and pain. A baby was something she wanted more than anything in the world, and it would be the shining star in her life. As she lay in bed next to her husband, she smiled at the fact that George was now ready to start a family. If all went well, she would be pregnant sometime after mid-January. She had counted all her fertile days. They had planned accordingly, and come next month, she wanted to hear the news that she and George were expecting. But first, they had to get past the trial of Sam.

★★★

Limon, Costa Rica

Domingo had been keeping up with the news regarding the kidnapping trial of Sam McAllister over the past few months. He was now living a peaceful, carefree life in Puerto Limon, where his sister lived. He had purchased her a beautiful home—not too big, not too small, and a hundred times better than the home she'd lived in before, which had been basically a hut. He had been living with her since his escape. But it wasn't going to be for too much longer. His ultimate plan was to settle in Europe, take on a new identity, and perhaps get married and raise a family.

Domingo had told his sister, Anna Maria, everything about his former life, which he had been forced into by Raul. At first, she had been angry, but ultimately, she had been happy to know that she had a little brother and that he was now free. Domingo and Anna Maria shared the same father but had different mothers. Both his parents were dead. Anna Maria's mother was still alive and lived with Anna Maria; however, she was incredibly old, could barely see or hear, and suffered from dementia. She knew nothing of Domingo or his existence in their lives.

"After the trial is over, you're flying off to Europe? Where in Europe, Domingo? Why not live in another Latino country?" she asked her brother as she flipped over a tortilla on the stove.

"I get what you are trying to say, because I would blend in nicely in a Latino country. I don't know. Perhaps France or England. I would love to go to America, but it would be too risky for me. Too much immigration checking and harassment. Listen, wherever I go, I will always keep in touch with you, Anna Maria. Don't worry, okay?"

"Now that I have learned I have a little brother, I have no choice but to worry and wonder, especially after what you've been through. Please stay in Costa Rica for a little while longer. I doubt they will come looking for you here. Raul is dead. You've destroyed his compound and every shred of contacts in his warehouse. Change your name if you must, but stay. Stay put right here, my brother," she begged.

Domingo took his sister's hand and replied, "Okay, Anna Maria. I will stay for a little while longer, but you must know that if the authorities somehow find out I have a sibling here in the country, they will come for me, and I don't want you to be caught in the crossfire. That's why I want to leave."

"Just don't leave without saying goodbye, okay?"

"Okay, I won't forget."

★★★

Chicago, Illinois
Christmas morning, Sunday

Sierra and George woke up early to hear Eddy laughing it up downstairs with his daughter and grandchildren. It was a joyous sound, and it was the last time Sierra would hear Eddy's voice, for tomorrow morning, he was leaving with his daughter and her family for Miami. It had been a pleasure to have them there for the past few days. She was going to miss Eddy something terrible but would be forever filled with joy in knowing he had finally found his daughter and was going to spend his last years with her.

George's mother was also up, preparing breakfast. She looked a little down and rightfully so. Sam's trial would be starting soon. No one could imagine how Ellen truly felt. She and Sam had been married for more than thirty-five years, and losing him to prison was devastating. George walked up to her as she flipped pancakes and gave her a hug. She smiled as she watched the kids rip the paper off their presents to see what Santa Claus had brought them. For a minute, George imagined the day when he and Sierra would watch their own children on Christmas morning. He was hopeful, because last night, he and his wife had had the most intense lovemaking. George would just have to wait and hope, come the end of January, for a missed period.

Later that day, Sierra's family stopped by to wish everyone a merry Christmas. They stayed for dinner, and then, just like that, Christmas was over with.

The next morning, Eddy and his family bid farewell to Sierra and George. She cried, of course, and sent blessings of peace and love, and that was it. The man who'd helped them escape hell was gone. Now it was time to prepare for George's father's trial, which was January 15.

The house was strangely quiet after Eddy's departure, almost creepy. Sierra went back to work full-time the following day. She did not like being home all alone with George at work and Eddy and Ashanti gone. She had quickly become comfortable with them in her home. Plus, having them there had been a protective shield from the mental hell she was going through because of the abduction. Eddy and Ashanti had made her feel secure. She missed them both, but it was time to get back to her livelihood. Everyone was glad to see her back on the scene. It was the start of her returning to her normal life before the kidnapping. She had one more hurdle to get over: the trial of Sam McAllister. It was all over the news, making headlines everywhere across the nation and even the world. It was a big story because of the name of corporate giant Samuel McAllister.

New Year's Eve was approaching. Sierra did not want to be out in the public eye to celebrate, as she feared public harassment, especially now that the kidnapping had been reported through newspapers, television, the internet, and radio.

★★★

Chicago, Illinois
Thursday, December 30, 8:00 p.m.

George and Sierra were enjoying a nice, quiet candlelit dinner at home. He was trying to convince his wife that they should go out and have a good time with his friend Jim and his wife, Liz.

"Honey, it will only be for a few hours. We can leave at midnight and come back home. Babe, you cannot allow what happened to you to stifle your life, or you'll never be free or at peace. You're here. Accept that you are a survivor. You survived a horrible thing that took place in your life, and I know you are traumatized. I feel you, babe. I do. It was painful for me not to know what had happened to you. I suffered too."

"You did not go through what I went through, George. It's one thing to imagine it, but to actually live the horror—you cannot even begin to understand or feel my pain or fear. I love you, George, but please don't force me to rehabilitate overnight. I still have nightmares on a regular basis, and yes, therapy is helping somewhat, but it has not stopped the fear. Just be patient with me. I am afraid still. You expect me to just snap out of it or just bounce back like it was nothing."

"No, babe, I don't. I just want you to try not to allow what happened to you and the ladies to stop you from living. That's all. If you don't want to go out tomorrow night for New Year's Eve, okay. I ain't mad at you. We'll celebrate together in private," he said, reaching across the table to hold her hand.

154

Sierra smiled lightly and looked into his eyes. "I'm sorry, George, if I spoiled your plans. Um, don't just cancel yet, okay? I mean, you're right; I can't allow this thing to destroy my mind and my life."

"I meant it, babe. If you don't want to go, we can stay home, and if you change your mind, I promise we'll leave right after midnight."

"So where is the party going to be?"

"At Jim's brother's restaurant. He invited two other couples. Grace and William will be there from the office. I know how much you love them. The other couple I don't know. Friends of Liz's, I'm told. Look, babe, the Rainforest Club is an exceedingly high-scale place."

"I know, darling; you don't have to tell me what type of people frequent there. I've been there before with the girls. Very nice indeed. Okay, so, um, looks like we're going out tomorrow night. Bring in the New Year with hope and positivity, right?" She smiled.

"Right, babe. Don't worry. I'll be by your side the entire time."

December 31st, Glen Hills

Snow fell heavily that night as they slept; however, only three inches accumulated, not enough to stop the city from celebrating the upcoming New Year. George went to work the next morning but was home by noon. Sierra met with the girls for lunch. Each planned to celebrate that night with loved ones. Chloe was spending it with her parents. Lisa and Marquise, who had reunited, were planning on remarrying. Sierra didn't know how she felt about that situation, but as long as Lisa was happy, she would try to be supportive. She prayed Marquise would treat her right this time, but overall, Sierra was happy for her, even though she didn't like him. Finally, Jenelle and her husband were planning to celebrate New Year's at home. She was never the party girl anyhow.

★★★

Green Terrace Café, Glen Hills
12:30 p.m.

"I'll have the salmon," said Sierra to the waitress, "and a glass of chardonnay. Thanks."

"My pleasure, ma'am, and I'd just like to say I'm glad you all are safe," replied the waitress as she took the menus, and she walked away.

"See what I mean? The whole world knows now. I'm serious. We're about to be scrutinized and stalked over our ordeal. I don't like attention, and the trial is starting in four days!" exclaimed Sierra.

"Unfortunately, we have no control over it. People are going to approach us. Thankfully, I wasn't fired. I still work for the news station, and let me tell you, already I've been approached by talk show hosts to appear after the trial," Chloe said.

"Did you agree to appear, Chloe?" asked a frantic Sierra.

"No, I didn't. I feel the same way you do, CeCe. Not going to be put in the public eye any more than I already am! Bad enough I've been taken off the anchor team," she said.

"What!" the girls said together.

"Chloe, no," Sierra whined softly.

"Yes. I told you a while back I was off the team. Joel sentenced me to programming. I can't be mad, because actually, I sort of hinted I was not ready to be out there in the field again. It's okay. At least I still have a job."

"How are things going for you since you've been back home with your parents, Chloe?" asked Jenelle.

"It's been somewhat challenging. Sometimes overbearing. Especially my father. He won't stop hovering over me, and I get it, but let me breathe a little on my own. However, I'm not ready to move back into the penthouse alone."

"I'm sorry, sweetie," said Sierra. "What can we do to help?"

"Nothing, really. Remember I told you about Scott Graham, the guy who works in editing? And how he's been after me for the past year to go out on a date?"

"Yes, and?" asked Jenelle, smiling.

"Well, we're dating!"

"Oh, that's wonderful!" the girls called out.

"It is. I mean, he's been incredibly supportive and just a real friend. He's always been kind and—"

"Attracted to you?" Lisa smiled.

"Yes, that also. I just enjoy the companionship right now."

"Have you two—you know? Knocked some boots?" teased Lisa.

"No! Not yet." Chloe laughed as she bit into her prosciutto and provolone panini. "Who knows? Might happen soon."

"Okay, we want more info! So are you two hooking up tonight for New Year's Eve?" asked Sierra, excited to hear her friend finally had found a mate.

"As a matter of fact, we are. We are having dinner at the Rainforest, and then off to his place for—"

"We're having dinner there tonight also!" exclaimed Sierra, laughing.

"Really? I guess I'll see you there." Chloe smiled.

"Yes, then I can meet this Scott Graham."

After a nice long lunch, the ladies hugged and wished each other a happy New Year before departing and going their separate ways. The next time they all saw each other would be at the courthouse.

"See ya, Lisa! See ya, Jenelle! See you all on the other side of time!" Sierra called out. "Chloe, I'll see you tonight."

"Okay, my friend. Later." They hugged.

★★★

Rainforest Club
December 31, 10:30 p.m.

While Sierra and George were getting ready to bring in the New Year with friends, his mother, Ellen, was home alone, crying. Her incarcerated husband was in his cell, crying. Every year for the past ten years, after a big Christmas celebration with family, Sam and Ellen had taken off to Palm Springs, California, to ring in the New Year with their closest friends, the Griffins and the Powells. They were in Palm Springs again that year, living it up, but the McAllisters were alone and miserable.

Ellen had lied and told her sons she was going out with the ladies, but when George saw his mother's neighbors, whom she'd claimed she was hanging out with that night, at the Rainforest Club, he knew his mother had made up a story to stay home. The Rainforest was crowded, and people were having a great time, eating, drinking, and socializing. Sierra and George sat at a private table on the platform with a few other notables. They were nibbling on appetizers and sipping champagne.

"What's the matter, George?" Sierra asked.

"Mom. She's home alone. She told me she was going out with friends. Well, her friends are here at the club, over there dining together. Where is she?" He pointed them out.

Sierra stretched her neck to see. "Mom's home alone?"

"Yes. Um, CeCe, I think we should leave and go be with her. Is that okay with you?"

"That is perfectly fine with me. Let's go," she said as she gathered her purse and cashmere coat.

George made an excuse that he wanted to be making love to his wife come midnight. Their friends laughed and whistled. They knew George and Sierra were on a quest to make babies.

"See you all on the other side of time, my friends," said George, and they scurried their way through the crowd and out the door and headed west to Ellen McAllister's home, which was fifteen miles away, near downtown Chicago.

When they arrived, the house was dark, with only the entrance light on. Ellen's car was in the driveway. However, John's car was parked next to hers. *So he came to wish his mother a happy New Year, eh?* George thought. Just as George pulled into the driveway to park behind his mother's Benz, John exited the house.

"John, is Mother okay?"

"Yes, she's doing fine, George. Sad, as expected, but overall, she is okay. I wanted to stop by to wish her a happy New Year. With our father being in jail and all, I'm sure this is not a happy holiday season for her. Look, I've been trying to convince her not to divorce Dad. Do you think you could convince her not to? Not for yourself, George. I know you hate him, but for our mother. Can you at least—"

"You've got to be kidding me. Yes, I despise him, and hell no, I will not try to convince our mother to stay with that criminal. Did he think about love for her when he committed a criminal act of conspiracy and kidnapping? Did he?" George yelled, and he walked away.

Inside, Sierra was sitting next to Ellen by the fireplace, when George walked in. He was solemn and feeling empathy for his mother. For some strange reason, she seemed at peace. She told George she had been meditating and doing a lot of thinking about her future, and she viewed that night as the start of a new life.

★★★

11:40 p.m.

"George, I haven't told your brothers, but when I file for divorce on Monday, I, um ..."

"What is it, Mother?" asked George, holding her hands. He looked her straight in the eye. Something else was bothering her.

"Well, I've decided I am going to put this house up for sale. I don't want to live here anymore. Too many memories. Fond ones, of course, but also bad ones. When you let go, you must let go completely."

George smiled and kissed his mother's hands. "It's okay, Mother. I know this house has meaning. You've been living here since you got married. Raised a family here. I remember the day you first planted a garden out back. I was seven. How I enjoyed watching food grow from the ground. Remember I used to help you water the garden?"

Ellen smiled with tears in her eyes. "Yes, I do. But one time, you overwatered, and it was disastrous!" She laughed.

"Mother, this house has a lifetime of memories and rightfully so. Thirty-five years is a lifetime. After all that's happened, especially with you filing for divorce, I couldn't see you continuing to live here, and it's okay. Time to turn the page in your book of life to a new chapter. Even through the hurt and pain, it's okay to move forward. As a matter of fact, we must. You have to think about your happiness and survival now. Sierra and I will be here every step of the way!"

"That's right, Mom Ellen. We've got you," added Sierra.

"I know you do, my darlings. But let me be clear on one thing. I am not going to live with you and be a burden. I have been looking at those penthouses near Arrington. They're for seniors over fifty-five, and they are eloquent!"

"I've seen those. Mother, they are absolutely beautiful," said George.

"Or I was thinking about buying a small cottage in Creekside. I'd be closer to you and Sierra. Over there on Mason Lane. I actually fell in love with it, George. It looks like something right out of a storybook. Very quaint, but the inside is very modern, with state-of-the-art appliances, and I love it. And Mason Lane is a particularly good neighborhood."

"And it's only ten minutes from George and me." Sierra smiled.

"Well then, let's purchase it for you! I think it would be a great start to your new life. Mom, I love you, and everything is going to be okay. Trust in the Lord, and everything will be okay. Do you believe that?" asked George.

"Yes, my son. I trust in God, and I pray all will be okay." She smiled.

Thirty seconds later, they were doing the countdown, and just like that, they were on the other side of time. It was a new year. George and Sierra stayed up until one o'clock in the morning and made sure Ellen made it to bed and was okay. They set the security alarm and decided to stay the night. George and Sierra always kept extra clothes at George's parents', and they slept in George's old room. *Happy New Year, world!*

★★★

Chicago, Illinois
Monday morning, January 3

Ellen McAllister was up early and on her way to her attorney's office to officially file for divorce from Samuel McAllister, her husband of thirty-five years. She had dried her tears after a long two months since finding out her husband, the father of her children, was responsible for his son's wife's disappearance and had paid criminals to kidnap Sierra to be sold off into human trafficking.

It was cold as ice that morning. About four inches of snow covered the ground. Ellen's car was kept in a garage; however, she worried that when she pressed the remote to open the garage door, she would not be able to leave. To her surprise, her entire driveway had been plowed. She took a deep breath and exhaled, smiling. She did not want anything to deter her from her appointment with her attorney. This divorce was going to happen. Her mind was made up. She might have forgiven other mistakes and moved on but not orchestrating a kidnapping and potential murder. That was the epitome of evil, and she was not having it as a Christian woman. Sam had cheated on her quite a few times, and she had forgiven him and carried on, but this was unforgivable, and only God could give him a pass.

As she drove toward the city, she reminisced about her entire life with Sam. When they first had met, she'd been only eighteen. They'd had a short courtship, gotten married, and made a family, and she'd watched him climb the ladder of success with his business. Through the good and the bad, she had been there and had stayed, regardless of his faults. She cried again.

★★★

161

Bluford, Resnik, and Kemp law office, downtown Chicago

Ellen was escorted by secretary to see Joel Kemp, her attorney. He offered her coffee and doughnuts. She sat down and sipped slowly on the hot coffee, feeling somewhat nervous but trying hard to hide the pain of the moment. She couldn't believe she was actually getting ready to end her long marriage to a man she had known since she was a kid.

"Thank you for coming, Ellen. I know this has to be one of the most difficult things to do, but sometimes it's necessary. I just want to say I'm sorry this has happened to your marriage. I'm going to be straight. The whole world knows about the kidnapping, and we here at the firm give our deepest apologies. The good part is, they all survived."

"Yes. Thank you, Mr. Kemp."

"Call me Joel. So let's get started. First thing we'll do is prepare the documents to file for divorce. And before we actually send these documents to be filed and recorded at the courthouse, we'll need to go over everything you are seeking or demanding. Assets, stocks, bonds—everything down to Great-Grandma's candy dish," he joked lightly.

Ellen looked at him and told him, "Let's get this done."

★★★

Meanwhile, at the county jail, Sam McAllister was in his cell, sulking. He was upset his attorney had not yet been summoned. The guard told him his lawyer was not scheduled to come until Wednesday. The trial was set for January 15. There were things they needed to discuss and witnesses and other issues that needed to be handled before the trial. Sam was confident he would beat this rap, despite the overwhelming evidence against him. Because he was filthy rich and had connections everywhere in high places, he was sure he would not be sentenced.

His lawyer was busy gathering information and trying to

locate those who had been associated with Raul. Even Sam's mistress, flight attendant Madeline Benson, would be questioned and perhaps arrested, for she had redirected hotel and flight plans and slipped mickeys into the women's orange juice that morning. Domingo was the main person of interest at that point. They knew finding him would be like looking for a needle in a haystack, because with the fire and death of Raul, all information and records had been destroyed along with him. The fish warehouse, the mansion, and the holding house all had gone up in smoke. For Sam, it was good if Domingo could not be found. It was bad for Sierra and George. When Sam got word around the cell block that Raul's men had practically vanished off the face of the earth, he rejoiced loudly. He knew at that point he was not going to serve time ever. However, he forgot about Eddy, Madeline, and the two pilots from Trak Airlines.

Chapter 6

Glen Hills
Thursday, January 6
6:00 p.m.

"How can this happen, Steve? Are you telling me there is a strong possibility Sam will walk? We have enough information that he set this whole ordeal up!" George yelled. He paced back and forth in his living room before standing in front of the fireplace.

Sierra was quiet, in shock. They had just finished dinner with their attorney.

"George, yes. We have information that he changed the flight and hotel arrangements, and we have proof he paid a flight attendant and pilots to redirect the flight to Brazil. That's it!"

"Well, there you go! We have phone records, notes, and phone logs. How can he get arrested based on all these things and still walk?"

"Because we need direct proof that he had interactions or conversations with Raul Serranos and his men," Steve said.

"We do! He spoke to a Raul on his cell phone. Jess retrieved his cell phone records from Tevron Communications and found that my father had at least five or six conversations with this asshole! What more do we need?" yelled George.

"George, it's not that simple. We can't mess this up. We have to get this right the first time going in, or you are looking at a mistrial. Someone could have posed as Raul, or he could have had one of his men speak on his behalf. Listen, I'm in your corner. I believe you! I believe your father is responsible and had dealings with Serranos, but we don't have proof that it was in fact his personal cell. That number came up as unidentified. It was a disposable phone. He used a disposable phone for each of those calls. Raul was a very intelligent man. Concrete evidence is what we need. Right now, Jess is looking into the flight attendant and the pilots to see if they knew anything directly related to Raul."

George sat down on the sofa next to his wife. "Then what?" he asked more calmly.

"We gather all the intel we can from them. I'll say it again: it is imperative that we find this Domingo character or someone who knew Raul well in order to bring your father down. There is no retrial. We have only a little more than a week left before the trial to find them and question them."

Sierra suddenly interjected. "Darling, what about Eddy?"

"No, Sierra. We can't do that to him. He was merely a slave in Raul's holding house. A cook, for crying out loud! What could he know?"

"Eddy was his slave for many years! He may know something or know someone who would be helpful to us. And I honestly believe Eddy would do everything in his power to help us. Doesn't hurt to try," Sierra said with hope.

"I think it's a great idea," Steve said. "He could be extremely helpful. We have to exhaust all our resources here. We're running out of time."

"Listen, I don't want Eddy testifying up on the stand in his condition. He is an old man. A not-so-healthy one at that. He just found his daughter! Let him be," George stammered.

"Okay, McAllister. Have it your way, but if I were you, I would try and convince this Eduardo Montenegro to talk. Otherwise, we are grabbing at thin air with nothing to hold on to. Think about it. The trial begins in nine days. I'll leave you to discuss it with your wife and this Eddy guy. Call me, and make it soon. Time is of the essence," said Steve as he gathered his hat and coat, and he left their home.

The wind whistled, and snow blew harshly against the windowpane. The sound of the fire crackling was intoxicating and inviting. Sierra was wrapped up in her husband's arms as they discussed Eddy. They didn't want to involve Eddy, but he was the only one left, aside from the others Domingo had allowed to escape, who'd lived and worked in the holding house. Eddy had to know something. They decided to call him, and he was more than willing to help with the investigation and trial—anything after their assistance in his finding his daughter and escaping from Raul's reign of hell. Eddy felt indebted to Sierra and George, so it was no problem to help them out.

Eddy remembered Domingo and Carlos well. Both men always had treated Eddy with respect. Eddy would prepare them their favorite dishes and starch their shirts and pants. He'd pick fruits from the trees, clean them, and make fruit salad, Domingo's favorite. Although they were criminals, thugs, and henchmen, they'd treated Eddy with kindness, maybe because he was an old man or because they knew what Raul had done to his daughter.

***

Domingo had hated Raul from the beginning. When he'd smoked his ass, he'd felt as if he'd died and gone to heaven. He was now in France under the alias Jason LaSalle. Although he was Latino, he could pass for white, Italian, or even French. Plus, he spoke French fluently. Domingo was living well. He'd left his sister in Costa Rica and begun his new life with $5 million to his name. He'd bought himself an elaborate but not overly dramatic fully furnished flat located in town for $350,000 US and a Mini Cooper. His plan was to lie low but introduce himself to the community enough that folks would not deem him suspicious, unapproachable, or antisocial. He was especially careful of the women he met or planned to date. He had no idea, let alone concern, that he was being sought for questioning, but he knew all about the trial, for it had made worldwide news.

Domingo, a.k.a. Jason, sat back in front of his sixty-inch television, watching the update on the news. Outside, he could hear horns honking and folks out and about the town, shopping and dining. Domingo had just finished a plate of chicken, potatoes, and green beans. He held a glass of wine in his hand, studying the news with intensity, when suddenly, his name was mentioned, and an old photograph appeared on the screen. Gently, he squirmed in his seat with his eyes fixated on the television screen. The photo showed him looking scruffy and unkempt. Now he was shaven, with a slight mustache and a five o'clock shadow. His long, curly hair was cut short, close to his scalp. He looked different. Clean cut.

There was no mention of Calderon, Carlos, and the others, just him. *Why?* he thought. Immediately, his thoughts went to the flight attendant chick, Madeline Benson. There was no mention of her either. Then he finally realized it had to be Eddy.

Domingo knew it would take a really skilled individual to track him down. His credits were tight. His Social Security number was tight. His identity was secured. He had everything under control. All records and information about anyone related to Raul had been destroyed in the fire. Eddy was George and Sierra's last hope to bring Sam McAllister down. They might not even need Domingo, he thought.

His cell rang. It was a woman he'd met at a café the other day. Her name was Celia Downing. She was in her midthirties and single with no kids. She was a gorgeous brunette with long, flowing curls and was built like a brick house at size twelve. Domingo answered her call and invited her over.

It was on after that. They had a few drinks and then went straight to the bedroom to bang the headboard until it broke. He hoped Celia was not interested in love, commitment, and all that lovey-dovey stuff, because he wasn't down for it. Not now. Perhaps not ever.

Celia made breakfast the next morning, gave him a goodbye kiss, and left shortly thereafter, happy and satisfied until next time. Domingo had to admit she was a sweetie. Pleasant. Poised. Not a pushy type of woman. She was educated and sophisticated, and she had a great career. She was vice president of Mon Amie Textile Industry in Paris. She was independent but somewhat submissive in the most important way: in the bedroom. The sex was rated five stars according to Domingo, and that was all he cared about for now. Celia was a sexy, sweet woman, and he'd been lonely since he escaped Brazil.

He wasn't too concerned at the moment regarding the manhunt, because he believed he had dodged law enforcement. Still, he wanted to keep a close eye on the news. He had a computer but never used a search engine to get information regarding Sam McAllister's trial or Raul's death. He did not want that on his hard drive. Mostly, he used the computer for nonsuspicious stuff, such as ordering food or reading novels online. He planned to take a trip to the bookstore soon to purchase some books and periodicals to pass the time.

★★★

Cook County Jail
Saturday, January 8, 10:00 a.m.

A fight broke out in the chow hall during breakfast, and Sam McAllister and a few other inmates were indirect victims in the line of fire between two rival prisoners who had been beefing for weeks over a snitching incident. Sam tried to get out of the way when the fight started, but he wasn't quick enough. His aching, arthritic knees would not allow him to fly like a gazelle. So he took a breakfast tray to the forehead. He was taken to the infirmary, treated, and released back to his cell. His roomie at that time was an older man who was awaiting trial for an assault on his girlfriend, who he claimed had cheated on him with his brother. Lockdown was in effect.

Sam had been promised a phone call. He wanted to contact his wife. Divorce papers had been served to him yesterday during his meditation time. Sam was shocked and devastated, and he even cried.

"McAllister, you okay, man?" asked his cellmate, Horace, a fifty-five-year-old black man from Chicago's west side.

"No. Not at all. My wife is filing for divorce. Over thirty-five years of marriage. And now she is calling it quits."

"Yeah, that's how them bitches be. You catch a little case, and they wanna fuck you up by leaving."

168

"No, you've got it wrong. Don't you ever refer to my wife as a bitch! The only fuckup is me! Ellen is pure and good and faithful, and she's been by my side for a lifetime, but this time, I guess she said, 'That's enough.'"

"Well, are you gonna fight it?"

"No. I'm going to give her what she wants—her freedom so she can be happy for however many years she has left. She's put up with me and my dirt long enough."

"You're too hard on yourself if you ask me, bro. What you in here for anyhow?" Horace asked as he stretched out on his cold, hard cot.

"Kidnapping."

"Who you kidnap? Some sexy chick and try to hold her ass hostage somewhere?" Horace laughed.

"Basically, yes. I conjured up a plan to try to get rid of my son's wife because of what her father did to my brother's company thirty years ago. I wanted revenge, and when I found out my son married his daughter, well, that was perfect reason to get revenge. Hate. It's full of pain, ugliness, and evil. And I had all that for a man who only tried to stand up and do what was right. Now here I am, sitting in this rathole, and he's living high on the hog in a beautiful luxury home on the South Side of Chicago."

"Man, that's some stupid shit. Jealousy is a mafucka. I know! I beat my girl over being jealous. What was your plan after she had been kidnapped? That's crazy—over company bullshit? Dayum! You rich folks are evil!" He laughed.

"Her father caused my brother to go bankrupt and die of a heart attack!"

"Was it worth you sittin' up in here facing a potential thirty years at your age?" asked Horace, now serious, thinking about his own crime he had committed.

"Hell no, it's not worth it. Look what I lost. My family. My wife."

"Got that right. I'm fifty-five years old. I lost my damn temper over some bullshit act that involved my brother too."

"Yeah?"

"Yeah. He betrayed me—slept with my woman."

"Why'd you beat her? Should have kicked your brother's ass. Women are a dime a dozen. You only get one brother. Now, was your shit worth it?"

"Fuck no. Still, I got to pay the piper. My attorney told me I could do three years in the pen."

"For slapping a woman?" yelled Sam.

"No, for beating up a woman. Two black eyes, and I knocked her teeth out. And, um, I fractured one of her ribs," he added sorrowfully.

"Damn. Still, three years sounds like ice cream compared to thirty. I'm sixty-five. I may as well plan my funeral now. Trial starts on Tuesday. Not feeling greatly confident."

"Yeah, well, good luck anyhow. I'm black. My ass is grass regardless. You're rich, and you're white. You have a better chance of being free than me."

"Oh, come off that bullshit. What's color got to do with crime?"

"Man, get the fuck outa here! You know damn well the system is biased as fuck when it comes to race and money. Don't say another mafuck word to me, McAllister. I hope they fry your ass."

Two days later, Sam's cellmate found out his daughter-in-law was black. He ripped him a new asshole after that. Horace spent forty-eight hours in the hole. Meanwhile, the trial of Sam McAllister began.

★★★

Courthouse, Glen Hills, Illinois
Friday, January 14, 10:00 a.m.

It was snowing heavily outside when the entire McAllister family arrived at the courthouse for day one of the trial of Samuel McAllister. Sierra was nervous, but she promised herself she would endure it to the end to hold accountable the man who had meticulously tried to have her vanish from the face of the earth. Ellen sat on the left side of George, with Sierra to his right. John and Mike sat on Ellen's left with their wives. The jury already were seated. Minutes later, the bailiff walked in with Samuel McAllister. He was handcuffed and wearing an orange jumpsuit. Ellen immediately pursed her lips and put her head down as a single tear fell from her eye. Sam looked at his wife for a quick second, as if he wanted to say he was sorry. It was too late now. Even John and Mike had tears falling from their eyes, but George and Sierra did not. She was angry as hellfire yet kept her composure so she didn't get kicked out of the courtroom. It was packed. All the girls were there with their husbands, and Chloe was with her boyfriend, Scott.

"All rise!" the bailiff said loudly as the judge entered the courtroom from a side door.

He was a tall black judge about sixty years old with salt-and-pepper hair cut close to his head, and he wore thick-rimmed glasses. His presence commanded power. John and Mike squirmed in their seats with fear at the sight of him because he was black. They felt their father was not going to have a fair trial because of it.

The bailiff announced, "Department one of the Chicago Superior Court is now in session. The Honorable Milton Stivers presiding. Please be seated."

"Good morning, ladies and gentlemen. Calling the case of the people of the State of Illinois versus Samuel McAllister III. Are both sides ready?" asked Judge Stivers.

Both the district attorney and prosecutor replied that they were ready. Then the judge asked the clerk to swear in the jury.

"Will the jury please stand and raise your right hand? Does each of you swear you will try the case before this court and will return a true verdict according to the evidence and instructions of the court, so help you God? Please say, 'I do.' You may be seated."

Next came the opening statements from the district attorney and the prosecutor, who was the attorney George had hired, Steven Highlander, the best prosecutor in the state.

"Your Honor and ladies and gentlemen of the jury, the defendant has been charged with the crimes of kidnapping, extortion, and bribery with the intent to sell his daughter-in-law Mrs. Sierra McAllister into the sex-trafficking world. The evidence will show that Samuel McAllister not only orchestrated the entire operation to have Sierra McAllister sold off into human trafficking but also was the driving force in having her kidnapped, using his own personal resources and connections to carry out the crime committed. The evidence I present will prove to you that the defendant is guilty as charged."

Thus, the trial began. It was a long day. They broke for lunch at one o'clock, and Sierra and George didn't get out of there until five thirty. The first day consisted mostly of identifying all the people involved and evidence from Sam's binders and telephone calls to Trak Airlines. George could tell it was going to get ugly right from the start. Steve wanted to present motive first, and he had it. He presented strong evidence of motive and dug hard into Sam's racist persona. There was also information regarding the steel mill case, which gave even stronger motive for Sam's hatred and revenge toward Sierra. It was only day one, and George was feeling confident that his father would not get away with what he had done to his wife and her friends.

Ellen was exhausted both mentally and physically. Thank goodness they had the weekend to rest. On Monday, it was back to court.

The only downfall for George was being away from his company. However, his colleague Jim Melton was holding it down, and George was able to do some work from home. No one knew how long the trial would last, but Steve assured them it was not going to happen overnight. With the severity of the crime he'd been accused of, Sam's trial might last a few months or longer, Steve said. Thankfully, all the witnesses who'd experienced the kidnapping were alive. Sierra's and the other ladies' testimonies were going to be the key to seal the deal. After all, Sam hadn't expected them to survive, let alone escape and live to tell the story. Then there was Eddy Montenegro, the only true witness to prove there was a connection between Raul and Sam. Although Eddy hadn't known who exactly was responsible for the girls' kidnapping, he had been part of Raul's world for many years as his chef, confidant, and record keeper. He'd kept a manifest and done most of Raul's paperwork because he was wise and trustworthy, unlike the flaky females at the front desk of the warehouse. Eduardo was ready to defend Sierra against Sam McAllister.

Ellen decided to stay the night at George and Sierra's home. She didn't want to worry her son, but with Sam incarcerated, she was lonely and was going through deep separation anxiety. Even though she was in the process of selling their home, she found it heartbreaking and sad to continue to sleep there every night. She missed her husband. All the memories she'd shared in that home were alive and vivid. She cried a lot. In two weeks, she would be moving into the charming little cottage not far from George and Sierra. John and Mike had begun to put things in storage; however, most of her belongings would be donated to charity. There were some items she had held on to forever, but since forever didn't truly exist, she wanted them out of her life.

★★★

George and Sierra's home
7:00 p.m.

"I don't know if I can be present every day of the trial, kids. This is too much for me already. To sit there and listen to Sam being judged and accused of this horrible crime. Even though I know he did it, I just can't sit there and listen to it! I'm sorry!" she exclaimed, wiping her tears with a tissue.

"Mother, we understand, and you don't have to. As a matter of fact, I don't think you should be there at all. It was a long day, and most likely, they all are going to be long and weary. It can tear you down. If you ever want to see what's going on, the trial is being televised live. You can watch some of it, all of it, or none of it from the comfort of your home," said George.

173

"Speaking of home, do you know when settlement is for the cottage?" asked Sierra, handing her a cup of hot tea with lemon.

"Two weeks from now, on a Wednesday," Ellen replied, smiling.

"Mother, I think this is a whole new wonderful beginning for you. I'm glad you chose the cottage over that senior living place. Reminds me of living in a dorm. Too many people too close for comfort," said George.

"I'm happy about it too, Son. New memories. A new beginning. I am looking forward to a new life."

★★★

Chicago, Illinois
Sunday, January 16

Ellen, George, and Sierra attended Sierra's church together for the first time. It was different from what Ellen was accustomed to. She was Catholic. Sierra was Baptist, and she was black. Black churches didn't skip, hop, sing a quick note, and send people out the door in less than an hour. It was more like two or three hours, if the Spirit didn't move them. Thankfully for Ellen and George, the service lasted for only an hour and a half.

Afterward, they all trekked to Sierra's parents' home for Sunday dinner. Ellen always felt at home in the presence of Sierra's family. They made her feel like family too. She could kick off her shoes, lean back, and fall asleep in the recliner if she wanted, and no one bothered her. As a matter of fact, that was what she did. It was only Sierra's immediate family, but it felt as if an entire football team were there! Kids were running around, laughing and playing in their Sunday best; the adult men watched a game on television; and the women prepped the meal to be served. It was a feast to behold: glazed ham, fried fish, fried chicken, potato salad, baked mac and cheese, red beans and rice, collard greens, and biscuits. Lord, Ellen felt as if she were at an all-you-can-eat buffet. She smiled from ear to ear.

They sat down to eat around three o'clock. Everyone was full of love and happiness. There was much energy at the Jackson dinner table, and conversation was golden. They talked about everything, but there was no talk of the trial.

Around six o'clock, George and Sierra headed home with Ellen. As he drove, he asked his mother if she wanted to stay for a few more days. She told them no. She asked him to take her home so she could finishing putting things away. She said her good friend Gayle was coming by to help. Besides, it was starting to snow again, and she didn't want to be trapped at George's home without any clothes or personal items, especially her medication.

★★★

Ellen McAllister's home
8:00 p.m.

Gayle had been helping her friend pack for the past several weeks. They had just finished five boxes. Ellen separated everything by what she would keep and what she would donate.

Flopping down onto the sofa, Gayle said, "I'm so happy for you, Ellen. I think you're going to love Creekside. I absolutely love that cottage. And Mason Lane is a great neighborhood. What are you—like five minutes from George?"

"Something like that. You know, I look around at this home, and I never imagined in a million years I would be leaving it because of divorce. I thought this was where I would die," said Ellen, holding an old photo of herself and Sam when they were young.

"I bet. Life doesn't always end up the way we want or imagine it will. We can create a beginning but never an ending, because we never know what the future holds. But life isn't over with yet, Ellen. We're only in our early sixties. Starting over may not be the long-term plan, because we've married and had children and now grandchildren, but we can look for a better, brighter new day ahead. I think you've got a great new start, lady. I know you are heartbroken over Sam, and I'm so sorry for that."

"Not sorrier than I. I have nightmares. Sometimes I wake up in the middle of the night and expect Sam to be right next to me, and I start to cry from the emptiness and the reality of the situation. Then I get angry and want to bash his head in and can't. Then I realize he did this to us. This is all his fault. And you know something else?"

"What?"

"I don't feel sorry for him for where he is. He deserves to be in prison for what he did to our beloved son's wife. All these years, you think you know a person, but then he does something so out of character and so bizarre and unbelievable that you stop and think, *My God, who is this person I shared practically all my life with? Who is he?* Sam McAllister is a monster."

"Perhaps he's always had this personality all his life, but you just never saw it or wanted to see it. Racist people are hate-filled people, Ellen. Remember that. They're not kind or gentle. Their thought process is not rational, loving, or positive. They are filled with animosity and nothing but hate. I do believe Sam always loved you, Ellen. I do. Whatever possessed him, you had no control over it. You're going to be all right, my friend. And don't let anyone convince you to forget about him like he is a stranger you met and passed by in the night. He was your husband for thirty-five years and the father of your children. Grieve. Because your situation is equal to a death. You know what I mean?"

"I do know what you mean, and you're exactly right. Well, it's getting late, and it's snowing again. You'd best get home!"

"I only live next door, Ellen. Hello!" she teased. "Actually, if you want me to stay, I will."

"No, no. Go on home to your children."

"Children? They're all over twenty-one. Grown! Not babies. I'll sleep in Mike's old room."

"Okay. I'm kind of loving the company right now. Thanks, Gayle. I hope you visit me often over in Creekside."

"You know it!" Gayle smiled.

"Good. Now, how about some of my pineapple upside-down cake and another cup of hot tea?"

"Sounds good. Let's watch an old movie until we get tired."

"I'm tired now, but I will stay up as long as I can, Jane Fonda!" teased Ellen as the two friends closed in on their evening.

★★★

Miami, Florida
Monday, January 17

Eddy was enjoying a wonderful, peaceful day with his daughter and a friend named Blake from next door under the beautiful Miami sun. Carmelita had a beautiful home with her husband, and his grandchildren were the lights of his soul. It was midafternoon. There was a slight breeze off the ocean. Carmelita lived close to the water in a beautiful, sunny four-bedroom ranch-style home. Her husband was at work. The children were at school. They were enjoying cool drinks outside on the patio. Tiny lizards leaped all about them, when he got a call from George's attorney, Steve.

"When do I have to be there, sir?" Eddy asked.

"We'll be calling witnesses the second week in February. But listen, if you are unable to make it due to your health, we can always do a virtual one."

"I'm afraid that may have to be the case, sir. I'm not well enough to make the flight. I'm doing okay, but that would be too much for me."

"No worries. That's perfectly okay and acceptable, and I'm glad we got this settled early so we can put you on the schedule. Enjoy your day, Eddy. And take care of yourself."

"Thank you. I will." He hung up the phone. Carmelita was sitting next to him on the terrace, under the awning.

"Was that the attorney, Papi?" she asked.

"Yes. They are calling witnesses the second week in February.

Basically, I told him I cannot make such a flight at this time in my life. It's not a problem because they're going to set up a virtual appearance. I have no idea how that works!" he exclaimed, slightly nervous.

"It's easy as pie, Papi. All you need is a computer, and that we have. Jerron is an expert with computers. Not to mention your grandchildren. Are you okay being a witness and giving testimony regarding all this? I mean, I can also be a witness, because Raul kidnapped me years ago. I have some evidence to share."

"Carmelita, I don't want you to have to go through the torture of reliving what that monster did to you. It was a very dark day for you and for me. If your mother had been alive, she would have never survived losing you like that. I was tortured every day in my mind while working and slaving for Raul. I am glad he is gone forever. I don't want you to go through that pain all over again, Carmelita!"

"Papi, I'm okay. My life is good. I am at peace. That girl he took over twenty-five years ago died. Her spirit died and was reborn once I escaped. You know, we both escaped because of someone's love and trust in us. Sierra and her friends trusted you, and I trusted Paola. And look where we are!" she cried, holding Eddy's hand.

He kissed his daughter's hand and shed a tear. "And I am grateful to God for sending us to safety."

"I want someone to pay for what happened to all of us from Pueblo Azul. That Sam McAllister made a deal with the devil when he chose to try to sell his daughter-in-law to that monster! Now, I don't know any of these women, but I want to help any way I can. If it weren't for you, she wouldn't have found me. You both helped each other. She brought my papi to me. *Te amo*, Papi."

"I love you more, my dear daughter."

Carmelita contacted George and Sierra's attorney and asked to be put on the witness list. She didn't know Sam, but she knew Raul and all his dirty dealings. Steve was happy. She would be an asset to the case. If only they could find Domingo, they'd have a sure shot to a victory.

Eddy wasn't doing well, and four weeks seemed far away. He was struggling with his health but didn't want to alarm anyone, especially his daughter. In his heart, he knew he didn't have much longer to live, so each day with Carmelita was a blessing and treasure from heaven. However, if he could help Sierra out after what she had done for him, he would do it with his dying breath.

The escape had taken a lot out of him. The night out in the cold, wet, dangerous jungle and the lack of sleep had taken a toll. He would always be thankful to the Lord for allowing him to make it to freedom, because now, after all those years, he was sitting next to his beautiful daughter, whom he hadn't seen since she was fifteen. If he died that day, he felt he would die the happiest man ever, for at least he'd had the chance to be with his child one last time. But he didn't want to die yet. He prayed to last a few more years so he could enjoy his grandchildren a little longer. Miguel was the eldest at fourteen. In three years, he'd be graduating from high school. It was a long shot with Eddy's health, but perhaps he would last long enough to see at least one of his grandchildren graduate from high school, since Carmelita never had made it past ninth grade, thanks to the evil Raul. She had been captured right before entering tenth grade. That day was still vivid and fresh in his mind.

Carmelita had been tending to the chickens, gathering eggs from the shack. Her friend Paola was helping because she wanted to grab a dozen eggs for her mother. They were laughing and joking, when all of a sudden, mayhem happened. Raul's men stormed the village and ransacked the villagers' homes and small gardens and farms, ripping through the yards, disrespecting everything the homeowners owned and cherished. Carmelita and Paola heard the commotion and fled to hide in the shed, but one of the men found them and snatched them.

Eddy came racing to the shack, trying to protect the girls from being taken. He fought off two of the kidnappers. He managed to hit one in the head with an iron crowbar, knocking him out. The girls were kicking, screaming, and fighting back as best as they could, but then two more men came in, and the girls and Eddy were overpowered. Carmelita and Paola were taken away in a black jeep. Eddy could hear his daughter's voice yelling, "Papi! Help me!" until he could hear her no more. He fell to his knees, crying out, looking up toward the sky, asking God why he'd let that happen. He cried so hard his stomach was as tight as a knot. Minutes later, two masked men whisked him away in another jeep. Unexpectedly, they knew who he was, calling him "that chef from the restaurant." Many jeeps came and took away women, young girls, and young boys that morning. The girls were used as sex slaves, and the boys became henchmen for Raul.

Everyone knew of Raul and his evil ways, and everyone always prayed he or she would not be his next victim. Horrifically, some of the local authorities were in cahoots with Raul. The people didn't know whom to trust. If the villagers had enough money and resources to escape Pueblo Azul, they would do so, but most were poor. Many worked long hours for pennies a day just to eat and survive. August 25 was a day of mourning, hurt, and pain, for it was the day Eddy's soul died after he lost his one and only child, Carmelita Montenegro, to evildoers.

Now, finally, this day was a day of jubilation, for Raul and his people were in hell, suffering for their crimes against those they'd made suffer for many years.

Chapter 7

Versailles, France
Friday, January 21

In France, Domingo, a.k.a. Jason LaSalle, had been keeping a close eye on all that was going on in America. Law enforcement were pleading for him to come forth and promising he would not be prosecuted for the crimes he had committed. Because he was the sole witness who could bring Sam down for sure, they promised to make a deal with him. He knew that without his testimony, there was a strong chance Sam could walk away free. Domingo wasn't buying any of that bull crap. He knew he was wanted. He never would set foot on American soil—or Brazilian soil at that. Domingo had learned of Sam McAllister by accident. He was connected to Raul because of Sam's mistress, Madeline Benson.

It was late afternoon. The rain had stopped, and it was damp and cool in the city. He grabbed his overcoat and decided to take a walk down the avenue. It was Friday night. He was tired of being cooped up in the apartment with no one to talk to or have fun with. There was a little pub at the end of the street, on the corner. He decided to stop in to have a few drinks. His girl, Celia Downing, was out of town for a few days, visiting family. Otherwise, he'd have been in his apartment, working her over until the sun came up. But since that wasn't the case, he decided to have a few drinks and mingle at the local pub for a few hours.

After a couple of glasses of scotch, he began to relax. He found a seat at a table near a window and sat back and watched the locals come and go. It felt good to be free, he thought to himself. Thank goodness he had Celia in his life. She was becoming more and more of a keeper. His lack of trust in people kept him distant, though. He thought again of the law enforcement in America trying to lure him to come forth, promising he would not face charges. *Lie!*

How stupid did they think he was? Domingo was sure they knew he had killed Raul. What was he supposed to think—that they would plan a big celebration party in his honor? No, he was going to lie low for as long as he could, out of sight and hopefully out of mind.

Around midnight, just as he was getting ready to call it a night, a swarm of police and fire trucks raced past the little pub. Everyone went to see what the commotion was all about. An apartment building was on fire. It was Domingo's building!

Domingo was frantic. He rushed down the street to see what was going on. Police stopped everyone who tried to get past the yellow tape. There were two buildings attached to each other, separated by a breezeway three floors up. The fire was in the first building. Domingo's apartment was in the second building. *Thank God*, he kept saying to himself. Even though most of his money was in a safe-deposit box at the bank, he had at least $500,000 in small bills stashed in his apartment. However, his car, which was parked in front of the first building along with a few other cars, suffered smoke damage. He became scared when the police asked for everyone's ID regarding his or her vehicle. Domingo's info was tight, but he still didn't want the law to run his tags. Jason LaSalle was a law-abiding citizen with no record of any kind, but it made him nervous that he'd purchased the vehicle from a secondhand undercover car dealer who didn't care to check registration or insurance. But he did have those, for the record.

The police approached Domingo for his ID and info to check out, and they went back to their car to run the tags. He was nervous as shit. He wanted to take a dump right there in front of everyone. It took them a few minutes longer than it had for everyone else. Then an officer flashed a light on Domingo and his driver's license.

"He's good!" said the officer to his partner.

Domingo took a deep breath and exhaled slowly, trying not to look suspicious.

"Here's your information, sir. You'll need to take your car to a detailer to have it cleaned professionally. It could start a fire if you smoke," the officer said, handing him back his papers.

"*Merci*, sir. I will do just that," Domingo said, smiling lightly. "Are we allowed back into the building, Officer?"

"Do you live in this first building?"

"No, the second one."

"Yes, you can enter your apartment. Just keep all the windows open and air circulating."

"Thank you. Have a good rest of the night, Officer. Or morning, I should say," he joked, and he quickly headed to his apartment building.

When he walked into his apartment, everything was in order, but it smelled of smoke—not heavily but enough to open the windows for fresh air. He plugged in his cell and let it charge. Domingo was tired after all the excitement. He just wanted to sit back and have a cup of coffee. It was one thirty in the morning. If Celia had been there, he'd have been in bed by then after a good screw and in snore-land. He turned on the television and let it watch him until he fell asleep.

★★★

Saturday, January 22, 3:30 p.m.

Celia came home the next day and called Domingo later that afternoon. She had a proposition for him, an offer she hoped he wouldn't refuse.

"I was thinking perhaps you and I could purchase a house together."

Domingo was too stunned for words. They'd only been dating for three months, and she wanted to live with him? *No, no, no.* That was not a good idea. She knew nothing about him really, and living together meant she would find out things. He did not want to walk on eggshells or tiptoe around the tulips just so she didn't find out things. The answer was no.

She was disappointed but not upset. She sort of shrugged and called it a day. He liked Celia's nonchalance. Still, to offer to buy a house together and live like husband and wife had to come from a deep place inside her heart, he thought.

Sorry, Celia. I am not the marrying type. Perhaps I thought of marriage at one point in my life as a young man working in the fields in Pueblo Azul, but not now. Not ever. I'm spoiled. As in damaged goods. You don't want me like that. You deserve better. Perhaps it's time I let you go. Perhaps.

Celia came over that evening to have dinner with Domingo and spend the rest of the weekend with him. They toured the city on Sunday via a horse-and-carriage ride, did a little shopping, and had dinner in the city before coming back to his apartment to relax, make love, and relax some more. Domingo Rodriquez, a.k.a. Jason LaSalle, was living his best life. For some reason, he knew it might not last long. With practically everyone in the world looking for him, he knew deep down inside he couldn't stay too long in one place. In six months, he would look for somewhere else to live in France. Versailles was beautiful, and he loved it there, but he couldn't get too familiar with the area or with the people, especially the people.

★★★

It was mid-February. The kidnapping trial of Sam McAllister was still going strong. The State of Illinois was doing a bang-up job against him. The evidence was overwhelming. There had been at least half a dozen witnesses, including Eddy and his daughter, Carmelita. The final witnesses would be Sierra, Chloe, Jenelle, and Lisa.

That day, Madeline Benson was called to the stand. Her testimony was explosive. Madeline tried to plead her case that she'd had no idea about the kidnapping that was to take place once the flight was rerouted. She simply had thought that Sam was punishing Sierra because of her involvement with his son George and that Sam had made it look as if Sierra had stolen from his company or something like that. Even if that had been the case, going to great

184

lengths to reroute her flight would have been evil and hateful. She claimed she hadn't even known that Sierra was his son's wife. The prosecution wasn't buying it, and neither was the jury. Her speaking seemed sketchy.

It was heartbreaking for George and his brothers to hear the explicit details of their father's affair with this woman. Ellen refused to watch it live from her home on television. As a matter of fact, she and her friend Gayle decided to take a day trip to the casinos. She wanted nothing to do with the trial or her soon-to-be ex-husband's affair with another woman. She had enough heartbreak to last her for the rest of her life. That day, she was doing her! *To hell with Sam McAllister*, she thought.

The next day, the two pilots from Trak Airlines took the stand to testify against Sam. Pilot Jefferson Bailey and copilot Blake Norwood had already lost their licenses and their retirement with Trak Airlines and would never be able to fly another airline again. However, their sentences had been shortened because their attorneys had cut deals. Like Madeline, they claimed they had not known about a kidnapping. Pilot Jefferson Bailey remembered Sam laughing and calling it a joke just to reprimand Sierra. However, there had been no plan to make sure Sierra and her friends reached their original destination, Aruba, once they landed in Brazil. The pilots had let them exit the plane to fend for themselves.

Pilot Bailey apologized to Sierra and her friends, as did copilot Blake Norwood. He even had tears in his eyes. He hadn't had tears when he accepted that $250,000 check from Sam, though. Both pilots and Madeline Benson had been sentenced to one year in the county jail. It could have been worse if they hadn't cut deals with the prosecution, because they had been looking at five years in the state penitentiary. Still, their lives were ruined. Perhaps once they were free, they could get a job at a grocery store, bagging or stocking shelves, if they were lucky.

★★★

Ellen McAllister's new home, Creekside, Illinois
Monday, February 25

The trial was taking a break until next week because of the heavy snowstorm that had occurred a few days ago, and everyone, including the McAllister family, was stuck in his or her home. Two feet of snow had fallen over the city, and state officials worked overtime to clear roads, trying their hardest to get the city up and running again as soon as possible. Ellen McAllister had successfully moved into her beautiful little cottage in Creekside, four and a half miles from Sierra and George. She felt like a new woman at the age of sixty. She was alone, but she was doing okay.

It was late afternoon. Snow fell lightly. Ellen had retired to the sunroom to sip her coffee and watch the snow fall. It was cozy and warm inside the sunroom. She was surrounded by windows and could see her entire backyard. It was her favorite place to sit and meditate.

Her cell rang next to her. It was her eldest son, John, calling to check to see if she was okay.

"I'm fine, John! Really, I am. How are you and your family?"

"We're fine, Mother. I wish I could drive over there, but the roads are so bad still."

"No worries, Son. I've got everything I need here. I'm good!"

"You sound it, Mother. That makes me happy. Listen, I know you don't want to discuss Father or the trial, but the trial is expected to last a few more weeks, and it's pretty much a done deal. Looks like he will be going to jail for a long time, Mother. I'm only sorry for you. Sierra and her friends will be the last to testify before Steve makes his final closing statements."

"Well, how do you feel about all this, John? I know you and Sam were awfully close as father and son."

"To be honest, I feel horrible. I'm truly sorry for what he did to George's wife. I am, Mother. You must believe me."

"John, I never accused you of hatred toward Sierra. I'm glad you are apologetic regarding what happened to your brother's wife, because it was the epitome of evil! And as much as I want to hate your father, I cannot do it, because that would be un-Christian of me. But I do despise him for what he did. I do. He separated our family through his hatred. I can't live with that. I love my daughter-in-law. She's a wonderful woman and a great wife to George. I can't make you or your brother like her or have love for her, but I don't ever want to hear or see you mistreat her or show hatred toward her simply because she is of a different race. She's part of the one race we all are part of: the human race."

"Mother, I don't hate Sierra, but what her father did to Uncle Ryan—"

Ellen cut him off with deep resentment. "Don't you dare! Sierra's father was an upright, hardworking, honest, and loyal employee at the steel mill! He only did what anyone would have done: fight for better working conditions. Your uncle died from greed. Sierra's father did not kill your uncle Ryan. I'm through listening to that bull crap, John. For your father to seek revenge for something that wasn't criminal from the beginning is despicable. Benjamin Jackson did not commit any crime by fighting for his rights. None. So don't ever say that to me again."

"I'm sorry, Mother. I apologize. I don't want to upset you. Listen, I want to try to make amends with our family. The reason I called was to invite you, Mike and his wife and family, and Sierra and George on a family getaway so we can try to reconnect as a family and to ask for forgiveness and begin a new journey, especially with George and Sierra. I mean it, Mother. I want to bury this pain that's been ailing some of us—all of us."

"I think it's a good idea with good intent, but are you really serious in your conviction that you want to start a new life with your brother and his wife?"

"I do. But not just me. All of us! I know you were never distant from George and Sierra, Mother; I'm not speaking of you. More so myself and Mike. Actually, the way you showed unconditional love toward Sierra, I applaud you. In fact, Mother, you are my inspiration."

"Have you run all this by George yet?"

"No, not yet. I wanted to see how you felt first. Mike knows. He's the one who suggested a getaway."

"I don't know about the getaway part. Sierra has issues now with traveling. She's been severely traumatized by what happened to her. Not sure that's a good idea. But do talk soon with George."

"I plan to call him right after I get off the phone with you."

"No, no phone calls. Say it to him in person. You understand, John?"

"Yes. Yes, Mother, I understand exactly. Love you, and I will talk to you later." John closed his cell.

When John phoned his brother George, he was somewhat apprehensive but felt good about his intentions because they were coming from an honest place, somewhere real. John said he wanted to meet with George in person, as their mother had suggested. However, the snowstorm had stifled everyone. John had a nice large pickup truck and was determined to meet with his brother regardless.

George accepted his request to come visit and speak with him and Sierra in private.

John's wife, Bethany, had been on pins and needles lately. After all, she had been the one who posed as Sierra to cancel their hotel reservations in Aruba under Sam's direction. Next week, a representative from the hotel was going to testify on behalf of Dolphin Lagoon Resort. If it got out that Bethany had been part of Sam's scheme, it would end her marriage to John. No matter how much John disliked Sierra's being in their family, he would never have teamed up with his father or anyone else to have his brother's wife kidnapped or killed. He was not that ruthless. Greedy and selfish, yes. A murderer, no.

Sierra had just finished putting the dinner dishes away, and she and George sat down to talk about John, who was fifteen minutes away.

"I'm not trusting John at this point, George. I mean, he and his wife have shown me nothing but ugliness from day one. Sometimes it's just too late to make amends."

"I agree, but at least we can listen to what he has to say. I'm almost certain he wants to apologize to you and to me. To us. Anything after that, well, it's most likely a ploy to try to wipe the guilt off his soul."

"Then he should talk to God and ask him for forgiveness. I'm not the one. Just because he didn't have anything to do with the kidnapping doesn't mean he's not an accomplice to his father's hate toward me and my father, and I don't know if I can sit here and listen to him talk shit to us after the many years he and Bethany treated me so badly! I can't. I'm sorry."

George wrapped his arms around his wife as they sat on the sofa in front of the crackling fireplace. "No, don't be sorry, darling. Your feelings are justified. Simple as that!"

Just then, there was a knock at the door. George went to answer it, and it was John, all bundled up in a long cashmere overcoat, a wide-brimmed hat, and a wool scarf covering his neck and mouth. He rubbed his leather gloves together as George escorted him inside, taking his coat and hanging it up. They shook hands, and then they walked into the living room, where Sierra was still seated in front of the fireplace. John stood alongside George and greeted her with a simple hello. Sierra looked at him and said, "Hey," in a dead-toned voice. However, she offered him hot coffee. John smiled lightly, accepted, and watched her breeze past him, heading toward the kitchen. Minutes later, she came back with coffee for everyone and sat down next to George.

"So, John, what did you want to talk to my wife and me about?" asked George as he slowly sipped his coffee while looking John directly in the eye. Sierra never looked his way. She kept her head turned toward her husband.

"Well, thank you both for allowing me to be here in your home. I want to apologize to you first, Sierra. I am truly sorry for what you went through by my father's mad, evil doing. What he orchestrated was horrific, ugly, and humanly demoralizing. You may not believe this, but I was in shock when I found out my father was arrested for such a crime. A crime that directly involved you, a family member. And you *are* a member of the McAllister family, Sierra. I know I haven't treated you as such over the years, and I am extremely remorseful for that. You have been through a lot with our family. I apologize for how I treated you. I do. I apologize for how my wife treated you. If you're questioning why she's not here, well, I didn't want her to come. This is something I wanted to do alone. I'm asking for your forgiveness. And if you can't find it in your heart to do so, I totally understand. Totally.

"George, my baby brother, I ask for your forgiveness for not being the brother you deserved. I should have been someone you were proud to claim, look up to, and even emulate. I was none of that. I failed you because I was stuck so far up our father's wallet that I forgot to be human. I forgot to be your brother. You deserved my love and protection. There are so many things I've done wrong. So many. Somewhere along the way, I lost my dignity and let foolish pride step in and reign over my being.

"I'm here because I want to start over with you both. Dad has done something unforgiveable in my eyes. No matter what, Sierra, I would never, ever condone what he did. I didn't want to believe it at first because I idolized him! I didn't want to believe he would do such a thing. I loved him. I still do. He's still my father. But I don't like him, and I want nothing to do with him. Samuel McAllister III is going to prison for the rest of his life. This I feel in my heart. As far as I'm concerned, my father will be equal to someone who is dead. I can't speak for you, George, or even our brother, Mike. Just know I love you, George, and I'm sorry for everything. Another thing, George: I am stepping down from all of our father's businesses and entities. I plan to offer it to either you or Mike. And if you two don't want it, I will sell."

George and Sierra looked at each other in a state of shock.

"Well, I can tell you right now I want nothing to do with anything that Sam owns or has in his possession. Count me out!" said George.

"I'm not surprised, but I wanted to make the offer anyhow," John said.

"As far as everything else goes, John, I forgive you, but it's going to be hard for me to just bounce back and act like nothing ever happened to us as brothers. I was hurt by all of you when I first married Sierra and the way you all treated me. Mother was the only one who didn't chastise me or show any type of animosity toward my black wife. Yes, I said it: *black*. I married a black woman whom I fell deeply in love with eleven years ago. And I almost lost her a few months ago because of our father's wickedness. I do believe you had nothing to do with it. For that, I am grateful, but it doesn't change the fact that you and I have to work on building an entirely new relationship as brothers. But I am willing to try."

John was near tears. "That's all I can ask for, and I am more grateful to you than you'll ever know. Thank you, George. Sierra?"

Sierra wasn't as quick to extend an olive leaf or accept one. She still felt hurt, angry, and bitter toward the entire McAllister family, except their mother.

"I'm sorry, but my forgiveness still has to be earned. You all put me through hell the past eleven years. I don't trust any of you. I don't. I remember practically breaking my neck to be accepted by you all in the beginning. I got ignored at every family event and every business event. Never did you include me on invitations to anything! The invite always said, 'George McAllister and guest.' Guest? You never accepted the fact that I am his wife! The way you treated me was simply ugly and hateful. I cried many nights because of how you and your wife treated me. Mike and Linda sort of played follow the leader with you and Bethany. To me, they didn't have a backbone. Linda would be all nice and sweet when it was just the two of us, but as soon as you all appeared, boom! She treated me like the plague. So I distanced myself from you all. And now because your anchor, Sam, is not present to dictate to you all, you want to run to me and offer an apology? I'm a Christian woman for the most part. I am supposed to forgive, so I have to forgive you, but I don't have to ever be part of your life. Not now. Not ever."

"And I accept that and fully understand, Sierra. I will do everything in my power to rectify all the wrong I've done to you. I was going to offer a family getaway after the trial. Sort of a healing vacation to try to bring us together."

Immediately, Sierra cut in. "I won't be part of it. I don't want to travel anywhere for a long time. I'm good."

"I don't think it's a good idea, John. I know you probably mean well, but no, not for me either. My wife and I are on the same team. I don't do anything without her approval when it comes to my family."

"No problem. Perhaps it was a little premature to even think about offering something like that. Listen, I'm gonna get going. It's horrible out there, and driving at night in all this snow can be tricky. Just know I plan to live up to my word of trying to make it right with you both. Will you both be at the trial next Tuesday?"

George and Sierra nodded. Next week was a big week for the trial of Sam McAllister. The hotel would produce records of the phone call they'd received to cancel the reservations in Aruba, possibly exposing Bethany. Finally, the testimonies of Sierra and her friends would be heard.

John grabbed his overcoat and headed to his truck. It was snowing again but not as much as the day before. He made it home safely about an hour later.

Bethany greeted him in the kitchen, holding a cup of hot tea. "How did it go?" she asked casually.

"I'd say it went pretty much as I expected, given the history of all that has occurred with Sierra, George, and me—and you. George was modest in accepting my forgiveness. Sierra was not at all really, but she wasn't like cursing me out. More so, she was so hurt it was hard to forgive so quickly. I felt it went well, considering."

"Well, big day tomorrow. Are you going to be available for any of the meetings for McAllister Industries? I have major meetings tomorrow at work with two big distributors regarding the Allen Cove deal," Bethany said, pacing back and forth.

"No, dear. I have to meet with George's attorney. He said he had information regarding the hotel Sierra and her friends were supposed to stay in during their vacation. I'm just interested in why

Dolphin Lagoon would be testifying. What is their involvement in all this? The prosecution sure has some tricks up their sleeves. At any rate, I'm tired. I'm going to bed, love. Good night." John kissed his wife on the cheek and headed upstairs via the kitchen side steps.

Bethany sat up for another hour, thinking about tomorrow. If Steve Highlander, the attorney for the prosecution team, really did have explosive evidence to present to the court by way of the hotel, Bethany would be summoned to court and likely would be punished by the law. It would show she had been in cahoots with Sam, whether she had known his plan to kidnap Sierra and her friends or not. The small part she'd played was big enough to bring charges for aiding and abetting. Bethany Juliann McAllister was done.

★★★

Downtown Chicago
Tuesday, March 5

The time had come for Dolphin Lagoon's testimony. Sierra was anxious to hear the hotel's reason for messing up her reservations. No one had any idea it all had been part of Sam's scheme. The hotel manager had previously handed over two audio recordings of conversations between Sierra and the clerk. The first one played, which featured Sierra confirming reservations she'd made weeks before the incident, was in fact Sierra's voice.

"Hello. This is Sierra McAllister. I am calling to confirm reservations I made yesterday for four people beginning on October 20. It's for five days."

"Mrs. McAllister, yes, we have you confirmed for October 20 through October 25 for two suites here at the Dolphin Lagoon Resort. They are our most exclusive rooms we have available. All the amenities are included, along with pool passes and a daily yacht cruise to Pino Island for lunch. We have you marked for early check-in, and we've received your credit card confirmation. You're all set, and we apologize for the delay yesterday, as our system was down. But you are set for October 20. Is there anything else I can help you with?"

"No, I think we're good! Thank you!"

"Thank you for choosing Dolphin Lagoon."

The prosecutor continued. "Ladies and gentlemen of the jury, as you can tell, Sierra McAllister did in fact make the reservation for herself and her friends. The initial reservations were made in September. However, right before her trip, she wanted to confirm that specific rooms would be available, so she called the Dolphin Lagoon Resort on October 18. Their computer was down, and she was told to try again later or the next day. She then called the next day, October 19, hoping those special suites were available, and the clerk said yes and confirmed. Sierra and her friends were confirmed to be there on October 20, per the evidence we just presented to you. Now, the problem occurred when George McAllister didn't hear from his wife the day she was to arrive at the hotel. When he called to check on her, a clerk said there had been no reservations made! We know Sierra made the original reservations in September, and we clearly heard her later confirm with another call on October 19. We call Diana Hunt to the stand."

Diana Hunt was the manager of Dolphin Lagoon. She had taken the call from George and told him there had been no reservations made for a Sierra McAllister party of four. It got intense. Steve drilled Ms. Hunt like mad until she broke down and said she'd been paid $10,000 by Sam to cancel Sierra's reservations and state that none ever had been made. He never had given Ms. Hunt a reason; he'd just said that if she could do the favor for him, he would pay her $10,000. She dropped her head and cried. The court murmured. Then Steve played the most crucial tape of all: the audio that suggested Sierra had canceled the reservations.

"Hello. This is Sierra McAllister calling again. I'm sorry, but I will need to cancel my reservations with you all. There's been a change of plans. I am unable to visit Aruba, as I have a family emergency."

"Oh, I am so sorry, miss! Well, I must tell you there is a penalty fee for canceling so late. I don't understand. Yesterday you called to confirm! I'm sorry for whatever reason you're unable to make it to Aruba. We will cancel the reservations but can only refund you half at this time."

"No problem! I understand. And don't worry about a refund. I'm sure I inconvenienced the hotel by doing this at the last minute."

When Sierra heard the voice, she cringed and nearly burst into tears. George was in a state of shock, but most surprised of all was his brother John. They knew instantly it was Bethany's voice.

"Oh my God, George! Bethany was in on it," Sierra whispered to her husband, holding her hands over her mouth in shock.

"Now, that voice you just heard, ladies and gentlemen, was not the voice of Sierra McAllister but of Bethany McAllister, Sierra's sister-in-law. Very obviously two different voices here. Bethany helped in the plot to rid Sierra McAllister from their family under Sam McAllister's orders and directions."

The court was in an uproar. The judge called for order in his courtroom. He immediately called for recess for one hour. The defense team were pissed. They knew they were losing at that point. The clerk who'd taken the $10,000 was charged with bribery. However, it was Bethany's participation that turned the whole trial upside down.

John was livid and in a state of shock. He broke down in tears in the courtroom and walked out. His beloved wife, the woman who had given him three beautiful children, had a black heart. Sierra almost felt sorry for him, but she was too angry to feel any type of empathy for George's siblings, because of the way they had treated her for so long. She just shook her head and walked away. George was over the top with anger toward Bethany. At that point, contrary to his wife's feelings, he felt bad for John and their children. Bethany was on her way to jail as well—however, they couldn't find her. She had skipped town that morning after the kids were on the school bus. Now there was a manhunt for her.

Bethany booked a flight under an alias to Canada. She was scared, and inside, her heart was crying out for forgiveness and wishing she never had been part of Sam's plot to kidnap Sierra. She'd known nothing about a kidnapping, just that she was supposed to cancel her vacation reservations at the hotel in Aruba.

When John arrived home, their children, who were six, thirteen, and fifteen, were crying that their mom had left them a note. John immediately consoled them but said nothing about their mother being part of the trial regarding their grandfather. With the exception of the youngest, they were old enough to know what it was all about.

The worst thing Bethany could have done was run. She'd made it worse for herself by doing so. The best thing would have been to stay, face the court, tell her side, and let the judge decide if she had been in cahoots with Sam regarding the plan to kidnap and sell her sister-in-law into the sex-slave industry. By running, she'd made herself look guilty.

By the end of the week, Bethany was captured and taken to the county jail, where she was held for questioning before being arrested for obstruction of justice. The following week, the second week in March, she took the stand, telling the court what she had done but claiming she'd had no knowledge of a kidnapping plot. She cried the entire time. Sierra looked at her as if she were the devil himself. When Bethany cried out in court that she was sorry to Sierra, Sierra just shook her head in anger. She kept her mouth shut once more to prevent being held in contempt. She wanted to break every bone in Bethany's skinny body!

Bethany was handcuffed and escorted by the bailiff and placed behind bars downstairs until it was time to transport her to the county jail, where she most likely would spend six months for her part in Sierra's kidnapping. An upstanding businesswoman who'd never even had a parking ticket was now going to spend six months in jail. Her position with McAllister Industries was over. All because of her dislike toward her sister-in-law.

John was devastated and in complete shock at what his wife had done. He was numb, heartbroken, and sad. The McAllister family was falling apart at the seams. John called his mother, and she told him to come over and bring the girls. He arrived in Creekside with his daughters and flew into his mother's arms.

"It's going to be all right, John. Come in, Son. Have a seat. Kylie, Megan, Susana, take your things into the guest room. Grandma has dinner ready."

"Okay, Grandma," they said sadly.

"The girls are heartbroken, Mother. They are devastated that their mother has to serve time in jail for her part in their aunt Sierra's kidnapping. This is awful! I had no idea, Mother. None!"

"I know, John. I believe you. I also believe Bethany regrets doing what she did, because honestly, I don't believe she had knowledge of your father's scheme. She got caught up because of her dislike for Sierra."

"I love my wife, Mother. I love her, but I am so angry over what she did. I feel like she's someone I never knew. I mean, we didn't treat Sierra very well over the years. We were wrong for showing ugliness toward her just because our brother married a black woman. Sierra never deserved any of that. I don't know what to do."

"What do you mean, Son?"

"I don't know if I can live with what Bethany did to my brother's wife. I'm thinking about divorcing her. Now I know what you went through when you found out about our father. How are we supposed to get past this, Mother?"

"We pray for peace and accept that this is something out of our control. The only thing we can do is try to move forward. Take one day at a time, because in life, that's all we're given anyway. But do know that we as a family will get through this. You and the girls are welcome to stay here as long as you want. Come. Let's have some dinner."

★★★

Chicago, Illinois
Saturday, March 20

It was the first day of spring. Two weeks ago, there had been a major snowstorm, and now it was seventy degrees. Although there were remnants of winter lingering, with small patches of snow here and there, the sun was slowly warming things up. Spring was a sign of new beginnings.

Yesterday Sierra and her friends had had a difficult day of testifying and reliving their experience of being kidnapped at the direction of Sierra's father-in-law, Sam McAllister, formerly one of America's wealthiest and most powerful businessmen. His money and power now had been stripped from him indefinitely. The three-month trial successfully proved Sam McAllister was guilty of all charges against him, along with his accomplices. They never had found Domingo, who was still hiding and living large in France. As far as he was concerned, it was over. He was free and in the clear. Next came closing arguments, and then it was time for the jury to render their verdict.

After Samuel McAllister was found guilty, the judge sentenced him to twenty-five years with no chance of parole. That meant he would be nearly ninety years old before he could even think about an appeal. Case closed.

That day was a day of mourning for Ellen, John, and Mike. George, in his own way, also mourned his father, but he was relieved Sam would pay for orchestrating a horrific act that most likely would have killed his wife.

Two days later, Sierra burst into the house after a checkup with the doctor. She was pregnant—with twins! George rejoiced like a church choir on Sunday morning. Ellen was over-the-top happy and cried joyful tears. Immediately, she began to dote on Sierra. Ironically, Sierra was due on October 20.

George's brothers, John and Mike, sent their congratulations to him and Sierra. John's fifteen-year-old daughter Megan immediately volunteered to babysit later on down the road. Sierra was so happy that for a brief moment, she forgot her husband's siblings' behavior over the years and accepted John's invitation to have a special celebratory dinner party with all Sierra's family and friends at the posh Jasmine Room in downtown Chicago.

Everyone got dressed up that evening and pigged out on a spectacular buffet of fine food. They danced and laughed and forgot all about their troubles, except for John, George, Mike, and his wife, Linda. John and Mike made a special speech regarding family ties, forgiveness, and making all their wrongs right. Sierra's family were moved by their speech, and for the first time, John and Mike hugged Sierra with genuine concern. They even shed a tear or two. At that moment, Sierra felt sorry for John and his daughters. Bethany had been taken away from them for her part in the kidnapping. Sierra felt the most empathy for their young daughters. At the end of the night, John promised to never disrespect family again and made a pact to always show love and togetherness.

Around midsummer, George and Sierra received a call from Carmelita in Miami. She told them Eddy had passed away, but he had been surrounded by family. Sierra cried hard that morning. She, Chloe, Jenelle, and Lisa flew to Florida for his funeral. Sierra was six and a half months pregnant. At first, George did not want her to go, fearing she should not fly in her condition, but her doctor said it was okay for her to go. After the funeral, the four friends stayed in Miami with Carmelita for a few days before flying back to Chicago. The man who had saved them was gone for eternity.

In France, Domingo heard of Eddy's passing via the news. His death made headlines in connection with the trial of Sam McAllister since Eddy's testimony had led to McAllister's conviction. Domingo always had liked Eddy. He had been a gentle old soul who treated all the men at the holding house with kind regard, and he'd fixed them meals at the drop of a dime if they requested it. Domingo said a prayer and moved on with his life. He would never go back to being Domingo Rodriquez. He was forevermore Jason LaSalle. In the end, he wound up marrying Celia Downing in early September. *What the heck?* he thought. He was free and wanted to finally see what it felt like to live like a normal human being. They decided to travel the world before settling down with children.

On October 20, exactly a year after her kidnapping, Sierra McAllister gave birth to a boy and a girl, naming them Ellena Marie, her mother's middle name, and Geordan Benjamin after her husband,

George, and father, Ben. Sierra and George were the proudest and happiest parents in the world. Destiny had been fulfilled.

Sadly, John divorced Bethany and decided to raise his daughters alone. Ellen insisted they come live with her, and they did until John found another home in which to start over with his girls.

Now that Sierra had been gifted the one thing in life she'd longed for, motherhood, she could positively move forward with her life, but she would never forget the panic in the jungle and the miracle through which she'd survived and lived to see another year. October 20 would always be a day of both joy and pain, sunshine and rain.

It was time to begin another chapter of life.

About the Author

Lena Lee is a native of West Chester, Pennsylvania. As a patented inventor, she created dolls of no race or nationality called the Lollipop Tots. Having loved writing since she was a child, she has penned thirteen non-published short stories. She also has a patent pending on a multi-functional laptop. In her spare time, Lee enjoys drawing, sketching and designing and spending time with family.